PAGAN

PAGAN

by
W. F. Morris

CASEMATE | uk
Oxford & Philadelphia

Published in Great Britain and
the United States of America in 2017 by
CASEMATE PUBLISHERS
The Old Music Hall, 106–108 Cowley Road, Oxford OX4 1JE
and

1950 Lawrence Road, Havertown, PA 19083, USA

Series adviser: Elly Clark

Paperback Edition: ISBN 978-1-61200-464-8
Digital Edition: ISBN 978-1-61200-465-5 (epub)

A CIP record for this book is available from the British Library

Printed in the Czech Republic by FINIDR
Typeset in India by Lapiz Digital Services, Chennai

For a complete list of Casemate titles, please contact:

CASEMATE PUBLISHERS (UK)
Telephone (01865) 241249
Fax (01865) 794449
Email: casemate-uk@casematepublishers.co.uk
www.casematepublishers.co.uk

CASEMATE PUBLISHERS (US)
Telephone (610) 853-9131
Fax (610) 853-9146
Email: casemate@casematepublishing.com
www.casematepublishing.com

PREFACE
BY
DICK BARON

THIS is a record of a holiday spent in the Vosges in the early autumn of 1930 by Charles Pagan and myself. It is, however, more than a mere record of continental sightseeing; indeed Pagan maintains that the series of coincidences of that holiday were too remarkable to be attributed to mere chance. And it may well be that he is right.

Certainly he is not a superstitious man, nor is he a religious one in the church-going sense. It is true that the letters C. of E. were engraved between his name and regiment on the identity disc he wore round his wrist during those far off war days when first we met, but were he pressed to make a confession of faith, the resulting rudimentary creed would, I fancy, defy classification into any of the recognized forms of dogmatic religion. A vague but none the less sincere belief that "what is to be is to be"— that one cannot escape what is coming to one—is probably the principal article of that creed; and that again is a legacy of the fatalism of the now almost forgotten war days and of this dramatic holiday in particular.

However that may be, he will have none of it that chance was the determining factor, and that but for an idle action of his he and Clare and I would never have known. "And will you maintain," he demands, "that it was chance also that led me to take that holiday in Alsace of all places and stumble upon the one person in the whole world that it concerned?"

Put like that, it does sound convincing, and one hesitates to deny that he is right and that the apparent coincidences of that dramatic holiday were not the preordained dispositions of a higher power. Perhaps, after all, he is right, and in the words of the national poet he is fond of quoting, "There's a divinity that shapes our ends, rough-hew them how we will."

CHAPTER ONE

THE hardy veteran of the Jungfrau and Monte Rosa will despise the Vosges. Tramp their eighty rugged miles from north to south, you will find no frosted canine tooth like the Matterhorn, no giant's winter slide like the Mer de Glace. At no point do the bare round *ballons* rise above five thousand feet. To the south-bound traveller as he rattles down the line from Strasbourg to Basle they are but hills that make a pleasant picture, framed by the window of his comfortable dining-car, pleasant, sunny, vine-shod hills, with ancient villages nestling at their feet and mellow castle ruins crowning their low green bastions. Behind, rise higher, thickly wooded slopes, and occasionally perhaps against the sky is glimpsed the bare round purple hummock of a distant *ballon*. But hills they are—no more, less mysterious and menacing than the distant purple switchback line of the Schwartzwald, framed in the windows on the other side of the train.

But higher up those pleasant valleys, beyond the vines and cosy villages, blinding snowstorms rage in winter, and the wind howls among the bare white domes like the ghosts of lost projectiles. And in summer, too, when dark clouds hide the sun, and rain lashes the grassy slopes, those cols and scarps above the forest line are bleak and desolate as many a knapsacked holiday tramper can testify.

Two such trampers found them so one evening in early autumn. They were trudging wearily up a steepish slope in single file, their feet slipping on the sodden grass, their faces wet and ruddy from the driving rain. They were barely three thousand feet above the sea, but they might have reached the summit of the world, so close above them like a ceiling hung the great grey clouds. The grassy slopes on either hand ran up and disappeared in wreaths of drifting vapour, and through the drifting murk behind them appeared and disappeared, like pictures on a screen, patches of a dark wooded hillside that lay far below, beyond an unsuspected abyss.

Dusk was falling. The grey watery light died slowly in the low hung clouds. The colour faded from the wet grass underfoot. There was no sound except the lashing of the rain and a metallic clinking from the haversack of one of the travellers.

The leading figure, Charles Pagan, tilted his head so that a miniature waterspout cascaded from his hat down the front of his already sodden mackintosh. "Are you wearing spurs or what?" he demanded.

Baron trudging stolidly in the rear, gave a hitch to his rucksack and produced a clink louder than any of its predecessors. "It's that confounded enamel mug rattling against the handle of my tooth brush," he said.

"You sound like a ruddy knight in armour," declared Pagan.

Baron moved his neck uncomfortably within the clammy upturned collar of his mackintosh. "I *feel* like a ruddy damp night in a ditch," he growled. "And I shall not be sorry when we reach this pub—that is assuming that it still exists and you haven't made an utter box up of the map reading."

Pagan's snort of disgust blew a shower of drops from his dripping face. "That was the most unkindest cut of all," he quoted in tones of injured virtue. "Didn't you and I go to war together God knows how many years ago? And didn't I lead my trusting fellows all over France with the unerring skill of a born leader of men? And you suggest that in my old age I can't read a map! It's enough to make poor old Melford turn in his grave."

"All right; Kamerad! There's no need to stop and argue about it," retorted Baron, whose bent head had come into contact with the other's wet shoulder. "But Heaven help you, Charles, if that pub does not materialise pretty soon."

Pagan stepped out again. "Barring fire, tempest, earthquake or other act of God," he answered cheerfully, "we shall see it in a minute or two when we are over this col."

Baron made no reply at the moment. "The proof of the pudding is in the eating," he growled sceptically, at last.

"You put it pithily and with great originality," retorted Pagan. "But likewise it's a hell of a high mountain that has no public-house."

They trudged on in silence. The ground grew almost level for a short distance and then sloped gently downwards. A rough track ran through the sodden grass and rocky outcrops. On either hand the enclosing slopes loomed darkly through the gloom. The wind was rising. The rain came in sudden, driving gusts that buffeted the faces of the travellers and beat a muffled tattoo upon their sodden hats and mackintoshes. Darkness enshrouded them.

Low down to the left a light appeared suddenly. It was but a dull yellow blob in the darkness, and it was impossible to say whether it came from close at hand or lay on the far side of an invisible valley, but Pagan pointed to it confidently. "*Voilà!* The local Pig and Whistle." The sound of his voice swept by on a rainy gust. Baron grunted a non-committal reply, but quickened his pace hopefully. The blob of yellow light glowed more brightly with each step. A long, dim, grey line wavered uncertainly below it. The gable end of a building took shape dimly against the dark sky, and quite suddenly they found themselves looking across whitewashed wooden palings at a curtained window in the darkened wall of a house.

No gate was visible. Pagan moved off to the left to look for one, but stopped abruptly when he found the ground descending steeply beneath his feet. The foot of the palings had risen nearly to the level of his face. To his right was the dark, almost perpendicular earth bank on which they stood; ahead was darkness and the indefinable sense of nothingness that had pulled him up short.

"Anything down there?" called Baron.

"Nothing except a large pile of air with mountains round it," remarked Pagan as his head rose again above the level of the palings. "Scout off to the right, old thing, and see what happens."

They stumbled off along the palings past the lighted window. The flat front of the house came dimly into view behind the gable end and lengthened slowly. The palings took an abrupt turn to the left; the wind died suddenly in the lee of the dark length of the building. Baron found a gate, and they splashed across an enclosure on which the water stood an inch deep to a shadowed doorway. There were windows, on either side of it, but the shutters were closed and only from that on the left did a faint gleam of light escape.

Pagan fumbled for a bell, and finding none, rapped upon the panels of the door with his stick. Then he shook himself like a dog, scattering water around him like a garden spray, and banged his sodden hat upon his knee. "A little more moisture inside and a little less out, that's the programme," he murmured. "And then sleep that knits up the ravelled sleave of care."

"And fodder, Charles," added Baron. "Don't forget fodder. Food that fills up the rumbling voids that were."

"Crude but true," conceded Pagan.

The grating sound of bolts being withdrawn brought his face round again to the door. A perpendicular beam of light slit the darkness, and a shadowed face appeared behind the narrow opening.

"*Wer ist dort?*" It was a woman's voice and the question was repeated in French. "*Qui est là?*"

"Wise men from the East," answered Pagan cheerfully.

The owner of the voice had opened the door no more than five or six inches, and Baron, dubious of the effect that this announcement in a foreign language might have upon her, hastened to explain in his halting French. "*Deux voyageurs, madame. Voyageurs Anglais—très humides et très fatigués. Nous désirons seulement quelque chose à manger.*"

"Yes, that's the idea," chimed in Pagan boisterously. "*Beaucoup abendgessen, bitte. Swei zimmer and twa wee bocks.*"

"Easy, Charles," warned Baron. "Don't frighten the woman with your fearsome jargon."

"It has done the trick, anyway," retorted Pagan as the door swung slowly open.

"It has. She probably takes us for a couple of delegates from the League of Nations," remarked Baron dryly as he stepped across the threshold.

The door was closed behind them and they found themselves standing in a long, brick-floored room lighted by a single lamp that hung from a low beam. Three or four bare deal tables and chairs occupied the greater part of the floor space, and in one corner was a rough wooden counter or bar, semi-circular in shape with a few shelves containing bottles fitted to the angle walls behind it. Here, where they stood, the ceiling was low, the black uncased beams being but a foot or two above their heads, but the other half of the room was nearly twice as lofty, the ceiling level there being the same as that of the rooms above. At the far end an open staircase in the room itself led up to a kind of indoor balcony protected by a wooden balustrade that ran along one wall on the level of the ceiling of the other half of the room. Two doors, leading presumedly to bedrooms, opened on to this balcony. The room evidently stretched the entire length of the building, for there were two shuttered windows on either side of the door by which they had entered, and one in each of the end walls. The other wall was blank except for a door near the bar and a large fireplace under the balcony in which a wood fire was burning.

Baron slipped off his pack and dumped it on the floor. "Well, it's a poor heart that never rejoices, Charles," he said, rubbing his hands. He crossed towards the fire, leaving behind him on the brick floor a pool of water from his sodden mackintosh.

The woman who had opened the door to them picked up the pack. In the light she was revealed as a young girl of eighteen years or thereabouts, solidly built, with a broad, unbeautiful face, that had nevertheless a pleasant expression.

Pagan slipped off his own pack and dripping mackintosh. Keeping now exclusively to the workaday French that had served its purpose in the far off war days further north, he asked if they could have a meal and two beds for the night.

Although the expression of the girl's face was amiable enough, there was a slight hesitancy in her manner and a hint of uneasiness in her honest eyes that was in strange contrast to her general air of rustic frankness.

During his conversation with her the door near the bar opened and a broad, well-built man dressed in working clothes came into the room. He bore a strong resemblance to the girl, but though his face, like hers, was honest, he glanced somewhat suspiciously at the two travellers as he murmured "*Guten abend.*" The girl turned to him at once and spoke rapidly in German, of which Pagan understood nothing except the one word Englander, and as she pronounced it the man's eyes sought his, he thought, none too graciously. The look perhaps was more speculative than hostile, as though its owner were embarrassed by the presence of his visitors and were trying to make up his mind whether they were genuine travellers or not.

However, the result of the conversation was satisfactory, for the girl picked up Pagan's pack, which he immediately relieved her of, and bidding them follow her, led the way down the room and up the staircase at the far end. She threw open the first door on the balcony and told them to wait while she got a light. A moment later a match flared up within the room, and she called in English, "Come 'en, Messieurs."

"Oh, ho, you speak English, M'selle!" cried Pagan striding in. "French, German, English—that's pretty good!"

"A leetle," she answered with a slight flush; and added in French, "But M'sieu also speaks all three languages." And then for the first time she smiled.

Baron guffawed. "By Jove, Charles," he cried. "I believe she is pulling your leg."

Her smile faded as quickly as it had come, and with an expressive gesture towards their wet garments and the packs, she asked if they had a change of clothes. On hearing that they had she ordered them to change at once and to put their wet things outside the door. She would have them dried. Then she passed through an inner door connecting to another room, lighted a lamp and returned. Some food would be ready, she said, as soon as they had changed. She left them, but was back again in a minute with two cans of hot water; then she went out and shut the door behind her.

Pagan took off his damp coat. "If ever I marry, Baron, which God forbid, it will be a little Alsatian wench like that. She would not get a place in a beauty competition, but she would keep the house as clean as a new pin, and she would have a first rate meal ready for me in five minutes at any hour of the day or night. If ever I came home canned, she would carry me upstairs and put me to bed; she wouldn't blue my hard earned pay on cocktails and erotic smelling cigarettes, and if I made love to her she would stand stolidly like a cow till I had finished and then would go on with the dusting."

Baron kicked off his wet shoes. "What you are thinking of, Charles, is an electric dumb waiter; not a wife. Personally I should prefer somebody with a little more sex appeal."

"A good leg isn't everything, my bold, bad Baron."

"Perhaps not, but it's well on the way to it. Which billet are you going to have anyway?"

Pagan stood up and with his braces looped down over his hips like an ostler, looked about him.

It was a fair-sized room. The dark weathered joists and floor-boards of the garret above formed its ceiling, and the floor was composed of thick narrow planks, scoured and polished to the colour of an autumn leaf. It was uncovered except for two small mats. The walls were of plain white plaster, a little yellow with age, and undecorated except for one crude coloured print of Heidelburg Castle in a worn red plush frame. A large maplewood bed stood against the wall on the left behind the door. It had solid wooden panels at head and foot and a wooden valance reaching to within an inch or two of the floor. It was covered with a fat red quilt. A large wooden press stood against the wall at its foot. In the wall facing the door was the window. It was hung with heavy curtains of dark red. Before it was a plain wood table dark with age, supporting a cheap swing mirror. In the corner was an enamel washstand with a receiver beneath it. In the middle of the room was a small table covered with a knitted woollen cloth of various bright colours on which stood the oil lamp. Against the fourth wall stood a rough wooden chair, and near it was the other door leading to the inner room.

Pagan passed through the door to inspect the other room. It was an exact counterpart of the first. Each room had the one connecting door in common and one door opening to the indoor balcony. In the second room, however, the bed and press were of necessity on the right of the door, and the place of the enamel washstand was taken by a low, marble-topped chest of drawers bearing a basin and jug of an old and very ugly pattern.

"I had better have this one," said Pagan. "I am accustomed to marble and art crockery."

"No, you jolly well don't," retorted Baron. "We will toss for it. How the deuce could I wash in that tin gadget in the other room?" He produced a coin and spun it.

"Heads!" called Pagan. Heads it was. "Well, that's all right, since you don't wash, anyway," he remarked as he coolly picked up the coin and pocketed it. "And now, my dear Baron, perhaps you would have the goodness to retire to your own apartment."

They changed into dry clothes and slippers and came out upon the balcony. Another lamp had been lighted in the long room below them and one of the tables had been covered with a cloth and laid for two. An appetizing smell of cooking food drifted up to them. Pagan leant his arms upon the balustrade.

"Stalls rather empty to-night," he remarked, surveying the vacant tables and chairs below him. He twisted his neck and glanced at the two doors behind him. "But what a setting for the Birth of the Heir," he grinned. "Picture it— all the local bigwigs assembled down there—mayor, town band, and village postman, all registering tense emotion and watching these two doors. Doctors with black bags trot up the stairs; nurses tiptoe importantly along this balcony. At last the door opens and a triumphant nurse displays bawling triplets to the enthusiastic crowd. Then everybody has free drinks while they drown the carbon copies in a bucket."

"Or better still a French farce," suggested Baron. "Bearded husbands and naughty wives popping in and out of doors."

Pagan turned upon him a look of withering contempt. "Popping in and out of doors!" he exclaimed in disgust. "Sounds like a public lavatory."

The girl appeared below carrying a tray. She looked up at the sound of their voices and announced that the meal was ready.

"We are coming, Juliet," answered Pagan from the balcony.

"Juliet!" She puckered her brows. "My name is Bertha," she answered.

Pagan struck a stage attitude. "What's in a name? A rose by any other name would smell as sweet."

"And so would Bertha, eh?" grinned Baron. "But its culinary smells I'm interested in at the moment, Charles. Suppose we go down."

"May I take you in?" asked Pagan offering his arm. And they went down the stairs together.

Bertha waited upon them and served a really excellent meal as Pagan had prophesied.

"What are we going to drink?" asked Baron as the large steaming tureen that had held enough soup for six ordinary persons was removed.

"Bock Tigre," suggested Pagan.

"You have vulgar tastes, Charles," Baron told him. "Why not experiment with the local wines?"

"I like Bock Tigre," asserted Pagan. "When I was a little boy at school I learnt that the tiger was a fine and very fierce animal. And when I drink Bock Tigre *I* feel a fine and very fierce animal."

After the meal they had hot coffee brought to them in tall glasses, and they smoked their pipes by the fire under the balcony. The man did not appear again, but Bertha brought her needlework and sat sewing at a table under the lamp. Otherwise the long room was deserted, though it was clear that it fulfilled all the functions of restaurant, bar and living-room.

Baron stretched his slippered feet luxuriously before the blaze. "That tramp through the rain was well worth it for the sake of that meal and this fire. It's a funny life: you have to be beastly uncomfortable before you can appreciate simple joys."

"Wisdom falls from your lips like pearls, O Baron," Pagan agreed. "Personally I am finding the thought of that big bed and fat red eider rather attractive."

Baron yawned in sympathy. "Bed at an early hour is indicated," he agreed.

Pagan heaved his body reluctantly from the chair. "I feel like the cove in the play 'Who with a body filled and vacant mind gets him to rest crammed with distressful bread'—and not too distressful either," he added as an afterthought. He walked over to Bertha who had raised her head. "We are turning in, Bertha. *Nous sommes relentirant dans*," he said with a grin. "We promenadered far to-day and we shall probably promenader further to-morrow. Brekker—that's *petit dejeuner*, and not too petit either mind you—at *huit heures et demie, s'il vous plaît. Bon soir et bon rêves*." And he made her a bow in the correct French manner.

She answered, "*Bon soir, Messieurs*," in her stolid fashion. Baron said good night and they went upstairs although it was barely nine o'clock. Before turning in to his room, Pagan looked over the balustrade, and there below him, alone in the long brick floored room, sat the enigmatic Bertha, her shingled head bent again over her work.

In the warm lamplight, the twin bedrooms with their simple massive furniture, mellow walls, and dark ceiling timbers, had an engaging air of rustic peace and comfort. Outside, the wind still moaned and whimpered, and the soft pad of rain sounded now and then upon the window behind the thick red curtains; but within the house itself quietude reigned.

Pagan, in pink pyjamas, was sorting the contents of his knapsack upon the bed. The connecting door between the two rooms was open. "Reminds one of the really good billets we got occasionally in the bad old days," he said.

"Just what I was thinking," answered Baron from the other room. "I had a billet rather like this those few days we were at Vaux just before the Somme started. Poor old G. B. had the room opposite, across the passage."

"Yes," said Pagan reminiscently. "I had a damned good billet too—in that cottage at the cross roads, with Twist and Hubbard. And I remember how sick I was when my platoon had to go up to man the corps o.pips, and you lazy devils in A Company were left behind."

"Only for a couple of days," retorted Baron. "Then they pushed us up to dig toc emma pits at Carnoy."

"Happy days," said Pagan.

"Well, we certainly did enjoy those spells in rest."

"And the leaves," added Pagan.

"Leave! By gad, yes! Fourteen days freedom from the gory old fracas; plenty of money to burn; Blighty—London! I tell you, old Charles, you and I will never see their like again."

"'Fraid not—unless there's another war; which heaven forbid."

"Not even then. We are not exactly nonagenarians yet, but we are getting on, Charles, you and I. We were very young in those days, and that was half the secret, I suspect. No—it would not be quite the same—ever."

"I suppose you are right, Dicky." Pagan climbed into the comfortable bed, under the warm red eiderdown. The lamp was on the table beside him, and he had an interesting book. "Still—old soldiers never die!"

"No. And we haven't even yet begun to fade away," answered Baron who also was now in bed.

CHAPTER TWO

Pagan became interested in his book, and half an hour flashed by in silence, broken only by the turning of pages and the gentle rustle of bedclothes as he shifted his pipe from one side of his mouth to the other. Presently, however, Baron's voice came from the other room. "Where do we go to-morrow, Charles?"

Pagan blew a cloud of smoke upwards and answered without raising his eyes from the page. "Down to one of those old fortified villages guarding the valleys— Kaisersburg or Riquewihr. I haven't decided yet."

"Got the map?" asked Baron.

Pagan looked up and glanced around the room. "Yes, it's somewhere about. Oh no, I left it in my mac. pocket. Bertha has it downstairs."

"Oh, damnation!" came Baron's explosive exclamation from the next room.

"Well, you can go and get it if you want it," Pagan retorted amiably as he turned over upon one elbow and resumed his reading.

Silence settled down again to be broken a few seconds later by the creaking of a bed in the next room. A series of slight thuds followed and a muttered exclamation. Then Baron appeared in the doorway connecting the two rooms.

"Energetic cove!" murmured Pagan with a yawn.

"I can't open my door," said Baron as he crossed the room in thin leather bedroom slippers. "It's stuck or something; so I'm going to use yours."

"Use the window and the chimney if you like," murmured Pagan amiably from the bed.

Baron turned the handle, but the door refused to open. "That's curious," he said. "Both doors stuck!"

"What's that?" demanded Pagan lowering his book.

"Yours has stuck as well. Or else they are both locked," explained Baron as he prepared for a lusty heave on the handle.

Pagan slipped quickly out of bed. "Here, hold on a moment. Are they really locked?"

"Looks like it," answered Baron. "They won't open anyway." And he prepared again for a heave.

Pagan caught him by the arm. "Shut up. Don't make a row," he exclaimed. "This is interesting. I thought there was something fishy in that girl's manner—and in the old boy's too."

"But damn it, they are not going to lock me in," retorted Baron hotly. And he prepared for an onslaught upon the door.

Pagan restrained him. "But don't you see, you chuckle-headed old lout, that we want to find out what the game is; and if you go making a row, we shall find out damn all. Come over here and let's have a powwow."

Baron allowed himself to be led away from the door, and he sat down on the bed. Pagan refilled his pipe from his pouch on the table by the lamp. "Let's approach the problem logically," he said. "If they have locked us in, it means that they don't want us to get out."

Baron assumed a mock expression of amazement. "Really, Charles, you ought to be at Scotland Yard," he said in tones of deep admiration.

Pagan ignored the interruption. He repeated firmly, "Don't want us to get out—for some reason or other. And I want to find out that reason." He shifted his pipe across his mouth. "The fellow is obviously a Bosche," he mused.

"Oh yes, he's a Fritz all right—an Alsatian Fritz at any rate," agreed Baron. "And we were probably potting at each other on the salubrious Somme fourteen odd years ago. But that doesn't explain anything, Charles. The Jerries are not hostile to us now—on the contrary."

"Well," said Pagan with a grin, "he's an innkeeper, and he may think it's up to him to live up to the old reputation of his profession and murder us for our gold!"

"Then he's not only an innkeeper but an optimist," put in Baron dryly.

"I agree with you that the theory is unlikely," grinned Pagan.

"Very," asserted Baron. "The simplest explanation is that having seen you, Charles, he is afraid for the honour of the beauteous Bertha, since on your own showing Bock Tigre makes you feel a fine and very fierce animal, and he has locked the door to prevent any tigerish cave man stuff."

"My dear old Baron," protested Pagan in pained tones, "allow me some rudiments of taste. Bock Tigre forsooth!

Believe me, it would take a whole Bock zoo to place the bashful Bertha in danger."

"But you said yourself that she was just the sort of wench you would marry, if ever you did marry," insisted Baron maliciously.

"Oh, pardon me, thou bleeding piece of earth, that was only what I praught," retorted Pagan. "And you don't think I'm fool enough to practise what I preach, do you?"

"Well, why is the door locked, anyway?" demanded Baron.

"Ah, that is the question, as laddie Hamlet said. And we were getting on with it nicely till you butted in with your facetious remarks about the seductive charms of Bertha. Now, as I was saying, I thought there was something fishy about those two. Instead of swooping down upon us like a couple of vultures as any well conducted landlord and daughter would, they didn't seem a bit glad to see us, and retched at one another in German before they condescended to take us in. And now they lock us in our rooms—which, as the Army Act says, is conduct to the prejudice of good order and landlordly discipline."

"All of which may be true, but nevertheless doesn't answer the question Why?" yawned Baron.

"I'm coming to that," said Pagan patiently. "They have locked us in because there is something going on that they don't want us to see."

"But . . ." began Baron.

Pagan raised a judicial hand and went on. "They know, of course, that we could break our way out, but we are not likely to do that, and anyway it would give them time to hide whatever it is." Pagan walked up and down the room as he warmed to his subject. "They think that we are tired and are asleep."

"They are bound to think that with you lumbering up and down the room like a tank," commented Baron dryly.

Pagan sat down abruptly upon the bed. "They think that we are in bed and asleep," he went on imperturbably. "But to make quite sure that we won't stick our heads out of the door and see what is going on in that room down there, they have locked the door. They calculate that if we do by any chance want to get out we shall try the door, and then finding it shut, pull away at the handle and make a devil of a row just as you would have done if I hadn't stopped you. Then mine host downstairs would have hidden whatever it is, run upstairs and opened our door oozing with apologies and regrets at the strange way doors have of sticking in old houses. And we should have seen damn all. Whereas now—"

"Whereas now," interrupted Baron, "you're sitting up in your little pink jimmy-jams enjoying the children's hour. Anyway, you have a wonderful imagination, Charles; I will say that."

"Imagination!" echoed Pagan indignantly. "What about that locked door: is that imagination?"

"Well, is it locked?" asked Baron. "We are not sure."

"Then if we are not sure, let's jolly well make sure," cried Pagan springing up.

They crossed to the door and examined it. Pagan peered through the keyhole and cautiously tried the handle. Then he fetched his penknife from the dressing table, opened it, and with the door handle turned, slipped the blade between the door and the jamb. He slid it slowly downwards till it hit something with a metallic click. He withdrew the blade and inserted it lower down. He slid it upwards, and again it clicked and stopped. He shut the knife and threw it on the bed. "Well, there's proof," he said. "The door is locked, and the key is not on the outside either."

Baron turned from the door and walked slowly across the room. "Granting that there may be something in what you have said Charles, what are we going to do about it?" he asked.

"Well, we want to know what is going on, and to do that we must get out without making a row."

"Yes, that's all very well; but how?" insisted Baron.

Pagan scratched the back of his head. "Skeleton key," he suggested.

"Oh, I know that's the way it's always done in the penny shockers," retorted Baron caustically. "But personally I've left my burglar's set of keys at home, and if you have never tried to open a door with a bent nail, I have; and I can tell you that it's about as easy as opening a tin of bully with a fork. And we haven't a bent nail, anyway."

"It's only your cheery optimism that keeps me from despair," grinned Pagan. "But what about the window?"

"Now you are talking sense," admitted Baron. "The only snag is that we should then be outside, and we want to see what is going on inside."

"True, o King, but once we are outside we might be able to get a squint through the lower windows."

Baron nodded. "It cannot be much of a drop anyway."

"Are you game then?"

"Yes—I suppose so; though it's all damn nonsense."

"Right 'o! Then we had better get some clothes on first."

Baron went back into his room, and Pagan hurriedly pulled on his clothes. Baron returned, buttoning his coat about his uncollared neck. "Which window shall we try?" he asked.

"It makes no odds," said Pagan. "This one will do. But we must put out the light in case there is anyone about."

They shut the door leading to Baron's lighted room, switched on a flashlight, and turned out the lamp in Pagan's room. Baron pulled aside the heavy red curtains. The window glass was still wet, but the rain had ceased. The moon hung clear, but a low vapoury cloud rushed upon it, and its brightness died away in a prismatic rainbow glow.

They opened the casement cautiously to avoid any creaking, and Pagan put his head out. At the same instant the moon sailed out across a narrow rift in the scurrying clouds and was gone again. But during the few brief moments that it hung undimmed in the narrow lane between the fluffy pearly edged clouds, he saw the dark line of a hill crest take shape against the sky across a black abyss, and far below twinkled a cluster of tiny lights. He withdrew his head.

"The drop is not much," he said. "Twelve or fourteen feet at the most, but the confounded pub is built right on the edge of the hill. You can see the lights of a village in the valley below."

"Fourteen feet," repeated Baron; "that's all right."

"But the devil of it is," objected Pagan, "there is no level ground at the bottom. It slopes right away from the wall—and pretty steeply too. If we hung by our hands and dropped we should be sure to go over backwards, and then by the look of it, we should not stop rolling till we reached the Rhine."

"Well then, we shall have to hang something out of the window and shin down it. But the question is 'what.'"

"We might tie sheets together," hazarded Pagan.

"My dear Charles, what is it you read?—*Little Folks?* And besides, if this is to be a secret stunt, how are we to explain the crumpled and dirty sheets?"

"Well, we had better put on the light and have a look round," said Pagan.

They closed the window, drew the curtains and relighted the lamp.

"Doesn't seem to be much here in the way of a rope or ladder," remarked Baron. "I suppose, at a push, we could use sheets."

Pagan was thoughtfully filling the inevitable pipe, and at the same time casting appraising glances round the room. Suddenly he jumped up and walked in a purposeful manner towards the window. He pulled aside one of the heavy red curtains and from behind it produced in the manner of a conjurer the short red tapestry rope that was used for looping back the curtains in the daytime. "*Voilà!*" he exclaimed in triumph.

Baron pursed his lips judicially. "Hardly long enough," he remarked.

"But there is one on the other side of the window," said Pagan; "and probably two more in your room." He took the other one from its hook and returned from Baron's room with another pair. They were each about three feet in length and when knotted together formed a rope some nine feet long.

"That's all right if we could hang it straight out of the window," said Baron. "But we shall have to loop it round something and that will make it too short."

Pagan looked around for further material.

"How about the bell pull," suggested Baron.

Pagan looked blankly at the bare wall behind the bed. "I didn't know there was one," he remarked testily.

"Neither did I till this moment," answered Baron. "It's over there by the press—at least the iron gadget at the top is."

Pagan dodged round the foot of the bed to the big press that stood against the side wall, and there in its shadow and partly behind it hung an old fashioned bell pull of the same material and colour as the curtain loops. Evidently the bed and the press had at some date exchanged places.

Pagan mounted a chair and with great care detached the rope from the ornamental iron lever from which it hung.

"Go on; pull it off," said Baron. "You never knew one of those things to ring by any chance, did you!"

"Not when you wanted it to," replied Pagan as he stepped down from the chair. "But everything makes a row when you don't want it to—even you."

The rope was about seven feet long, and when joined to the one they already had, brought the total length up to between fourteen and fifteen feet.

"It is long enough this time," said Pagan as he tested the knots. "Now what are we going to tie it to?"

"The bed is the obvious thing. But we should have to pull it across the room, and that would make too much row."

"Quite out of the question," agreed Pagan. "But if there is another bell pull in your room, I believe the rope will be long enough to reach the bed where it is."

"Yes, and when we get our weight on to it the jolly old bed will come skating across the room after us like a pet tank," retorted Baron.

"Well, damn it all, we must hitch it to something; unless you like to hold it between your teeth like the strong man in the circus."

"As a member of the strong men's union I cannot work after hours," grinned Baron.

The press and the bed were the only pieces of furniture massive enough for their purpose. The press suffered from the same disadvantage as the bed and had the additional disadvantage of possessing no legs round which the rope could be tied. They gazed hopefully at the simple furniture and at each wall, but there was nothing that would serve their purpose. Pagan even tested the thin brass hook to which the curtains were looped back in daylight, but it was obviously unfitted to bear the strain they would have to put upon it.

Baron gazed at the ceiling in despair, and then suddenly with a muttered exclamation, pointed upwards. In one of the dark weathered joists that supported the uncovered floorboards of the attic above was an iron hook that had probably been used at some time to support a hanging lamp. It was opposite the window and about six feet from it.

"Good man! That's where the old boy hangs his victims, I suppose," grinned Pagan as he pulled up a chair and mounted it.

"Any good?" asked Baron.

Pagan placed both hands round the hook and cautiously bent his knees till his feet were clear of the chair. He swung for a moment and then dropped back on the chair. "It would hold a battleship," he announced.

"Good!"

"The only thing is," said Pagan as he regained the floor, "that being on the ceiling it shortens our rope by a good eight feet or more. It's about fourteen at the moment. It is twelve at the very least to the ground; add eight: that's twenty and a bit more for tying—no it won't reach to within less than eight feet; and that's being optimistic. And I don't fancy a drop of even a couple of feet on that slope."

"Well, there is probably another bell pull in my room," said Baron. "The rooms are so alike I can hardly tell t'other from which."

They went into Baron's room and found another bell pull beside the press. Pagan mounted a chair and detached it. "I have always hated pairs," he said as he stepped down again. "Hated 'em from pictures of Highland cattle to twins, but after this I swear by 'em."

They added the second bell pull to the rope and tested the knots.

"Seems sound," said Pagan.

"Anyway, we shall soon find out if it isn't," said Baron grimly. "Hitch it to the hook."

Pagan mounted the chair and did so. He reached the floor again by sliding down the rope.

Baron picked up the end and coiled it. "Right 'o! Out with the light."

They turned out the lamp, drew back the curtains and opened the casement. Baron threw out the rope. Pagan peered over the sill. "It is within an inch or two of the bottom," he announced.

"Good! Who goes first?" asked Baron.

"As the rope was my invention and therefore mine, courtesy demands that I should grant you that honour," remarked Pagan politely.

"Not a bit of it," retorted Baron. "I wouldn't deprive you of it for worlds."

Pagan sighed and climbed cautiously on to the sill. "If I die it will be for an ideal," he remarked sententiously.

"Yes—curiosity that killed the cat," retorted Baron.

Pagan hooked his feet about the rope and gently lowered his body over the sill. "In case of accidents, hops are my favourite flowers," he murmured.

"Right—I will put a bunch on your grave, Charles; in a glass of Bock Tigre."

Pagan's head was now on a level with the sill. "Well, here goes and I sincerely hope that it will not be a case of 'Jack fell down and broke his crown and Jill came tumbling after.'"

"You can make your mind quite easy on that point," Baron assured him. "If you fall down I shall not come tumbling after—not me. Besides there will be those hops to be seen to."

Pagan negotiated the knots and slid gently down till his feet touched the steeply sloping ground. He kicked a foothold for his feet in the sodden grass and let go the rope. "Come on," he whispered. "But go easy at the bottom; it's damnably steep and slippery."

Baron's dark form came over the sill and moved slowly down the rope. A moment later they stood side by side their bodies leaning inwards and their hands pressed against the rough stone wall of the house, their feet poised precariously in the slippery footholds they had made. Far below them twinkled the tiny cluster of lights; around them was darkness and a scaring sense of emptiness. The damp night wind ruffled their hair.

"Which way?" whispered Baron.

"Right," answered Pagan. "Always keep to the right: it's the rule of the road on the continent."

"But there ain't no bloomin' road," growled Baron as he stepped cautiously sideways after Pagan. "And the bit of continent I've got my feet on isn't big enough to write home about."

The going was both difficult and dangerous. Pagan moved sideways with his hands pressed against the wall and his back to the black abyss, and before each step it was necessary to kick himself a foothold with his toe. Progress therefore was slow; but his right hand at length encountered the sharp angle of the wall, and he found before him a steep stone-revetted bank some four feet high surmounted by white wooden palings. With a whispered word of warning to Baron, he hooked his fingers between the palings and drew himself up. First his knees and then his feet found a narrow support on the top of the bank; then he scrambled over the palings. Baron followed.

To their left rose the dark gable-end of the house with the one ground floor window. Pagan stole towards it. Baron followed and blundered into something that fell with a metallic thud. He muttered "damnation" and rubbed his bruised shin.

"Clumsy lout!" hissed Pagan. "Why didn't you bring a gong or a motor horn!"

The moon sailed out across a cloud rift and revealed the obstacle as a little iron table and chair that lay overturned on the sodden gravel. Beyond the palings the abyss showed black and empty, and the dark line of the opposite hill crest took shape against the sky.

Pagan reached the wall of the house and flattened himself against it in the narrow wedge of shadow. "Moon, moon, serenely shining," he sang softly. "Please go in quite soon." And as if in answer to his wish the silver radiance died away.

They sidled along the wall to the window. A narrow strip of light escaped from either edge, but the curtains were drawn too closely to allow even a glimpse of the interior of the room. Pagan moved on and reached the angle of the wall. He slipped round it to the front of the house. From the first window a strip of light escaped, but it was impossible to see anything of the room within. The second window likewise was carefully curtained. Baron laid his ear against the glass while Pagan went on past the door to the two windows that lay beyond it. These too yielded no results, and he turned back to find Baron bobbing towards him with long slow steps in an absurd parody of a stage tiptoe. "Shush!" he said in a loud stage whisper, with upraised finger and a broad grin.

"Shut up, you fool!" hissed Pagan. "Could you hear anything?"

"Nothing," answered Baron with a grin, "except rumblings in my own tummy."

"What, after that enormous meal! You must have an inside like the Albert Hall," exclaimed Pagan in disgust. "And if you go about rumbling like an earthquake, how the blazes do you expect to hear anything! Let's go and reconnoitre the other end of the house, anyway."

They moved off past the remaining two windows beyond the door and reached the angle of the wall. Pagan put his head round it. The low roof of outbuildings and stabling showed dimly against the sky. "Hope to blazes there isn't a dog," he whispered. And then remembering that no dog had barked on their first approach to the inn, he moved on boldly round the corner.

On his left was a window, the other end wall window in the long room, but this again was so heavily curtained as to render fruitless his efforts to see inside. Opposite him was a low outbuilding, built out at right-angles from the end wall of the house. The front was open, the roof on this side being supported on two wooden posts which he discovered by blundering into one of them. The floor was of brick, and the structure formed a covered way from the house to the outbuildings, for there was a door under cover in the wall of the house.

Pagan listened at the keyhole and cautiously turned the handle but the door was bolted or locked. They made a cursory examination of the exterior of the outbuildings and returned to the front of the house.

"We might manage to open a window," said Pagan hopefully.

"We might—and then again we might not," answered Baron.

"Anyway, we will have a shot at it. It must be one of the end ones. They will give us a view of the whole length of the room, whereas from the others we should be able to see only a bit. And it must be the end one at the other end, on that terrace arrangement where you threw the chairs and tables about: it's nearer our base of operations and gives a shorter line of retreat with no door to pass."

"Really, Charles, you were wasted with B. Company," chaffed Baron. "The War would have been over in '16 if Haig had had you as Chief-of-Staff."

Pagan led the way back to the other end of the house where the two tantalizing strips of light escaped from the window. He examined the casement carefully and inserted the blade of his knife between the frames. Baron watched him in silence. "You will never make your living as a burglar, Charles," he said at last.

Pagan withdrew the knife in disgust. "For two hoots, I'd smash the glass," he growled. "Here, you have a go."

Baron took the knife and tried. "You make enough noise to wake the dead," whispered Pagan. "Steady, man."

"But not enough to open the window," answered Baron as he withdrew the knife. "I'm afraid it cannot be done without a proper burglar's set. The only thing that I can suggest, Charles, is that you do one of your lightning change turns: put on a false beard, ring the front door bell and talk Chinese."

"If you can't talk sense, don't talk at all," retorted Pagan. And then suddenly he gripped Baron by the arm. "Did you hear that?"

Baron nodded. "Um—sounded like a door banging."

"Yes," said Pagan. "The one at the far end under the alleyway arrangement. Come on; but for the lord's sake, don't make a row."

They stole cautiously round the corner and along the front of the house. No further sounds reached them and they gained the far end without mishap. Pagan put his head round the corner inch by inch. All was dark there. He slipped round, and on tiptoe gained the shelter of the covered way where he paused to listen. No sound reached his ears except the faint crunching of Baron's toes on the gravel. The door was closed, and from it no light escaped.

As Baron's dim form moved up beside him he whispered, "Let's scout off along the outbuildings. If anyone came out they must have gone that way or we should have seen them."

They moved off silently in single file past a stable, a cart shed and a small barn. From the barn wall ran a fence with an open gate where their feet sank deeply in the churned up mud. Beyond the gate the ground rose steeply, and the dark line of the col crest showed dimly against the sky.

Baron moved slowly to the left along the fence and end wall of the barn; Pagan moved a few paces uphill and then stopped abruptly, listening. A moment later it came again, the sound of stealthy movement ahead, and then ceased.

A soft diffused light crept down the hillside before him as the moon sailed behind a thin mist of cloud. Twenty yards ahead a clump of bushes loomed indistinctly. On the margin of the clump something moved. The diffused light grew momentarily stronger and revealed dimly the blurred head and shoulders of a crouching figure. Pagan took a step forward, but his foot slipped on the short wet grass and he stumbled on to one knee. At the same moment a flood of clear moonlight slid like a flashlamp beam down the slope and was gone; and in that brief radiance the crouching figure turned its head.

Pagan, agape, remained motionless on one knee as though petrified, while obscurity again enshrouded the slope. Then the soft pad of Baron's feet on the grass roused him. He straightened his bent body and gripped Baron's arm. "There is something in those bushes straight ahead," he said in a low voice that quivered with suppressed excitement.

"Is there, by gad!" whispered Baron. "You go to the right; I will go to the left." And he started forward.

"For God's sake go carefully, Dicky," whispered Pagan as he circled to the right.

From either side the two men closed cautiously in upon the dim dark patch that was the clump of bushes. They met on the far side, and Baron turned and pushed his way through the clump. Pagan followed.

"Well," said Baron as he emerged on to the short springy turf, "there is nothing there. It was probably the local cow you saw, Charles, having a night out." He put his hand over his mouth and yawned. "I'm getting damned sleepy. How about toddling back to by-byes? I think we have done enough detecting for one night."

Pagan raised no objection, and they went back down the slope through the open gate and crept cautiously past the front of the house. Pagan said not a word, not even when Baron blundered again into the chair on the little terrace at the end of the house. They climbed over the palings and edged their way sideways step by step back to the knotted rope that hung against the wall. Baron seized it and swarmed up. His dark form hung heavily and kicking for a moment as he struggled over the sill; then it disappeared through the dark aperture of the window. A moment later his head reappeared. "Right 'o, Charles. Come on," he whispered.

Pagan swarmed up the rope and was lugged over the sill and into the dark room by Baron. Baron pulled up the rope, closed the window and drew the curtains. "A light, Charles," he said.

Pagan obediently struck a match and lighted the lamp. Baron set to work industriously untying the knots and restoring each part of the rope to its original place.

"I have been thinking over this locked door business, Charles," he chattered complacently as he untied the rope from the hook in the ceiling. "And I believe I have got the idea. Our friend the landlord is an ex-Bosche, and he is probably mixed up with some political party malcontents. Before the war Alsace was mostly anti-German, but now that it belongs to France it is probably anti-French. They are like the Irish—agin the government. That chap in Strasbourg said there were a lot of meetings and things going on *sub rosa*. I expect our gentle landlord belongs to one of these secret political clubs and had arranged a meeting here for to-night—I mean to say, what place could be more suitable? A remote spot on top of a mountain, . . . plenty of space in that room downstairs, and drinks available. Well, the pub being empty, he arranges that meeting for to-night, and then at the last moment we butt in and asked to be put up. We go off to bed early, but he locked our doors to make quite sure we shouldn't listen to his friends' Hyde Park stuff. That is what has happened, I bet you a fiver. And as far as I am concerned they are welcome to get on with it." He got down from a chair by the press where he had been re-hanging a bell pull. "I believe in self-determination; and if they want to make Alsace German, Swiss or Chinese I don't feel called upon to interfere. What do you say?"

Pagan, sitting on his bed abstractedly unlacing his shoes, shook his head. "No—I don't give a damn either way." He pulled off his shoes thoughtfully. "There may be something in what you say, Baron, but anyway it does not explain what I saw to-night."

Baron began to unlace his own boots. "But, my dear Charles, after all what did you see to-night? Some movement in a dark clump of bushes!"

"I saw more than that," answered Pagan. "It was light enough to see that the noise in the bushes was caused by someone crouching there."

"Well, there you are! It was one of our landlord's pan-Alsatian, or whatever they call themselves, friends. He probably thought that you were the gendarmes on his track."

Pagan shook his head. "No," he said as he took off his coat. "The moon came out brightly for a second or two so that I could see quite clearly; and in that second it turned its head."

"Well," answered Baron lightly, "who was it? Our seductive Bertha! Was it a face you recognized?"

Pagan picked up the crumpled pink pyjamas that had been thrown on the bed when he had slipped hurriedly into his clothes. "No," he answered slowly after a pause, "I didn't recognize it. You see, it hadn't a face at all—not a human face."

Baron gaped. "But, my dear old Charles . . ." he began after a pause.

"It only turned half towards me," went on Pagan slowly and abstractedly, "and I am sure it did not see me. But I naturally expected to see a face in profile—nose, chin and all that. But I didn't—it was just a dark, blunt blob like—like an ape. But it was as big as a man."

Baron stood up. "My dear old Charles," he said in business-like tones, "what is wrong with you is that you have been reading too much Edgar Wallace—or drinking too much Bock Tigre; I don't know which. What with those clouds hareing across the moon and causing the light to jump up and down like a stage storm, and the aforesaid Edgar Wallace, combined with too much Bock Tigre you imagine you have been seeing things. Now you go quietly off to by-byes and you will feel better in the morning."

Pagan who was already in pyjamas said nothing. He shrugged his shoulders and climbed into bed.

CHAPTER THREE

PAGAN was awakened by the sound of movement near him, and he opened his eyes to see Bertha drawing back the curtains and to find broad daylight streaming into the room. A steaming enamel can stood by the marble-topped chest of drawers, and his dried clothes hung across the chair beside the bed. At the movement of his head upon the pillow, Bertha said, "*Bon jour, M'sieu*," tapped on the connecting door and disappeared into Baron's room.

Pagan dressed leisurely. The rain and wind of the previous night had gone, and the sun shone from a cloudless sky. The view from the red-curtained casement was no longer dark and menacing with an air of mystery and emptiness; it was grand and inspiring. In the bright morning sunlight the opposite hill, which before had been glimpsed only as a wavy dark line against the night, was revealed as a green mountain side, clothed with thick leafy woods, towering to a bare grassy hump against the clear blue of the sky. The inn, as they had already discovered, stood upon the very edge of the hill, and sheer from the foot of the wall which stretched below the window, the ground sloped steeply in green grassy curves till the view was cut off some six hundred feet down by the broad swell of the hillside. Here the roofs of three or four cottages glimmered in the sunlight, and from their midst a narrow white road looped and twisted as it mounted upwards to disappear round another swelling slope to the right. But away to the left, where the contours ran inwards, the view extended far down over leafy sun-lit woods and cherry orchards to the toy-like roofs and chimneys of a considerable village in the valley bed nearly two thousand feet below.

Baron came into the room as Pagan stood by the window knotting his tie. He leaned over the sill and nodded downwards. "Yes, Charles, you were right," he said. "If the old rope had broken last night it would have been a long, long way to Tipperary."

They breakfasted off coffee and croisants in the long, clean brick-floored room, and Bertha waited upon them, neat, efficient and enigmatic. She presented the bill, which was gratifyingly small, and produced a packet of sandwiches which she had cut with her own capable hands, to help them on to *mittagessen* as she expressed it.

Baron put the packet in his pocket.

"If ever I found a chair of wifely science at Girton or Newnham," remarked Pagan, "you, Bertha, shall be its first occupant—though by then I hope, you will be married to a real nice German who will allow you to unlace his boots for him and stroke his stubbly hair when he has had too much lager." He struck an attitude. "Full many a gem of purest ray serene the dark unfathomed inns of Alsace bear: full many a flower is born to blush unseen and scratch its fingers on a German's hair!"

Bertha listened to this outburst in solemn seriousness unmoved, and then a flicker of a smile passed for a second across her stolid face. "M'sieu pulls the leg," she said in English.

Baron guffawed. Pagan shook his head and grinned. "No, no, Bertha," he said, "I suspect it is you who have been pulling ours."

They slipped on their packs and set out. They had decided to descend to the valley and make their way down it to the plain. Their route took them past the little terrace with its overturned chair to a narrow track that wound downwards round a bare grassy hummock. At the end of five minutes the inn was out of sight. To their right was the green valley with the houses of the township a shining reddish blur far below and the peaks of the opposite valley side ringing the sky; to their left rose the great bare grassy hump round which the track ran.

Baron stopped suddenly and pointed upwards On the summit of the hump above them, silhouetted against the sky, stood a tree; not green and leafy like those in the woods below them, but a bare pole of a tree with short ragged branches like a clothes prop. "What does that remind you of, Charles?" he asked.

Pagan looked up. "If I were in Picardy, I should know what to say," he grunted.

Baron nodded. "But as we are in peaceful Alsace and not on the Somme, it can't be," he urged.

"I don't know," murmured Pagan. "There was some scrapping in these parts, I believe—those Alpini fellows, you know. Anyway, I would stake my last bean that that tree up there is the twin brother of those splintered chaps on the Somme."

They went on again with many glances sideways at ragged tree on the skyline above them. A man was coming towards them up the track, and Pagan stopped him as they met. He was a dark, olive-skinned little man with an air of superficial grooming like a waiter. "*Bon jour*," said Pagan. And then with a sweep of his hand upwards, "Pardon, M'sieu, but unless I am blind, there is a dead tree up there of the kind we used to see a lot of on the battlefields further north. What about it?"

He spoke in English, and for once his guess was a good one, for the man answered with only a slight French accent. "But yes, M'sieu there are battlefields up there. Linge—Schratsmenele—very heavy fighting."

Pagan glanced at Baron. "We shall have to have a look at this."

Baron nodded. "But I expect there will be nothing to be seen," he objected. "They will have tidied it all up like the Somme—corn growing and new concrete houses."

The man shook his head vigorously. "No corn. No houses. All rocks. Too high." He held his arms wide apart. "Big abris—yes! Trenches, entanglements—yes!" He nodded again emphatically.

"Probably he is right," said Pagan. "It must be a good three thousand feet up. The land would be useless for cultivation and therefore it would be worth nobody's while to tidy it."

"Yes, but I know what you are like, Charles, once you get exploring on old bits of the line. We shall probably not get in till midnight."

The little man took up the word midnight. Night was a bad time to be on the battlefields, he said. He strongly advised them to be clear of the line before dark.

Pagan nodded. "And so we shall," he said. "My companion here, who has been crossed in love, exaggerates. And anyway we shall not break our necks falling into trenches or tear our innards out on the wire; we are used to that sort of thing."

But he did not mean that, the man said. They were battlefields, he explained. Many men had died there. And he shivered with pretended fear.

"Oh, I get you," said Pagan. "The very witching time of night when churchyards yawn and graves give up their dead!"

Baron laughed. "Spooks are about the only thing I'm *not* afraid of on a battlefield," he grinned. "Anyway we thank you for your warning."

The man raised his hat and continued on his way. Baron looked at Pagan. "Well, what about it, Charles?"

Pagan nodded. "I think so. A mysterious inn; now a haunted battlefield. Oh yes, I think so."

It was hot work trudging up the bare hill-side, but although the lone tree was now hidden by the convex curve of the ground, Pagan led straight towards it across the short, dry slippery grass. Behind them across the valley other and higher peaks appeared behind the hills that had ringed the sky at the inn. Pagan was ahead, and presently he pointed to a shallow, circular, weedgrown depression in the grass. "Shellhole," he grunted.

"Feels quite like home," murmured Baron.

As they toiled up the crest the dead tree came again into view, and with an entirely new vista. This bare hummock, which had towered above the inn and seemed to be the highest point of the encircling hills, was now seen to be but the lower end of a sickle-shaped ridge whose northern extremity rose another five or six hundred feet. The western side of this ridge descended as a bare grassy slope to a saddle between the hills—that which they had crossed in the murk and rain of the previous evening—but on the eastern side the ground dropped steeply and was covered with the bare shivered poles of a dead pine forest. Some hundred yards below them a narrow white road mounted this tormented slope, following the hollow curve of the ridge, and disappeared northwards over a col by a square blotch which Baron's binoculars revealed as a military cemetery.

Baron pulled out his map and looked around him. Through the tangle of trenches, brambles, boulders and wire that covered the crest there was no path, and the going would be difficult if not impossible. "*Passage interdit*, as the French say," he remarked. "The obvious thing is to get down to that road which looks as though it would take us bang through the whole bag of tricks." He consulted the map. "If we go back a bit round the shoulder of this hill and keep well to the left we ought to strike it."

They went back round the shoulder of the hill, crossed a col between grassy humps and found themselves upon the road. To the right the ground dropped several hundreds of feet to the head waters of a stream: to the left it rose steeply to the ragged sky-line of the ridge; and the whole mountain side from valley to crest was a wilderness of boulders, brambles, splintered branches and shivered tree trunks, furrowed with mouldering and half-obliterated trenches.

The road itself, mounting steeply through this devastation, was littered with fragments of dead wood, scraps of rusty wire, and twisted sheets of galvanised iron that were as full of holes as a cullender; and every few yards along the steep weed-grown bank to the left gaped the black entrance of a dug-out. In many of these time had rotted the supporting props and the great roofs of three and four layers of trunks and sandbags, crowned by a flourishing crop of grass and purple weed, hung aslant or had been precipitated half way across the road.

But many of the dug-outs, built with German thoroughness of reinforced concrete, looked as strong as on the day they were made; and clambering over the mounds of rubble and debris that blocked the entrance, Pagan and Baron found them occupied by broken frame wire netting bunks, rusty tins and rubbish. And on the battered slope above them also, projecting here and there from the young undergrowth, were the weed-grown sandbags and rotting logs of other dug-outs.

"By gad, I would like to explore this place," exclaimed Pagan. "But it would take a month. There must be thousands of cubby holes up there hidden under the weeds and debris."

They tramped on and reached the high-perched cemetery with its orderly rows of little wooden crosses. Here the narrow road turned to the left round the shoulder of the highest point of the ridge, and a narrow track led over this hump which rose another fifty feet above them.

By silent consent they took this track, which conforming to the windings of an old weed-grown communicating trench a yard or two to the right, brought them to the razor-edged summit of the ridge. Just over the crest, among the litter of dead-splintered wood, grey boulders, tangled wire and flourishing weeds, ran an old fire trench. It had been practically hewn out of the rock; for in most places the covering earth was not more than a foot deep, and here and there natural traverses had been formed by taking advantage of the big outcrops of bare rock. A little further down the slope beyond the loose rock parapet of this grim looking trench, the rusty protecting wire showed like a foul web among the long grass and weeds; and beyond that again was more wire and the ragged weed-grown parapet of another trench.

"That must be the old French line," said Baron. "And this solid stone arrangement the Bosche. As usual he had the advantage of ground and observation. And what observation!"

Indeed, from both aesthetic and military standpoints the view was magnificent. Every movement of the French must have been visible from this trench, and they could hardly have brought a man up that slope to their front line except under cover of darkness. Hills and valleys and woods stretched in a grand panorama before them; and behind them stretched the hills and valleys again, topped in the distance, beyond the invisible Rhine, by the purple line of the Black Forest.

"So if Brother Bosche was homesick he could sit up here and see his precious fatherland," commented Pagan. "Bit of an improvement upon the delightful scenery of the Salient, what!"

They followed the track along the ridge to the cliff edge of a quarry where the fire trench ended with an immensely strong concrete pill-box that commanded magnificent views in every direction. Roughly hewn steps led down to the quarry, on the far side of which ran the remains of a French trench.

"This must have been a sticky spot," said Pagan as he stood among the tangles of rusty wire on the quarry floor looking up at the precipitous steps and the frowning pill-box. "One can just imagine a dark night and half a dozen stout fellows with blackened faces creeping out from the trench through this wire and up those ramshackle steps in single file. Then one fellow loosens a bit of stone with his foot. Down it rolls. Up goes a Bosche light and then . . .! Yes, quite a health resort this must have been."

Beyond the quarry was a saddle in the ridge where the lines, French and German, approached each other and intermingled in a hopeless confusion of shell holes, half obliterated trenches, wisps of rusty wire and splintered tree trunks. Battered steel helmets lay here and there and the bent and rusted metal parts of rifles and equipment.

Pagan looked around him with raised eyebrows. "This is obviously where the French attacked to get observation on the other side of the ridge," he said. "Once more unto the breach, dear friends, once more, or close the wall up with your Gallic dead! And then of course the Bosche counter-attacked—and judging by the state of the ground, there must have been two performances nightly and the usual matinées. Nice cheery little spot!"

Baron nodded. "Very!" he agreed. "Well, which way now?"

The path along the crest had now brought them almost three quarters of the way back towards the lone tree at the southern end of the ridge; and on the opposite side of the saddle they were again faced by that trackless jungle of boulders, old trenches and tree stumps. On the French side of the ridge, however, the ground descended as a steepish grassy slope to a broad depression or col, through which ran a narrow track, and peeping above a grassy contour to the left were the chimneys and gable end of a house.

"That must be our mysterious inn," said Baron. "And that track down there must be the one we came along last night, little dreaming that this bit of the line was above us hidden by the clouds and rain."

Pagan nodded. "I had not realised that Bertha's pub was so close to this old trench system."

"And yet it must have stood all through the war," said Baron. "It is certainly older than that, though the roof looks like a recent addition. The contour of the ground must have saved it. Probably the Bosche couldn't lob a shell into just that spot."

"Or he had a pal living there," put in Pagan grimly. "You remember the miraculous escape of the château at Suzanne. That was German owned, I've heard."

Baron nodded. "Yes, that was certainly a sticky business."

"Well, what do we do now?" asked Pagan. "You are navigating officer for the day. Function as requisite."

Baron sat down and lugged out a map. "If we carry on as we originally intended, the only thing is to drop down to that track and so back past the Poilu's Rest or whatever Bertha calls her pub. But now that we are on top of the hill it seems a pity to go down. Possibly we might get across to Kaisersburg without having to climb any more."

"I don't give a hoot what way we go so long as you bring us to within reasonable distance of food at lunch time," Pagan told him.

Baron pulled out Bertha's packet of sandwiches. "Here, have a go at those. I never knew such a fellow for thinking about his belly. And with a view like this round you too!"

Pagan munched the sandwiches appreciatively. "The view is excellent," he agreed. "And so is the grub. I am nourishing both body and mind while you work out the march tables." He waved a half-eaten sandwich emphatically. "But mind there is a pub at the end of it. My heart is in the café there with lager, and journeys end in lovers' meetings."

Presently Baron folded up the map and struggled to his feet. "When you have finished hogging it we will start. I have worked out quite a good route."

"But are you sure that there is a lunch at the end of it?" persisted Pagan.

Baron sighed and reopened the map with an air of over-taxed patience. "We shall lunch by a lake," he said slowly and distinctly. "A shining blue lake."

"And very nice too—as far as it goes," conceded Pagan. "But you don't expect me to drink lake water, do you?"

Baron prodded the map with his finger. "Read!" he commanded.

Pagan put on an imaginary pair of glasses and read slowly, letter by letter, "A . . . u . . . b."

"Exactly! Auberge," retorted Baron. "Estaminet, albergo, inn, tavern, hostel, pot-house, bar or pub!"

"Why, so it is!" exclaimed Pagan in tones of mock astonishment. "What a thing it is to have the gift of tongues!"

Baron stuffed the map back into his pocket. "Well, are you ready?"

Pagan picked up his stick and sloped arms with it in military fashion. "Lead on, Macduff, and damned be he that first cries, 'Hold enough'."

They went back along the ridge northwards. It was hot going in the sun over the rough, broken ground, but they soon left the tortured earth and debris of the battlefield behind them. The path descended gently along the flank of a steep, wooded hill. It was cool and quiet beneath the trees, and although their feet made no sound on the carpet of pine needles which covered the track, their voices rang out clearly as though in a church. Lizards and occasionally a grass snake scuttled from their path, and to the left down cathedral-like vistas between the tall straight trunks they caught glimpses of the blue mirror surface of the lake that lay in the bottom of a deep green bowl, formed by the encircling wooded hills.

Their path emerged from the forest as a grassy track slanting round the green inner side of the bowl, and now close below them lay the lake, mirroring on its placid surface the sunlit grass and woods and clear blue sky. The track curved down to the level of the water where a dam of mellow stone, built across the narrow valley outlet, formed a terrace, with the lake on one hand and the bush bordered and boulder-strewn bed of a mountain torrent on the other. A narrow rustic bridge led from the track to the terrace, and beneath it the outflow of the lake slid green and glassy to cascade in a white foaming plume to the rocky bed of the torrent. Beneath the trees beyond the terrace stood a long, low, one storey building.

"Auberge, albergo, inn," said Baron laconically.

"Denoting lunch, lager and a luscious loaf," crooned Pagan as he leant on the low stone parapet and gazed into the greeny blue waters of the lake. "Do you know, Baron, I believe I should look rather well in a Beret—suit my manly bronze and military moustache—what!"

Baron leant on the parapet and found that their heads and shoulders were reflected in the calm water. "You are getting vain in your old age, Charles," he said. "But if you want to make yourself look like a Boulogne tripper, I really don't see why you should not."

They crossed the dam towards the auberge to find the long public-room crowded with feeding boy scouts whose bivouacs could be seen among the trees on the hillside above them. However, there was a bleached, weather-worn table beneath the trees outside, and here iced bock was brought to them as a preliminary of the meal. They dumped their packs on the bench and stretched their legs beneath the table.

The meal was excellent, and the landlord himself came to pass the time of day with them. Baron mentioned that they had just come down from the old battlefield, and added with a grin that they had not visited it at night.

"No," answered the man seriously, it was better not to be there at night.

"That's just what a fellow told us whom we met on the way up," said Baron. "In fact he warned us against it."

The man nodded. Pagan took a draught from his tall glass. "As *homme* to *homme*," he said. "What is it that is queer about this bloomin' battlefield?"

The man slightly lifted his shoulders. "*On dit, on dit*," he began. "They say that strange things are seen there at night."

"But what kind of things?" persisted Pagan.

The man spread out his hands in a French gesture and pursed up his lips. "Who shall say? I have not been there myself."

"But people will always say that an old battlefield is haunted—civilians at any rate," scoffed Baron. "But you— you have been a soldier I suspect; you don't believe this battlefield is haunted. You would go there any time?"

The man smiled. "I do not go to the battlefields," he said. "I have seen more than enough of battlefields."

"So have I," agreed Baron heartily. "But you would go if you had to?"

"If I had to go," answered the man, "I should go—but in daylight. Why not? In the army I have learnt—and you too, M'sieu, I expect have learnt—not to seek trouble. I do not believe every foolish tale I hear, M'sieu, nor do I scoff at anything just because it is strange. We in Europe are very clever, no doubt, but we do not yet know everything."

"In other words, there are more things in heaven and earth than are dreamed of in your philosophy, Baron," said Pagan.

As they shouldered their packs and again took the road Baron said, "Queer thing about this battlefield, Charles, but I believe mine host of the Poilu's Rest up there is at the bottom of it."

"How do you mean?" asked Pagan.

"Why, you remember what I said about the political business—some sort of secret Bolshy club that meets at the auberge. Well, probably they have had meetings up there on the old battlefield nearby, and it's their forms slinking about in the dark that has given rise to this haunted rumour. And probably they have encouraged the idea and played up to it in order to keep people out of the way."

"Sounds plausible enough, but it doesn't explain that thing I saw on the hillside."

Baron glanced sideways at Pagan. "But, my dear old Charles," he said, "you are not seriously going to maintain that missing link stuff, surely! A figure crouching in a bush at night, and clouds scurrying across the moon and throwing running shadows—I ask you! Why, you remember the queer tricks the Very lights used to play with objects out in no-man's-land. And that night at the pub, the conditions were much the same."

"But pardon me, thou bleeding piece of earth, it was bright moonlight for a few seconds, and I saw quite clearly."

"Then, my dear old Charles, you ought to have your eyes seen to."

"There is nothing wrong with my eyes," retorted Pagan. "They are better than yours and always have been."

"Well, are they?" queried Baron.

"Are they, my dear old son of an unbeliever! You know damn well they are. Weren't your field glasses in the old days eight mags? And hadn't I a pair of twelves? And there wasn't another fellow in the battalion who could use 'em. Are my eyes better than yours, forsooth!"

"All right, all right, I surrender," cried Baron. "They are. All I say is they must be so damn good that you saw something that wasn't there!"

"Anyway, I saw it," retorted Pagan. "Whereas you didn't see a chair that was there, and blundered over it—twice!"

"And if I do it the third time it's mine for keeps," grinned Baron. "It's too hot to argue, anyway."

The little valley they were following curved suddenly to the left between steep wooded slopes and began to descend rapidly. The brook gurgled noisily over the pebbles and hurled itself in a series of foaming cascades over a dozen rocky outcrops. But the narrow road continued its more gentle descent. It parted company with the rocky valley bed and slanted along the swelling flank of the hill which began to increase its distance from its wooded neighbour opposite. The valley widened rapidly and disclosed ahead a high wooded barrier of hills that proved to be the further rampart of a bigger, transverse valley, of which their own was but a tributary.

The narrow hill-carved road wound round the great green bastion that separated the lesser from the greater valley. A rank of feathery mountain ash protected its outer margin from the steep descent, and above the dusty wayfarers, great clusters of scarlet berries hung gala-like against the deep blue sky. Just below them in the valley ran a white, tree-bordered road with a broad shallow stream beside it. Beyond the road was a single line railway. Their own narrow road slanted down to join the valley where a double row of red-roofed, yellow-washed cottages formed a village. Behind them distantly among the hills sounded the whistle of an engine.

Pagan stopped dramatically, and seized Baron's arm. "Hark! Did you hear that?"

"Having the regulation number of ears, I did," said Baron. "A train."

"Where does this line go to?" asked Pagan.

"It runs down the valley to Colmar."

"Through Kaisersburg?"

"Yes."

"Well, my bold bad Baron, there you are!"

Baron gave a hitch to his pack. "Look here, Charles, I thought this was to be a walking tour."

"So it is," retorted Pagan. "But we are not walking round the world."

"Slackening of moral fibre, Charles."

Pagan scoffed. "Here we are," he cried, "two old crocks of the Great Fracas trudging down a mountain side on our flat feet, all hot and bothered, and a hell of a way to go; and along comes a perfectly good train at the right time and in the right direction—I ask you! And you look this gift horse in the boiler."

"Lead us not into temptation!" murmured Baron piously.

"You old Puritan!" exclaimed Pagan in disgust. "Ye gods, I believe you would call it temptation if you found yourself alone on a desert island with the Queen of Sheba!"

"No, Charles," grinned Baron. "That would be providence."

The little train puffed into view up the valley as they reached level ground on the white dusty road between the cottages. Pagan cast a thirsty look on the lime-washed front of an estaminet as they hurried past, but the fussy whistling of the engine was rapidly approaching and the little station was the other end of the village.

They sprinted the last fifty yards and boarded the train as it began to move again. Pagan dumped his rucksack on the seat beside him and lighted his pipe with an air of content. He nodded towards the dusty white road that ran beside the railway. "And you are the chap who would rather be legging it out there in the sun!"

Baron was leaning upon the rail of the little observation platform at the end of the coach. He turned his head and answered grudgingly, "I'm not denying that it's pleasant loafing here. Only I have a conscience."

Pagan threw back his head and blew a cloud of smoke upwards. "Thus conscience does make cowards of us all!" he complained. "I like loafing here in the sun while the engine does the work, and I am not ashamed to own it."

Baron glanced at his watch. "Well then, you can loaf right on into Colmar," he retorted; "and pick up our letters and washing. You will be able to get back in time for dinner. I will drop off at Kaisersburg and fix up at the hotel; it's called de la Cigogne according to the book of words."

"Right 'o!" agreed Pagan cheerfully. "I will fetch your little shirt and vest for you. Anything to encourage cleanliness, which is the nearest you will ever get to godliness."

CHAPTER FOUR

Outside the station at Colmar the afternoon sun beat down upon the white shuttered buildings that bordered the dusty road. The scalloped fringe of the green and white striped awning of the Café de la Gare hung motionless in the dry still air, and the aloes in their little green painted tubs threw hard brittle shadows upon the hot pavements. In the shade of the awning the white napkin of a waiter moved unhurriedly among the little tables.

Pagan yawned and glanced at his watch. In the station facing him across the sun-parched road an invisible engine was moving with slow, stertorous puffs, as though overcome by the heat. His train was not due to leave for a quarter of an hour, but on such an afternoon he would not take the risk of having to hurry. He picked up his hat and parcel of washing and stepped out into the sunlight. From a distance came indistinctly the strains of a quick-march played by a French bugle band. He crossed the road slowly and mounted the steps of the station. It was hot beneath the misty glass roof, but the subway was cool, and the far platform from which his train left was shaded and open to the air of either side. A number of passengers were already darting to and fro as though they had not a moment to lose, although the engine was not yet coupled to the train.

Pagan sauntered slowly up the long platform. Ahead of him a girl was talking to a porter. It was her voice that first attracted his attention, a low, clear, melodious voice speaking excellent French with a slow drawl and a slight English accent. From the voice he was led to take stock of the girl herself. She had her back to him. She was dressed in a simple coat and skirt, but it was beautifully tailored and fitted her like a glove; and he noted that the whole effect was right, absolutely right, from the close fitting little hat to the sheeny silk stockings and the trim shoes that were neither too-high-heeled and impractical nor too serviceable and dull. He was unable to see her face, but without staring too rudely he was able to catch a glimpse of it as he passed. That, too, was quite right, more right if possible than the clothes and the voice.

Half-unconsciously he slowed his steps and allowed the girl and her porter to pass him. Up the platform they went in single file, like figures on a nursery frieze: first the blue-bloused porter, short, fat and rubicund, carrying a morocco-leather dressing case; next came the girl, dainty and slim, moving with easy grace, her scarf ends fluttering behind her elbows; and then Pagan, a clean, well-knit figure in blue collar and grey lounge suit, walking with a slow, easy stride.

The short, plump porter passed along two-thirds of the length of the train, and then suddenly swung himself by the handrail up the two steep steps to the coach. He turned in the doorway to put a plump hand under the girl's elbow as she followed him nimbly, though of necessity displaying for a second, from ankle to knee, a very shapely leg. Pagan swung himself up slowly after her and followed at a discreet distance along the corridor where the motes hung like gauze in the sunshine.

Apparently she had reserved a seat, for her plump little porter, with much puffing and blowing, put his head into each compartment; and each time that he did so, the little procession came to a halt from front to rear in succession like a string of freight trucks, so that Pagan, taken at first by surprise, found his nose all but pressed against a close fitting little hat, and his mouth tantalisingly close to the nape of the neck that showed below it.

Presently, however, the porter announced the end of his quest by a Gallic click of the tongue and swung the dressing case on to the rack above a corner seat on the corridor side. The procession had, perforce, to halt once more, and Pagan, peering through the window as the girl stood in the doorway with her back to him, noted with amused disgust that all the seats in that compartment were taken. Before he could pass on to another compartment, however, the plump form of the porter backed out and blocked the corridor so that he had to wait whilst the girl took money from her bag for a tip; but she did not even glance at him, and only when the grateful porter, bowing and backing, bumped into him and filled the corridor with hearty deep-voiced apologies did her grave grey eyes rest for a moment on his.

In the next compartment he found a vacant corner seat, also on the corridor side, and he put his parcel on the rack and sat down.

He was amused at his own behaviour. "Charles Pagan," he said to himself severely, "here you are, a hardy old bachelor of some thirty odd summers, behaving like a callow schoolboy. Admittedly the girl is very pretty and chic and interesting looking, but you are no longer a susceptible youth and you are decidedly old enough to know better. I hope you are properly ashamed of yourself." And having decided half-heartedly that he was, he pulled an English newspaper from his pocket and settled down to read.

But not for long. He noticed that the windows of the corridor with the dark station behind them acted as mirrors, and that reflected in one of them was the provoking little hat and profile of the girl in the next compartment. And even as he made this discovery she left the compartment and climbed down to the platform. He put down his paper and went out into the corridor. With his elbows on the open window he watched her disappear among the crowd which had just descended from an incoming train.

He turned back to the corridor again. From where he stood he could see into her compartment. The morocco-leather dressing case reposed upon the rack above her vacant seat. The other seats were taken by some French children and a governess who were at the moment in the corridor staring out of the windows.

It was then that an idea came to him, an idea that caused his tanned face to crease into a grin as he eyed the dressing case upon the rack and the empty rack above the corresponding seat in his own compartment. Yes, it really was a masterpiece of strategy, he decided. And ridiculously easy. People returning to their seats past empty compartments usually identified their own particular compartments by their luggage. All he had to do was to move the dressing case from its present position and place it upon the rack above the vacant seat opposite his own in the next compartment.

The children and their governess were still gazing out of the corridor windows. It should be quite simple. "There comes a tide in the affairs of men," he murmured, and stepped into the compartment. The leather dressing case lay on the rack on a level with his face. A small label was tied loosely to one of the rings of the handle, the writing uppermost. "Clare Lindsey. Colmar via Paris and Strasbourg," he read. He liked the name Clare. It suited her, he thought. He swung the dressing case from the rack and turned quickly to the corridor, so quickly that he pulled up only just in time to avoid running full tilt into the plump, rubicund porter who stood there.

Now no hearty apologies came from the man. He made no attempt to move out of the way. For a moment neither moved nor spoke. They regarded one another in silence. In Pagan's eyes was startled surprise; in the porter's the unwinking stare of flouted authority. Then the man's eyes went down to the dressing case which he himself had placed upon the rack. He looked again directly at Pagan. "Is that your bag?" It was a challenge rather than a question.

Pagan smiled. "Is it mine?" he echoed amiably. He glanced down at it whilst visions of a French prison floated before his eyes. "Well, yes—in a way."

The porter folded his arms across his huge chest and nodded his head slowly. His voice was ominously quiet. "You assert that the bag belongs to you?"

Pagan maintained his air of innocence. "Yes—er—in a way."

The porter's eyebrows went up, and he pursed his thick lips. "So! A bag like that! Chic—petite—the bag of a demoiselle!"

Pagan smiled amiably. "It is true it belongs to a lady," he said. "To Mademoiselle Lindsey, but er . . ." The porter broke in with, "*Bon*! To the English Mademoiselle. *Bon*!" And then he added in tones threateningly polite. "And yet it belongs to M'sieu—in a way!"

Pagan nodded. "Yes. Mademoiselle—er—Clare, you understand, is my fiancée, and so well—what belongs to her, belongs to me," he ended triumphantly.

The man's conviction was shaken. It showed in his eyes, though the severity of his manner did not relax. Pagan was quick to follow up his advantage.

"We quarrelled, you understand, Mademoiselle Clare and I," he went on glibly. "A lover's quarrel. She would not allow me to explain. You, M'sieu, no doubt know how unreasonable are women. But in a train *tête-à-tête!*" He waved his disengaged hand towards the compartment behind him. "In a train one could talk, explain, is it not so? But her compartment is full. It is necessary for me to go to the next one in which there are empty seats." He waved his hand towards it, and went on in his literally translated French. "But will she come? No. But then I have an idea, a truly wave of the brain." He lifted the leather dressing case and patted it with his hand. "I put her bag on the rack opposite my seat. *Violà!* When she come back, she sit there, is it not so?"

The man was smiling now. Pagan had won. And he followed up his advantage by digging the porter familiarly in the ribs. "A good idea, my old one, is it not so!"

The man chuckled. "A good stratagem, M'sieu!" he boomed as his hand closed over the note that was pressed into it. He touched his cap. "*Merci bien!*" And he turned away chuckling, "*Un bon stratagème!*"

Pagan heaved a sigh of relief and picked up the dressing case which he had put down during the latter part of his romantic explanation; but as he turned again into the corridor, the outer door facing him opened and the girl herself climbed up. And her face as she rose above the level of the corridor almost touched the distinctive morocco leather dressing case which Pagan held in his right hand. Her eyes went down to it and travelled back to Pagan's face. "That is my bag you have," she said.

Pagan took off his hat with his left hand and nodded. "Yes, I know," he said cheerfully "And your porter very nearly arrested me for stealing it."

Her face gave no clue to her thoughts; only her eyes were calmly judicial. "You were not going to steal it then?"

Pagan shook his head vigorously. "Oh no," he laughed. "I was only going to put it on the rack in the next compartment."

Her brows met in a little frown of perplexity which Pagan found very charming. "I am afraid I don't understand the object of this—er—porterage," she said coldly.

Pagan smiled whimsically. "Well, you see, it was a brain wave of mine which your confounded porter upset. I thought you would come along, see your bag on the rack in the next compartment, and sit down there without realising that it *was* the next compartment."

Her eyes were still hostile, but a shade less so than at first he thought. "And why was I to sit in the next compartment when I had chosen this one?" she asked.

Pagan smiled engagingly. "Well, all the other seats here are taken by children, and I mean to say, children can be an awful curse on a journey—especially French kids. Whereas next door it's much nicer—no crowd—only one other person besides myself. I thought it was a jolly good idea," he confessed.

"Rather an impudent one, don't you think?" she asked coldly. But Pagan thought he detected a covert gleam of amusement in her steady grey eyes. "And I have only your word for it that you are not a thief. Do you expect me to believe you?"

"Well, the porter did," he answered blandly.

"So you told the porter this ridiculous story too!"

"Well, it wasn't quite the same story," confessed Pagan cautiously.

"Oh!" Suspicion awoke again in her eyes. "The whole story is all lies then!"

"Oh no, no," answered Pagan in tones of injured innocence. "What I told you is the truth—honour bright." He nodded his head earnestly.

"Then if the story you told the porter was different it must have been untrue," she persisted.

Pagan produced an expressive French gesture. "Well, I mean to say, he turned up in the doorway so sudden like that I was all taken aback. Is this a porter I see before me the handle towards my hand, sort of thing. I ask you—one minute there was nothing, and the next—well, there he was—all pink and peevish. I hadn't time to hoik old mother Truth out of her well. Lies come so much more readily in a crisis, don't you think?" he asked agreeably.

She did not venture an opinion upon that point. "What *did* you tell the porter?" she demanded.

For a moment Pagan hesitated. "Well, as a matter of fact, he asked me if it was my bag."

"Rather an awkward question," she commented.

"Yes; that was what I thought," agreed Pagan. "So I said, yes, it was—in a way."

Her eyebrows went up. "In a way! In what way, pray?"

"That was just what he wanted to know," answered Pagan dryly.

"Well?" she asked when he did not continue. "What did you tell him?"

"I . . . er . . . I persuaded him that it was mine—in a way."

Her brows contracted in that look of perplexity that he had previously admired. "You persuaded him that the bag was yours?" she echoed. "Why, he put it on the rack for me himself!"

Pagan nodded. "I know. It was rather a good effort on my part," he chuckled.

"What did you tell him?" she asked firmly.

Pagan looked embarrassed. "I ... er ... I ... well I proved it to him by logic, you know."

"What did you say?" she demanded.

Pagan regarded his finger nails solemnly and shot a covert half-comic look at her from under his lowered eyebrows. "I ... er ... well, as a matter of fact, I told him that you were my fiancée."

"What!"

"And therefore what was yours, was mine—in a way. Quite a brain wave—what! And," he went on quickly as she started to speak, "I said we had quarrelled, and I was going to put the bag in my compartment, so that I could explain and make it up. He was awfully taken with the idea. He called it a bon stratagem. I think it really was rather a good one, don't you?" he suggested modestly.

She was choking either with indignation or amusement; Pagan was not sure which. "Rather cheek on my part, I know," he murmured, "but you see I had to tell him something."

"*Rather* cheek!" she gasped. "Well! And what on earth made you think of saying such—such an impertinent thing?"

"Oh ... er ... I don't know. I expect the wish was father to the jolly old thought, you know."

She turned abruptly. "I think you had better put my bag on the rack," she said quietly.

Pagan put on his hat and moved towards the next compartment.

"This one," she cried firmly.

Pagan stopped. "Really? I mean to say—all those kids . . ."

"This one," she repeated firmly. "I like children."

"So do I," he agreed cheerfully. "Jolly little beggars—when they are not all smothered in jam and affection."

He put the bag on the rack, and paused with his hand on it. "You know," he said, "if that porter comes along and finds us in different compartments he will think we have quarrelled again!"

Her calm grey eyes met his. "Mr. . . . er . . ." she began.

"Pagan—Charles Pagan," he supplemented.

"Mr. Pagan," she said quietly, "in the circumstances I have treated you quite handsomely, don't you think? And now please we will consider this the end."

He raised his eyebrows and looked at her appealingly, but she met his beseeching gaze unflinchingly and nodded her head firmly. He smiled wryly. "I go and it is done," he quoted sadly. "M'selle, your bag is on the rack." He bowed and left her.

The train moved out of the station through the sunny vineyards towards the barrier of wooded hills that rose all green and golden in the afternoon sunlight. Through an ancient village at their foot it went by way of the narrow, winding main street, its bell clanging raucously and its slowly moving coaches so close to the yellow-washed walls of the gabled houses that Pagan could have rapped upon the old carved sun-bleached doors by merely putting his arm out of the window. He did not do so, however; he was too occupied in noting that the shadow of the houses enabled him again to catch provocative glimpses of the girl in the next compartment.

The reflection disappeared when the train left the narrow confines of the street and skirted the foot of a vine-terraced hill that formed one of the outlying bastions of the valley; and strong-mindedly he moved to the other side of the compartment and gazed out of the window. The train came to rest in a little tree-shaded station hard by the mellow weed grown walls of an ancient watch tower. He recognized it as belonging to the lower end of the village in which he was to spend the night, but since Baron had got out at the other little station at the upper end, he decided to do the same.

The train moved on again, puffing noisily uphill as it skirted the mouldering defensive walls of the village, and came to rest in the tiny station at the upper end. Pagan got out. He noted in passing that the girl was no longer in her compartment, and he smiled whimsically to himself as he turned on to the cobbled road into the village. It seemed likely that they would meet again, for evidently she had got out at the other station.

The combined porter, stationmaster and ticket collector informed him that the Hotel de la Cigogne was at the lower end of the village, and that he too should have got out at the previous station. He was doubly sorry that he had not done so. The village was a long one. The road twisted and turned unceasingly between the enclosing hills whose vine-terraced slopes rose close behind the ancient gables: and the round grey tower of a castle ruin perched upon a green hill shoulder appeared at times to the left above the jumbled roofs, at times to the right and at times directly ahead.

And the village itself was picturesque. Many of the houses had half-timbered upper stories with recessed balustraded balconies beneath the carved gables. Great stone arched doorways with massive timber doors gave entrance to the wine growers' cobbled courtyards, each with its ancient stone well and the pillars and carved balustrades of its wooden balconies draped in leafy vines. And all the odd shaped old chimneys were capped with a flat raised platform designed for the accommodation of storks' nests.

He crossed the boulder-littered bed of a stream by a fortified bridge with high loop-holed parapets and a fire step for archers, and found himself suddenly in a narrow cobbled square facing the church, whose tall, dome-capped tower rose tawny gold against the vivid green background of the vine-clad hills.

The hotel was at the lower end of the street beyond the church, and he found Baron lounging by an old stone well in the tiny tree-shaded courtyard. With him was a tall, slim, handsome youth dressed in plus fours and a pullover. Pagan planked the parcel down on the worn stone lip of the well.

"There is your clean bib and tucker," he said as he flopped into a chair. "And now for the love ye bear me, bring hither a drink cool as a cucumber and long as a loofah."

"This is Cecil Lindsey," said Baron, indicating the tall youth. "Charles Pagan—a thirsty soul as you have probably gathered from his shrieks for nourishment."

The tall youth nodded languidly without removing his hands from his pockets.

"As cold waters in a thirsty land, so is good beer in a far country," murmured Pagan. "You are not tramping up these awful hills, I hope."

"He is roaming round in a car," said Baron.

Pagan nodded approvingly. "Oh wise young man; how I do envy thee! Baron thinks it's virtuous to walk, even when there is a perfectly good train going the same way. But I am like you: I consider that a seven horsepower Austin is better than a two footpower Pagan any day—especially on an alleged holiday."

"You are dropping bricks, Charles," warned Baron. "Cecil runs a Bentley—about two squadron power."

"And this is not really a holiday," added the youth. "I have to see people in this part of the country on behalf of my firm; but I am taking a few days off to show my sister round."

Pagan merely nodded his head and said nothing, but he regarded the youth with sudden interest over the top of his glass.

"Anything interesting in Colmar, Charles?" asked Baron.

Pagan regarded his glass with a whimsical smile. "No—not now," he answered enigmatically.

Out of the corner of his eye he saw that a girl with a book under her arm had come out of the low arched doorway of the hotel. She wore no hat and was dressed in a light-coloured frock, but that peculiar air of grooming and daintiness was unmistakable.

Baron turned his head and saw her. "Hullo, Clare!" he cried. "My fellow hobo has returned. This is Charles Pagan—who helped me to win the Great War."

Pagan rose with a twinkle in his eye and bowed.

"But we have already met," she exclaimed in her low clear voice, as she held her hand. "Mr. Pagan was good enough to help me with my luggage at Colmar."

"I am glad you were useful if not ornamental, Charles," commented Baron.

Pagan smiled with becoming modesty. "It was really nothing," he murmured magnanimously.

"The stupidity of a porter," explained Clare with a twinkle.

"A little explanation put it right," added Pagan with a grin.

Baron guffawed. "What, in your 'no bon compree' French! Clare was pulling your leg, Charles. She speaks the lingo like a native."

Clare sat down in one of the deck chairs. "Dicky, you exaggerate," she admonished. And then with a glance at Pagan. "I assure you Mr. Pagan's French is equal to any emergency."

"Charles is equal to anything so long as it is talking and not working," agreed Baron.

Pagan changed the subject. "That libellous remark," he complained, "is because I insisted on taking a train this afternoon instead of walking. But I put it to you, Miss Lindsey, as one doomed for a certain term to walk this earth, that when a man has borne the heat and burden of the day down an exceeding high mountain and he arrives at a perfectly good station, who, I ask you would fardels bear to grunt and sweat another weary mile?"

"We are supposed to be on a walking tour," growled Baron.

"But Mr. Pagan prefers to sleep in hotels and take trains?" smiled Clare.

"Certainly," agreed Pagan stoutly. "Certainly—if there happens to be a train going the same way or an hotel in the dusky offing. Otherwise we go carolling along the highways of France like twin Tetrazzinis and lay our little heads in sleep beneath a simple bush."

Baron snorted.

"It sounds very romantic but terribly rheumatic," exclaimed Clare. "Where did you sleep last night—under a hedge or at the village inn?"

"At an inn—a strange and lonely inn!" cried Pagan in a stage whisper.

"Part of the night within the inn; most of the night without the inn," put in Baron.

"A most mysterious inn," continued Pagan.

"That's why we spent most of the night outside it—trying to solve the mystery," explained Baron.

"Look here," said Pagan sternly. "Am you telling this 'ere story or are I?"

"But you, my dear Charles, quoth he politely."

"Then there is no need for you to broadcast a running commentary," growled Pagan.

"Don't quarrel," admonished Clare severely.

"That will be the end of our running commentary," announced Pagan. "And Baron's Court is now closing down."

"And now we are taking you over to Pagan's restaurant to listen to dance music . . ." began Baron.

"Somebody kick that fellow in the stomach," commanded Pagan.

"Meanwhile I am dying to hear about this mysterious inn," sighed Clare.

"You shall," asserted Pagan with a fierce look at Baron. "Friends, Romans, countrymen, lend me your ears. It was a dark and stormy night upon the Caucasus."

"Vosges," corrected Baron.

"Vosges. Darkness was falling, rain was falling . . ."

"The barometer was falling," suggested Baron.

Pagan continued in tones of burlesque tragedy. "Upon a lonely mountain top thousands of feet above the sea, foot-sore, fed-up and far from home we were tramping through the night."

"Left, right; right, left; left, right," chanted Baron.

"We weren't fox-trotting you idiot," growled Pagan. "Mountains to right of us, mountains to left of us—invisible in the darkness. Minutes passed. Hours passed. A light appeared ahead. Was it a mirage of the desert or a miasma of the mountains? No. A shadowy building took shape in the gloom—an inn, dark and shuttered."

"Then the light was a miasma after all!" commented Baron.

Pagan ignored the interruption. "We rapped upon the door. It was opened a fraction of an inch and a voice, a woman's voice, demanded our business. I answered boldly that we were travellers in a strange land and craved a morsel of food, a mouthful of water and somewhere to lay our heads. She who had opened the door, one Bertha by name, provided all three."

"My dear Charles, we didn't lay our heads on Bertha," protested Baron.

"Provided all three," repeated Pagan firmly. "Though somewhat reluctantly I thought. We ate our morsel of food, drank our mouthful of water."

"Tasting slightly of bock," put in Baron.

"And went to our simple rooms—I to sleep, that knits up the ravelled sleave of care; he of the guilty conscience to brood upon a mis-spent youth. Wearying anon of this melancholy watch, he bethinks him of the map and the morrow's journey. But the map is downstairs in the pocket of my coat, which, because of its exceeding dampness, Bertha dries for us before the fire. He turns the handle of his door. It will not open. He tries mine; that, too, will not open. They are locked." He flung out his hands in an exaggerated gesture.

"Locked!" exclaimed Clare.

"Ay, lady, 'twas my word. Both locked—on the outside."

"That was strange," she said.

"Passing strange," agreed Pagan.

"And what did you do?"

"Do? Well, believing that there is some soul of goodness in things evil would men observingly distil it out, I restrained his vulgar impetuosity which would have broken open the door, and have alarmed the gentle Bertha and her sire. I decided to match cunning with cunning; to get a secret glimpse of the mysterious something that was evidently going on downstairs. In brief, we knotted the bell-pulls and curtain ropes together and climbed out of the window."

"Well?" asked Clare when Pagan paused. "What did you see?"

"Nothing, absolutely nothing," complained Baron. "The window blinds were all drawn so closely that we could not see in."

"But how terribly tiresome," exclaimed Clare.

"Terribly—we spent the night wandering about in the dark when we might have been in our little warm beds," growled Baron disgustedly.

"You forget the figure on the hillside," said Pagan soberly.

Baron shrugged his shoulders. Clare looked from one to the other. "Tell me about it," she said.

"Oh, Charles swears he saw a figure on the hillside. It had a queer face or no face at all according to him; but then Charles has a wonderful imagination."

She looked at Pagan. "I know that," she said with a ghost of a smile.

"Anyway," broke in Pagan, our doors were locked there was no imagination about that. And this morning when we started off again, the first thing we discovered was a haunted battlefield."

"Haunted! How did you know it was haunted?" she exclaimed.

"We had it on the word of two independent witnesses, both of whom warned us not to go there at night."

"And did you see the haunting, whatever it is?"

"No. Apparently it walks only at night. We were there this morning. But if you are interested in battlefields, it's quite a good specimen. And, mark you, within a stone's throw of our mysterious inn."

Clare nodded her small head seriously. "That certainly is an interesting coincidence," she said. "Of course you think that there is some connection between the two."

"Maybe," answered Pagan. "Anyway Baron has a theory—a poor thing, but his own."

She turned to Baron. "What is your bright idea, Dicky?"

"Not very bright, I'm afraid," said Baron. "But it explains the facts. It occurred to me that the existence of a secret political club, meeting at the inn, would account for our locked doors. You see, the landlord was obviously a Bosche—decent enough fellow to be sure, but almost certainly he was fighting on the other side in the war."

"But surely that does not prove anything," she objected. "All the Alsatians had to, whether they liked it or not. Though quite a number used to migrate to France, I believe, in order to avoid military service in the German army. I thought they were delighted to be under French rule again."

"They were pro-French before the war, I agree," said Baron. "But, like the Irish, they are always agin the government, I fancy. And many of them are pro-German now. You see, the Alsatian is an independent sort of cove.

He has been so chivied about between the two of them that at rock bottom he is neither really French nor really German: he is just Alsatian. And he is up against French or German, whichever happens to be top dog at the moment. And in these peaceful little villages there is a good deal of political intrigue going on *sub rosa*, I suspect. Don't you agree, Charles?"

"Well, methought yon landlord had a lean and hungry look, certainly," agreed Pagan.

"It sounds terribly plausible," said Clare. "You are depressingly matter of fact, Dicky, aren't you? Destroying all the spookiness and mystery!"

"He has the soul of a film magnate," said Pagan. "Fit only for treasons, stratagems and spoils."

At this moment a short, wiry little man wearing a chauffeur's cap came round the well and spoke to young Cecil Lindsey.

Baron stared at him for a moment, and then hastened towards him. "Gosh, it's Griffin!" he exclaimed.

The little man turned his head, and a broad grin overspread his face as his eyes met Baron's. He clicked his heels and saluted in military fashion.

"Well, well, Griffin," said Baron as they shook hands, "what on earth are you doing here? How often did I hear you say in the old days that if ever you got out of the army and out of France it would take a mighty big war to bring you back again! And here you are!"

The little man grinned. "What I always says, sir, is it's a pore heart what never rejoices. So when Miss Clare, that's the pore Captain's lady, comes along and says, 'Griffin,' she says, ''ow'd you like to drive a car for my brother?' I says, 'You jes try me, Miss,' 'me being on the dole at the time. And then Mr. Cecil, he says, 'Griffin,' he says, 'we're going to France.' And I ses, very good, so long as it's understood that I'm nootral in case we run across a war."

Clare made room for Pagan on the seat beside her. "Those two will talk war now for the next three hours. Griffin is always cursing the war and everything French, but Cecil said that when they came through Picardy he could hardly tear him away from the battlefields. I suppose you and Dicky are the same. Is that why you came here for a holiday?"

Pagan shook his head. "We discovered that battlefield up there by accident," he said. "And in any case Baron and I didn't function as far south as this. No, I have always wanted to see Alsace. One of the spots that have always appealed to me, you know—historic meeting place of square-headed Bosche and cheery old Gaul and all that. I saw the old Belgiques enter Brussels and I would have given a good bit to have been with the *poilus* when they ambled into Strasbourg."

"Yes. That must have been a great moment," she agreed.

"Like the finale of a cinema epic," he suggested.

She nodded her small, sleek head at him. "I'm glad that you are not too terribly modern to admit that you like that sort of thing," she said.

Pagan assumed an expression of alarm. "Am I being horribly old-fashioned then?"

"Not only old-fashioned but positively degenerate," she smiled. "Don't they tell us that patriotism and nationality are the root of all our evils!"

Pagan grinned. "Oh, you mean those coves who wax sentimental over an unwashed Hottentot but are not above hanging their relations on the nearest lamp-post! Oh yes, I admit I'm old-fashioned. If it comes to a scrap I'd sooner bash a Bashi Bazook than the local butcher any day."

"And you have a sneaking liking for dramatic pageantry?"

"Well, I mean to say, this country is simply made for it. Strasbourg itself and these old villages with their walls and towers and storks' nests. Anything might happen in them."

She gazed thoughtfully up the little street. "I wonder," she murmured.

"You wait till you have seen them," said Pagan. "This is only one. But there are dozens."

"I must certainly see some of them. Cecil is taking me up to Munster the day after to-morrow, and to-morrow if he can spare the time, we thought of going to Riquewihr—it's quite close, I believe."

"Quite," agreed Pagan fishing the map from his pocket. "And as a matter of fact," he fibbed, "Baron and I thought of going there to-morrow." He glanced at the map. "It is only in the next valley, and there is a track through the woods over the hill between. It ought to take"—he made a rapid calculation—"take—no more than a couple of hours or so. Lunch there; then saunter back. So if your brother cannot manage it, old Baron and I would be delighted . . ."

"What will I be delighted about?" demanded Baron breaking suddenly into the conversation.

Pagan kicked him surreptitiously on the leg. "Why, if Miss Lindsey will come with us to-morrow. I was just telling her that we had arranged to walk to Riquewihr to-morrow, and apparently she was thinking of doing the same. But her brother is a doubtful starter."

Baron looked at Pagan with a face like wood. "Did we say we were going to Riquewihr to-morrow?" he asked innocently.

Pagan delivered another surreptitious kick. "Of course we did," he cried heartily. "Don't you remember I said it would only take about a couple of hours and we could lunch there and stroll back afterwards."

"It seems highly probable that you mentioned lunch somewhere," conceded Baron. And then he added with a grin, "but highly improbable that you suggested walking anywhere."

"But what else would one do?" demanded Pagan. "These lovely woods and hills!"

Baron turned to Clare. "Charles is a great lover of nature. You would hardly believe it, but I have known him lie for hours out-of-doors on sunny afternoons, so rapt with nature that even his pipe has gone out. But come with us by all means; and there is one thing I can promise you: that so long as Charles is with us we shall get a good lunch. He loves nature in all her moods."

CHAPTER FIVE

I

PAGAN and Baron dawdled over their coffee that evening in the little outdoor restaurant of the hotel. It stood at the lower end of the street where the hills swept outwards to the fertile Alsatian plain in two castle-crowned bastions. It was little more than an auberge in spite of the faded gothic letters on its whitewashed gable-end vaunting it as the "Hotel de la Cigogne"; and it encroached upon the road at right-angles, so that, from their little table under the faded striped awning, they looked westwards straight up the cobbled street to the sun that was sinking slowly behind the thickly wooded hills.

Placed thus, the little outdoor restaurant of the Hotel de la Cigogne, separated from the street only by low, white, wooden palings, allowed its diners to share the life of the village. White fowls clucked soothingly while one ate, and craned their necks between the palings to peck at crumbs from the tables. Ducks waddled over the cobbles and squatted in the open culvert.

A cock was perched importantly upon the running board of a car which stood incongruously among the broad vine leaves that twined about the carved wood pillars of a sun-bleached balcony. A clumsy open framework waggon rumbled slowly and inevitably over the cobbles; beside it trudged a bony peasant from the vineyards, corduroys and battered hat all vivid green from the copper vine spray.

Pagan watched it idly. "Nice girl, Clare," he said irrelevantly.

Baron blew a cloud of smoke from his pipe and grunted.

"Rather a supercilious young pup, her brother though," added Pagan.

"Bit of a young cub," agreed Baron.

Pagan eyed an ancient dame wearing the black Alsatian head-dress, who was waddling towards the church. "You and Clare seem pretty matey. Known her long?"

"Since '17," grunted Baron. He took his pipe from his mouth and glanced at Pagan. "You find her worth looking at Charles, eh?"

Pagan pulled his pipe from his pocket and regarded the stork's nest that was perched like a Tartar cap on top of a peaked gable. "Well, I would rather look at her than at you," he answered guardedly.

Baron chuckled. "Yes, old Clare is certainly worth looking at," he agreed. "But you ought to have seen her in the bad old days of the great fracas when she was only seventeen. She was one of the seven wonders of the Great War." He tapped out his pipe and refilled it thoughtfully. "I hope you are not going to fall for her, old Charles—because, well you see, Clare is not the marrying sort."

Pagan laughed. "Neither am I," he said. "Still," he added a moment later, "she is a woman, therefore may be woo'd!"

"Wooed—but not won," corrected Baron. He shifted his pipe to the other side of his mouth. "You never knew Vigers, did you?"

Pagan shook his head. "Heard of him though. He got a V. C. or something, didn't he?"

Baron nodded. "He commanded a company in the battalion I went to at the end of '17 when I came out of hospital after that knock I got with the old battalion."

"Oh yes, I had forgotten that," said Pagan. "Let's see, where were we then?"

"Up at Arras. Our Lewis guns were in. I got my knock just after that trench raid when poor old G. B. came over and scuppered a lot of A Company."

"By Jove, yes—though we didn't know it at the time. Well, about Vigers—he was in this new push you went to?"

Baron nodded. "Yes, he was a dashed good soldier—rather G. B.'s type. And an artistic sort of cove too. He used to carve all sorts of gadgets out of lumps of chalk. Things were pretty quiet just then and it passed the time away. Why, I remember he carved a wonderful Norman arch round the doorway of the mess dug-out—you know, one of those recessed arrangements, all columns and zig-zags. Of course Jerry plastered it with whizz-bang splinters a few days later and we called it Pip-squeak Priory. However . . .

"Well, it was through Vigers I met Clare. If Clare is a sort of Anglicized version of Helen of Troy, Roger Vigers was her opposite number. But mind you, there was nothing of the kinky-haired flappers' delight about him. He was the finest-looking fellow I have seen, and of those who knew him, man or woman, I have yet to meet one that did not agree. And he was as fine a fellow as he looked." He struck a match and held it to the bowl of his pipe. "Clare and he made as good a pair as one could wish to see in a long day's march. Why I have seen a whole ball-room of people stand and stare, band and all, when they came in together."

Pagan nodded. "I can well believe it," he said.

"Well, as I was saying, Clare and Roger made a useful pair, and of course they agreed to make a match of it. It was at the beginning of '18, on Vigers' last leave that they fixed it up and became formally engaged. Then came the big Bosche attack of March when poor old Roger went west." Baron knocked out his pipe and refilled it thoughtfully.

"I shall not forget that show in a hurry. And I think that about the most vivid memory I have of that hectic morning is of my runner stumbling round a traverse with the news that Roger was mortally hit. That was the third officer within an hour, and it left me alone with the company. Later on, as what was left of us went back through the mist, I saw him for a moment in an old sand pit. Funny how some things stand out after all these years and others leave no trace! I can see that sand pit now, with the mist rolling over the edge like smoke. Wounded were being hurried back on stretchers and ground sheets, and I asked old Mac-Morland, our M. O., if Roger were there. He pointed to a crumpled figure covered with a greatcoat. 'Is he alive?' I asked. 'Just,' he answered. 'But he can't live, and he wouldn't want to if he could.'"

Baron stirred the cold dregs in his coffee cup absent-mindedly. "I knew that Clare would take it badly. She would not make a fuss—she is not that sort—but it would hit her hard. And it did. She was little more than a child in those days, and the years that followed have added, if anything, to her good looks. But although there have been men by the dozen who would have given their eyes to marry her, she has sent them all packing. She and Cecil are orphans, you know, but she has enough to live upon—a couple of hundred of her own and four hundred that old Roger left her. Anyway she won't have any of them. She is waiting, I fancy, for another like Roger: but there never will be another like Roger, and she must know it. But it has become a sort of religion with her now, if you know what I mean. Roger is her man, and she is his woman—and there it is."

Pagan nodded as he tapped his pipe upon the white palings. "Sort of wedded to his memory, eh! Poor kid! Still it seems rather a pity."

Baron shrugged his shoulders. "Women are like that," he said.

Pagan nodded. He watched an old peasant tether a cow by a halter to a ring outside the little *debit du tabac*. "I wondered," he said, after a moment, "whether—well, whether there was ever anything between you and Clare."

Baron laughed, and shook his head. "Good lord, no! I had other fish to fry—only it didn't fry."

"What young . . .?"

"Yes. Young Gurney's sister."

"Sorry, old thing."

"Not a bit. That's all finished with. No, Clare and I are just good friends. You see, I was rather a pal of Roger's—I was going to be their best man, in fact. I form a sort of link with him, that's all."

Pagan nodded. "And this comic chauffeur cove—where does he come in?" he asked presently.

"Griffin? Oh, Griffin was Vigers' servant. He had a bad time after he was demobilized, and apparently Clare ran across him by accident one day and signed him on as chauffeur to young Cecil. Quite a good chap; though as a matter of fact she would stump up half her kingdom to anyone who claimed to be a friend of Roger's."

Pagan rubbed the back of his neck. "She appears to be what you call a whole hogger," he commented. "Vigers was a lucky fellow."

Baron knocked the ashes from his pipe. "Yes, I suppose he was," he murmured. "He must have found life pretty good—while it lasted."

II

Young Cecil decided that he was too busy to go to Riquewihr, but Clare, Pagan and Baron set out soon after breakfast. Baron had the map and acted as guide, and he led them down a narrow cobbled alley between overhanging timbered houses to the bank of the boulder-strewn stream. They climbed the hillside in single file by a narrow path among the vineyards and passed around the back of the castle ruin. Baron halted by a sun blistered notice-board that stood beside the track.

"Put that pipe out, Charles," he cried sternly. "Or you will have all Alsace in a blaze."

Pagan, with his large briar pipe jutting from his teeth, and his hat cocked over one eye surveyed the notice which said that smoking was dangerous and forbidden. "I don't read French very well," he remarked innocently.

"Don't be a fool, Charles," protested Baron. "They probably use some inflammable stuff to spray the vines with."

"On the other hand, bold Baron, it's probably just eye-wash—the notice, I mean; not the spray."

Baron appealed to Clare. "Clare. Will you please make Charles behave. He'd smoke a pipe in heaven and strike matches on his harp if one let him."

Pagan cocked an eye at her appealingly. She smiled at him from under her close-fitting little hat as she leant upon her stick. She was very graceful, from her small dark head to her small well-shod feet. "Well, Dicky," she said in her slow, attractive drawl, "I was rather hoping that I myself might be allowed an occasional cigarette in heaven." Pagan grinned triumphantly. "But," she went on, "since it says that smoking is forbidden—and dangerous . . ."

Pagan removed his pipe from his teeth and eyed the nicely glowing bowl with a look of comic resignation. "Parting is such sweet sorrow," he murmured. "And to think that I had toyed with the idea of becoming a toiler in a vineyard—now it will have to be hops!"

Presently, however, they reached the shade of the woods, and Pagan was able to relight his pipe.

Two hours later they emerged from the woods on the other side of the hill to find themselves upon a narrow, white, grass-bordered road that followed the windings of a narrow valley. Close ahead the road passed under an old stone, gable-topped gateway, which, with its abutting walls, blocked the valley. At intervals above the walls rose low, brown, sandstone towers gable-topped and crumbling with age. The projecting rusty spikes of a portcullis cut across the segment of the arch under which the road ran, and on the worn stone of the low tower above was carved a coat of arms between two long arrow slits. Beyond the first arched gateway was a second with a lofty tower above, gable-topped and shingled, and surmounted by an alarm bell under a high peaked canopy.

"It is nice to think," remarked Pagan as they stood in the small walled rectangle between the two gate towers, "that if Baron's disreputable ancestors came down from the hills for a bit of sport and plunder in this village, they were unlikely to get away with it."

The outer or valley side of the lofty dolder was of plain red sandstone blocks pierced only by two long arrow slits and a large clock dial, placed there evidently for the benefit of the workers in the vineyards beyond the walls; but this frowning severity was relieved on the inner or village side by four wood and plaster storeys, black and white magpie pattern, each storey projecting a little beyond the one below it and the whole forming a kind of long panel let into the rough red sandstone wall of the tower. Immediately they passed beneath this arch they were in the main street of the little town.

"This is where I take over," said Pagan as they walked down the sloping cobbled roadway between old steep gabled houses whose chimneys were fitted with the inevitable stork's nest contraptions.

"Good!" said Baron. And then he added in a low voice to Clare. "Old Charles has got his work cut out. There does not seem to be anything in the way of a restaurant here."

Pagan strode along confidently, and presently he halted before an ancient lime-washed house which had before it a little cobbled terrace raised a few feet above the level of the sloping street. Low, white, blistered palings bordered the tiny terrace, which was furnished with a green bench and a table. One of the lower windows of the cottage displayed a few apples and some bottles of mineral waters.

Pagan mounted the worn steps and waved a hand towards the wooden bench. "*Asseyez-vous* and make your miserable lives happy," he said, "while I find the head waiter."

The place seemed unpromising enough, but Pagan's voice, which came to them through the open window as he chatted with Madame in that inimitable way of his that always worked miracles with the peasant women of France, sounded satisfied; and Baron assured Clare that in the matter of nourishment he was content to trust Pagan to the end of time.

The trust was not misplaced. A child of less than twelve years of age, dressed in a pink pinafore, spread a much darned but spotless white cloth upon the old, sun-bleached table. Madame herself followed with a large steaming bowl of appetizing soup, and there in the shade of the old gable house while the sunlight danced on the brimming surface of the ancient stone fountain opposite they ate what was unanimously voted to be an excellent meal. They even had the gratification of watching the purchase of one course of it by a smaller child in a smaller pink pinafore at the little butcher's shop across the street; and the butcher himself, knife in hand, came to the window and inspected them over his glasses before making the decisive cut.

"One, two—three nests!" counted Clare as her eyes roved over the alp-like skyline of ancient shingled gables above which the big black busby-like shapes of storks' nests showed against the sky. "What a lovely lot!"

Pagan eyed one of the macross the top of his iced drink. "The place is so stiff with them," he declared, "that I should not be surprised any morning to wake up and find twins on my pillow."

Clare laughed. "But that would be too terribly embarrassing," she said. "They would be almost as difficult to dispose of as the 'body'."

"I know," agreed Pagan gloomily. "I suppose I would have to shin up one of these pepper-box roofs and shove 'em back in the nest when nobody was looking."

"Anyway, that fellow seems to recognize you, Charles," grinned Baron nodding towards the absurd angular shape of a stork that was now silhouetted against the sky above one of the nests. The curious clacking of its long beak sounded clearly above the clucking of several hens in the roadway.

"What an eerie sound that is!" exclaimed Clare.

Baron dropped a neat spiral of apple peel upon his plate. "Something of that sort is probably the secret of our haunted battlefield," he remarked. "Anyway, storks are lucky; though I don't know whether haunted battlefields are. What do you say, Madame?"

Clare translated the conversation into French to Madame who was removing the debris of the feast. Madame shook her head emphatically. No, it was not lucky to see a spectre.

"Well, we haven't actually seen the spectre," laughed Baron. "We were up there yesterday in daylight—though Pagan here saw a—a thing—one always calls it a 'thing,' it sounds so much more ghostly—anyway whatever it was, it hadn't a face or was deficient in some important point according to him."

Madame's face had grown grave. "The apparition has appeared to M'sieu?" she questioned seriously. "On the old battlefield?"

"Well it wasn't actually on the old battlefield," corrected Pagan, "but it was pretty near it—the night before last."

Baron smiled at her solemn face. "Don't tell me," he cried in mock alarm, "that it's unlucky!"

"M'sieu has seen it once only?" she queried.

"Why what happens if he sees it more than once?" chaffed Baron.

"It is an omen of death," answered Madame seriously. "But M'sieu has seen it once only, is it not so? But yes, that is not so bad," she added more cheerfully. "It is when it appears the third time that it is serious. Then one dies within the week."

"Nice, cheery old dame!" commented Pagan when she had gone. But his face was thoughtful.

"It is all rot," asserted Baron. "And this proves it. She has got it all wrong. Her apparition violates all the laws of . . . well conducted ghosts. I have heard of apparitions haunting particular places and therefore appearing to anyone who happened to visit those places; and I have heard of apparitions—private spooks mostly—whose appearance foretells disaster or death to members of a particular family. The one is a sort of robot ghost, tied to a particular spot, that does his two performances nightly or whatever it is, and if you visit that spot at the proper time you see him, and if you don't, you don't; whereas the other is a much more intelligent cove who appears only at intervals for a particular purpose to particular people. Distance doesn't worry him: if he has something unpleasant to tell you, he will turn up all right whether you happen to be in Timbuctoo or Tooting. Now this vision of the Vosges does a bit of both, which is absurd—and against trade union rules. He warns people of their impending death and yet is tied down to one place, and a place, mark you, where visitors average about two per year. He has got to work in his three appearances and yet he can't leave his pitch! Of course it simply can't be done. And all the authority

Madame can give us for this is a rambling yarn about an old fellow who used to pinch firewood from the battlefield, saw the ghost—and after the third appearance fell down his staircase one dark night and broke his neck. I ask you!"

Pagan's face, however, was still serious and thoughtful, and Clare added her word of encouragement to Baron's. "I agree with you, Dicky," she said. "I really do not think that Mr. Pagan need make his will on account of such an inconsistent apparition."

"For this relief much thanks," laughed Pagan. "If Baron's ghost lore is sound, all I have to do is to keep away from that battlefield. But as a matter of fact I have every intention of visiting Bertha's pub again if I get the chance—and the battlefield. It interests me."

CHAPTER SIX

I

CLARE and Cecil departed the next morning in their car for Munster, and Pagan and Baron moved down to Colmar. They made a tour of inspection of the ancient town, called for their suitcases, which had been forwarded from Strasbourg, dined to music at the open restaurant in the Champs-de-Mars, and finished up at the theatre. The next morning, however, when the question of staying longer in Colmar was raised, they both voted against doing so.

"These old towns are delightful for a couple of days," said Baron, "but we came here to tramp the highways and hedges of the Vosges, and the sooner we get back to them the better, I say."

"O Baron, you have put into the poetry of words the secret thoughts of my heart," agreed Pagan. "But where shall we go? That is the question as laddie Hamlet said. High or low?"

"High," decided Baron.

Pagan lugged a map from his pocket. "Good. Your lightest wish is my command. High it shall be; silent upon a peak in Darien you shall sit." He studied the map. "We will go right up to the high ridge that forms the backbone of these blithering hills. There is a pass almost due west of us—the Honneck; that's where we will go."

"How far? How long?" asked Baron.

"A longish way on foot," answered Pagan, "but we can train part of the way—the uninteresting bit—as far as Munster; stay there the night and tramp over the ridge to-morrow."

Baron shot a shrewd look at Pagan. "Why Munster?" he enquired.

"Because, my dear old question mark," retorted Pagan, "we can't get to where we want to go without going through it. We can't tramp the Honneck in one day; therefore we must stop the night somewhere. And so it sticks out a mile that the thing to do is to train to Munster and tramp on to-morrow. You see, it lies bang in the middle of the hills where two valleys meet, and the main road up to the Honneck over the Schlucht Pass goes through it and up the northern valley."

Baron nodded agreement, but there was a sceptical twinkle in his eye. "All right, Charles. Your logic is almost too good to be true."

"And I don't know whether you realize it," added Pagan. "But the ridge immediately to the north is the one on which Bertha's pub stands; in fact they must have been the lights of Munster that we saw far below when we climbed out of that window."

Baron smiled at Pagan's earnestness. "And at what hour departs the train?" he asked.

"We pack kits and entrain forthwith," answered Pagan.

As the little train drew clear of the town they had a fine view westwards of the Vosges stretching in a purple barrier from north to south as far as the eye could see. The lower slopes, trenched with green valleys, encroached upon the fertile plain in humped wooded bastions, crowned with the brown crumbling walls of ancient castles; and in the valley mouths lay the old fortified villages, their walls and watch towers and high peaked roofs all golden in the morning sunlight.

Meandering inconsequently, it seemed, through sunny vineyards, the little train rounded the foot of a vine-terraced hill and bumped to rest at a tiny tree-shaded platform. Beyond it the sun-bleached walls and projecting angle towers of a small village nestled at the foot of a wooded slope. Gay wild flowers grew between the stones; moss and lichens patterned the mellow tiles on the peaked roofs of the towers, and a dry moat, carpeted with grass and gay with flower beds, encircled the walls. A shady avenue, crossing the moat by a balustraded causeway, led from the tiny station to the old portcullised gate tower, which was crowned by the inevitable stork's nest.

"*Mon cher, Seigneur,*" chanted Pagan in his best French. "*Voilà un nid!*"

"*C'est vrai, mon cher Mécréant,*" answered Baron; "*mais il n'y a pas des oiseaux.*"

But as the engine began to move again and float little balloons of smoke into the clear bright air, the two birds whirred overhead with a slow, strong beating of wings, turned into the wind like homing aeroplanes, and glided down to the nest.

The little train puffed its way laboriously up the valley. The hills closed in upon it and the vine-terraced slopes gave place to thick green woods. The hills grew higher and steeper, and up tributary valleys they caught glimpses of the bold, bare summits of the higher peaks beyond.

They reached Munster a little after midday. It lay in a natural amphitheatre where four valleys met. High wooded hills surrounded it, and behind them towered the bare, grassy *ballons*. Baron nodded upwards towards the great rampart of hills facing them as they walked slowly up the broad shady boulevard from the station. "There's our old friend the tree," he said.

Thick woods covered the lower slopes of the steep mountain wall that rose close beyond the outskirts of the little town, but the upper flanks were bare and grass-grown, and at one point where a huge grassy shoulder raised itself above the general level of the ridge, the familiar outline of a shell-shivered tree showed black against the sky, no bigger than a ragged match.

Pagan nodded. "True, o King. And that must be Bertha's Pub, two fingers left at eight o'clock," he added, indicating a brownish blur a little to the left and below the tree."

"By jove, yes," agreed Baron. "So on the whole, Charles, it is just as well that rope didn't break the other night!"

"If it had, we should have done Father Christmas down one of these chimneys all right," answered Pagan grimly.

Munster itself seemed strangely new and uninteresting till they recalled that it must have been almost entirely rebuilt, and that where they walked so calmly in the broad light of day by the clean new church, men had passed in terror of their lives, hurrying by the roofless walls only at night when the artillery observers far up there by the ragged tree were blindfolded by the darkness.

Superficially this town of clean new houses, tidy, evenly paved streets and unstained roofs was bright and prosperous; but it seemed characterless and out of place among those historic, soaring hills. It wore a tragic air of bravado, as though in spite of its bold and youthful front it was not unconscious of its past. But to Pagan and Baron, wandering sympathetically in the meaner street, it revealed the scars of that past: an old wall pock-marked fanwise by shell splinters, the blind walls of a gutted roofless house standing in a tangled garden, and some tell-tale humps in the pavé roadway where ancient shell-holes had been filled with bricks.

In the new main streets of the town the shops wore a very different air. Their windows were filled mainly with picture postcards and those numerous useless objects grouped under the general heading of novelties. Some of the locally made knick-knacks, however, were really beautifully carved, and for a few francs one could buy a stork's nest complete with father, mother and baby stork, a market woman in the wide Alsatian head-dress, or an Alsatian cottage with chimney, nest and storks on top.

Pagan was disappointed not to find Clare in the hotel. He made discreet enquiries, and learned that she had left that morning for Gerardmer, whither her brother had been called on business, but she was expected back within two days.

After dinner that evening he and Baron sauntered down to the little café by the station for coffee. It was a triangular piece of ground fenced off from the road by low wooden palings, and a few tables and chairs were set out under the half-dozen trees which were draped with coloured lights. The patron, a youngish man of military appearance wearing a beret, was an intelligent fellow, and spoke moderately good English, which he had learnt from fellow prisoners of war in a prison camp in Germany. At Pagan's invitation he joined them in a tall glass of the strong hot coffee.

All three had taken part in the Somme battles of 1916, and for a time the conversation centred around this topic. Then Baron enquired about the political sentiments of Alsace, and received confirmation of his opinion that there was considerable unrest among a minority of the population, who, it appeared, made up by their violence and the extremity of their opinions for their lack of numbers. The patron thought that an open outbreak was possible but unlikely; but were such an outbreak to occur, it might become very serious if not checked immediately, on account of its far-reaching political and international consequences.

Baron then brought up the subject of the haunted battlefield and expounded his theory that secret political meetings would account for the apparitions. But the man shook his head. There was more in it than that he thought.

Had they heard what form the apparition took? Baron admitted that their ideas on that point were distinctly hazy.

The man glanced around at his customers at the other tables and drew his chair closer. He lowered his voice. "I will tell you about it," he said. "Many people have seen this apparition, Messieurs." He held up his two hands with the fingers outspread. "Five . . . ten . . . perhaps a dozen in all. The accounts of it vary widely, as such accounts always do, but there is an agreement, very impressive, on certain points. It walks only by night. It has the body of a man and it walks upright like a human being, but there the resemblance ends. The face . . . well, the face is not human. Whether beast or devil"—he made an expressive movement with his hands—"opinions differ, but all are agreed that it is not human."

Pagan glanced at Baron, who, however, avoided his eyes. He took a gulp from his glass. "You really believe in this ghost then?"

The man laughed and waved his open palms before his face. "But, no! I do not believe in ghosts and spirits, I." And he laughed again.

Pagan stirred his glass thoughtfully. "Then you think it is all just nonsense . . . *sottise?*"

Again the man shook his head. He glanced round and drew his chair a fraction of an inch closer.

"I, I am from Bordeaux. I tell you, Messieurs, the Vosges are not like the rest of France. Strange rites were performed among these hills in days gone by—and still are, it is said. This country teems with folk lore; every valley has its own.

Strange tales of goblins, demons . . . half-men. Foolish, maybe, but there are so many of these stories and they have persisted so long that . . . well, where one finds so . . . so . . . ."

Pagan nodded. "Where there's smoke, there's fire, eh?" he suggested.

"But you said just now . . ." began Baron.

Pagan silenced him with a look. "And so you think, M'sieu," prompted Pagan, "that this . . . er strange apparition is . . . is . . .?"

The patron drained his glass. "What happened to that race of sub-men that inhabited Europe before our ancestors drove them out?" he demanded suddenly.

"Knocked on the head by our amiable ancestor, I suppose," grinned Baron. And then he added, "Good lord, Charles, he means what-you-may-call-um man—Cro-Magnon, isn't it!"

"No, they were the coves who did the knocking," replied Pagan. "It's Neanderthal man he means."

The patron nodded his head emphatically. "Yes, yes, Neanderthal. What happened to him?" He went on seriously. "I have studied history, Messieurs. Always the remnants of the early race are driven into the mountains or deserts. Your Britons in Wales, your Picts in Scotland, your Bushmen in Africa. And Neanderthal man also, yes? That is why the folk-lore of wild forests and mountains is always full of demons and half-men. And here in the Vosges, where that folk-lore persists so strongly . . ." He finished with an expressive gesture of his hands.

"Then you actually think," said Baron incredulously, "that the . . . the whatever-it-is up there is . . . is . . .?"

"A lone survival of that race, for evidences of which the scientists of all nations are hunting—and it is under their very noses," answered the man solemnly.

Pagan struck a match and held it to the glowing bowl of his pipe, but he made no comment.

As they sauntered back to the hotel Pagan said, "That's about the most amazing suggestion I have ever heard. I know that the miracles of Kew are the facts of Khatmandu and I could possibly believe in an ape-man in the dark interior of savage Papua, but in the heart of civilised Europe—in the Vosges . . . I ask you!"

"Don't ask me, old Charles," retorted Baron. "Most amazing rot I should say. But I would rather like to get to the bottom of it anyway."

Pagan nodded. "So would I." He walked on for a few steps in silence. "Suppose we put off the Honneck till another day and climb up to Bertha's pub to-morrow instead," he suggested presently.

Baron considered a moment and then he yawned. "Yes, suppose we do," he agreed.

II

In the course of the next morning Pagan discovered that the ancient motor van of a village carrier in a neighbouring valley ran into Munster every morning and returned each evening, crossing the dividing ridge by a col that was little more than a mile from Bertha's inn; and since, in his opinion, a tramp of a mile along the top of a ridge was infinitely preferable to one of three or four up the steep side of it, he contracted for the carriage that evening of himself and Baron as far as the col.

They retained their rooms at the Munster hotel for the following night and left there their suitcases and Pagan's pack, taking with them only mackintoshes and one pack containing pyjamas and washing kit. And before setting out, Pagan bought a powerful electric torch and half a kilo of candles. "They will come in handy if we go messing about dug-outs in the dark," he said as he stuffed them into the pack.

The ancient motor van proved to be an even more ramshackle affair than its unpromising appearance indicated. Broken places in the woodwork had been repaired with rough, unpainted boxwood, fastened with nails and string, and several broken or loose metal parts were held together by lengths of twisted wire. The gears rattled and scraped at every change, and the engine wheezed and knocked in a manner that raised grave doubts of its ability to mount the steep gradients ahead. The brakes doubtless were in the same crazy condition, and Baron regarded with a gloomy apprehensive eye the steep sharp zigzags by which the narrow road mounted the hillside. "If the box of loose scrap metal this optimist calls an engine conks out on one of those hairpin bends, Gawd help us!" he said gloomily.

"Amen to that," answered Pagan piously. "But you can't expect much of a ride for twelve francs, you know."

"Twelve francs!" echoed Baron. "It's rank robbery. Damn it, man, you could have bought an ounce of arsenic for five and committed suicide in comfort."

The seating accommodation was not as comfortable as they could have wished. The interior of the little van was cramped and low, and the floor space was occupied by a miscellaneous collection of packages, parcels and knobbly sacks. It is true that the carrier had arranged a plank across a couple of sacks as a seat, but the swaying of the van caused it to slide off every few minutes, and owing to the lowness of the roof and the violent jolting of the apparently springless body, they had to sit with their shoulders bowed and their necks bent forward in order to avoid bumping their heads. Finally Baron unshipped the plank in disgust and made himself a less uncomfortable seat on the floor among the sacks and packages.

His spirits rose, however, as soon as they were clear of the houses and the long steady climb upwards had begun. Uncomfortable though the floor of the van might be, it was certainly very pleasant to lie there in the cool evening air and watch the mellow sunlight gilding the great wooded mountain-side across the valley; and as the crazy vehicle twisted and turned on its tortuous path upwards his view extended now down the valley between green long-shadowed slopes, and now up the valley towards the great purple ridge behind which the sun was setting. And at the precipitous hairpin bends he caught glimpses of the town below, fast dwindling in size and already shadowed by the approaching dusk.

Pagan steadied himself on one elbow to apply a lighted match to his pipe. "Reminds one . . . of the old days . . . of lorry jumping," he murmured jerkily as he drew at the stem and the flame was sucked down to the bowl in a series of little swoops.

Baron nodded. "Do you remember the old box-body the Machine-Gun people used to take us into Amiens in?" he asked reminiscently.

Pagan pitched the burnt match over the tailboard. "The old bus Sweet Fanny Adams used to drive! Rather!" And he began to croon softly, "Pack up your troubles in your old kit bag and smile, smile, smile . . ." Baron joined in. One air led inevitably to another, and encouraged by the carrier in front, they went through their repertoire of old war songs, timing them all to the bumping of the car and the coughing and wheezing of the crazy engine.

The sun had set before they reached the top, and a bank of purple night clouds loomed dark above the ridge westwards when the narrow road finally straightened out and curved gently over the bare crest between two grassy shoulders. The carrier brought his steaming, rattling vehicle to rest. Baron threw out the mackintoshes and pack, and they climbed rather stiffly out.

The silence was almost uncanny when the van had driven off and dropped below the crest. Up there in the translucent twilight there was no sound except the distant tinkle of a cow-bell. The great vault of the sky stretched overhead and swept down, it seemed, almost beneath their feet. Westwards it was opalescent above the wine hued bank of clouds: eastwards the light had faded to a purple haze. Pale stars began to shimmer one by one.

Pagan slung the pack over one shoulder. "There's a long, long trail a-winding," he crooned, and they set off through the twilight, up the slippery grassy slope eastwards. There was no path to guide them, but they knew that somewhere ahead lay the depression down which they had tramped that first rainy night to the inn.

A cool breeze fanned their cheeks as they trudged at last over the crest; and although the last rays of colour were fast fading in the western sky behind them, there was light enough to distinguish the stark, bare stumps of the shattered wood on the sickle shaped ridge ahead.

"There's the old battlefield, anyway," said Baron. "Bertha's pub cannot be very far off now."

"Somewhere half-right, I should think," murmured Pagan with his eyes on the distant ragged stumps that showed black against the sky. "We shall see it when the next Very light goes up," he added with a chuckle.

"Shut up, Charles," growled Baron. "It's too damned like it at this hour. I swear my ears have begun to stick out in the old way, listening for the scream of a crump!"

"Funny how it all comes back to one!" exclaimed Pagan. "Half-right here, I think."

The ground sloped suddenly to a shallow, trough-shaped depression through which ran a narrow track that glimmered palely through the dusk. Baron turned down it confidently. "We know where we are now. And there's the pub," he added a moment later when the dark outline of a roof took shape against the sky. Five minutes later they were knocking at the door.

CHAPTER SEVEN

T HE door was opened by a tall clumsy youth whose big bony wrists and ankles protruded prominently beyond the limits of his rough, soiled farm clothes. He stared at them stupidly for a moment, and Pagan's exuberant French produced only a bewildered movement of his coarse, black-nailed fingers through his shock of dark hair; but as he stood just inside the doorway mumbling to himself in German, Bertha herself called from the kitchen to ask who was there.

Pagan stepped forward into the room. "Belle Bertha, Bold Baron, Charles Pagan, Old Uncle Tom Cobleigh and all!" he answered cheerfully.

Bertha appeared suddenly in the kitchen doorway, ladle in hand like an avenging goddess, but her fierce expression gave place to a slow smile when her eyes rested on Pagan standing there beneath the lamp. He dumped the pack upon the brick floor and made her a bow.

"*Bonjour*, Bertha, and likewise *guten abend*," he cried.

She dropped the ladle on a table and came forward, inclining her head to each in turn. "*Bon jour, Messieurs*," she said.

Pagan regarded her with arms akimbo. "I declare she doesn't look a day older than when last we met; does she, Baron?" he exclaimed.

"Well, you didn't expect her to have produced grey hairs and a family since Tuesday, did you!" growled Baron.

"*M'sieu dit?*" asked Bertha.

"*M'sieu dites* through his hat—*par son chapeau*," retorted Pagan. "And he's not nice to know—*nicht goot wissen*."

Baron groaned at this wholesale mutilation of three languages, but Pagan continued imperturbably, "*Mein lieber Bertha*, the question is—*le question vraiment brulante*—can you give us a meal? *Je*, I mean *moi*, and my boy friend here?"

"But yes, M'sieu, in one half hour."

"Goot! And rooms for the night?"

She nodded her head and answered in English. "Ye-es, se same two chambers."

"*Encore goot!*" exclaimed Pagan. "Bertha, your English gets better every day. Well, we will go and powder our noses—*mettre la poudre sur nos nez, vous comprenez*, while you get the meal, but mind it's a big one—*comme ca!*" He held his hands wide apart horizontally. "And big bock *aussi—comme ca*." He held them still wider apart but vertically.

The long room was empty of customers, but one of the tables was laid for one. "This pub is looking up," commented Pagan, nodding towards the table, as they mounted the stairs. "We have a guest—unless it's our friend with the mourning fingernails and the schoolboy complexion."

"What beats me," said Baron in an undertone, "is how they came up the other night and locked us in without our hearing them. Those stairs creak like the deuce."

"They may have come through one of those other doors there," said Pagan in the same low tones. "Evidently they lead to more rooms, and there may be a back staircase leading up to them."

These two other doors opened on to the indoor balcony, on that portion of it which turned at right-angles and crossed the room below like a bridge. Pagan tiptoed to the balustrade and bent over it so that he could see nearly the whole length of the long brick-floored room. "Coast is clear," he whispered. "Shall we have a look inside?"

But before Baron could reply, Pagan straightened quickly and turned the handle of his own door. "Well, here we are again," he said aloud, and then added in a whisper, "Bertha!"

Bertha came up the stairs with two steaming cans of hot water. Before leaving, she smoothed out a wrinkle in the gay patchwork counterpane on Pagan's bed and expressed the hope that he had slept well there.

"Like a log all night," he fibbed. "*Comme un grand morceau de bois!*"

She nodded her head appreciatively and eyed the huge old bed admiringly with her hands clasped before her. "*Mais oui, c'est vraiment magnifique,*" she said in an awed voice, and then hurried back to the kitchen.

Baron came in from his room next door and lounged on the bed which had so excited Bertha's admiration.

"How about having a peep at the other side of those two doors?" suggested Pagan.

Baron rested his head against the huge post at the foot of the bed and yawned. "The only thing is, Charles, that those rooms are probably occupied—or one of them at any rate. That table downstairs evidently means that there is someone else staying in the pub."

"Well, we can pretend we have made a mistake in the room," answered Pagan. "And it's a fifty-fifty chance which room he is in, anyway. You keep cave while I have a look-see."

"Right 'o," agreed Baron.

But when Pagan opened the door and stepped out on to the indoor balcony, it was to find Bertha laying a table in the room below, and they had no choice other than to walk straight downstairs. They seated themselves on the padded seat against the wall facing the staircase and ordered Martinis. The landlord himself brought the drinks and at Pagan's invitation joined them.

He seemed a simple, decent fellow, and during the conversation that was carried on in a mixture of French, English and German, both Pagan and Baron carefully avoided any reference to the real object of their return visit to the inn. The subject of the war cropped up inevitably and, as Baron had surmised, the landlord, whose name it appeared was Kleber, had served in the German Army but as a field hospital orderly. According to his own account he was pro-French, and quite satisfied with the present state of affairs, though he admitted that he had no grudge against the Germans.

"All this does not agree too well with your theory of a secret political club meeting here," Pagan remarked when Kleber had gone.

"No, it doesn't," admitted Baron. "Still, as far as these very moderate opinions of his are concerned, we have only his word for it, and if he really is a secret agitator, it is not to be expected that he would avow his real opinions to two chance strangers like ourselves."

"That's so," agreed Pagan. "Still, the fellow's appearance and manner rather support his account of himself."

"Well, what is the programme for to-night, anyway?" asked Baron.

Pagan tossed off the last of his drink. "Oh, have our meal. Keep a weather eye open meanwhile, and if nothing interesting happens we will take a stroll over the battlefield afterwards."

Presently Bertha bustled in with two large steaming bowls of soup, one of which she placed upon the table laid for one, and the other upon the table laid for Pagan and Baron. Then she retired and rang a cracked gong.

"That ghastly row is for the benefit of the other guest, I suppose," said Pagan. "I'm rather curious to see what he will be like."

"So am I," agreed Baron. "Though it is probably only another tourist on a holiday tramp."

Baron had half risen from his seat, but Pagan pulled him back again, for a door had banged on the bridge part of the balcony above their heads. They were too directly beneath it to allow them a glimpse of anyone standing there, but the remainder of the balcony, that part of it which turned at right-angles along the side wall past their own two bedroom doors to the stairs, was immediately facing them.

Footsteps sounded above their heads, and they watched that turn in the balcony beyond Baron's door with some curiosity.

Their first glimpse of the stranger was of a hand and a red and gold sleeve sliding along the top of the carved balustrade.

"It's a woman," whispered Pagan.

Then a figure came into view passing Baron's door, a graceful figure in a flimsy black frock and scarlet and gold bridge coat below a dark-dainty shingled head.

"Good lord, it's Clare!" exclaimed Baron.

At the sound of her name she turned and looked down at them. "Why it's Dicky and Mr. Pagan," she exclaimed in surprise. She paused and leant upon the balustrade. "And what, pray, are you doing here?"

"Come down, Juliet, and we will tell you," laughed Baron. "Though it seems to me a much more pertinent question is, 'What are you doing here?'"

She came down the stairs and they met her at the foot.

"Did you ever see such a person, Charles?" smiled Baron. "She comes down to dine in a lonely inn . . ."

"Upon a misty mountain top," put in Pagan.

"All togged up in fine clothes and soft raiment!" ended Baron.

"Like the lilies of the field," contributed Pagan.

"Which toil not neither do they spin," grinned Baron. "It can't be that she has designs on you or me, Charles, because she didn't know we would be here."

"Perhaps she has a secret passion for mine host, Kleber—or our awkward friend of the black fingernails," suggested Pagan.

"Perhaps it's just vanity," said Clare with a smile.

"Anyway, I think we ought to amalgamate these two tables," said Baron. "What do you say, Clare?"

"Of course," she agreed.

They transferred to their own table the knives, forks and spoons from the table laid for one. Then they sat down. Clare sat at the head with Pagan and Baron, one on each side.

"Are you here alone?" asked Baron.

Clare nodded her head. "Um-m!"

Baron assumed a severe expression. "You know, Clare, you really are the limit. You have no business to be here alone."

"Why not?" she asked innocently.

"Why not?" he echoed. "Because this lonely inn is not the sort of place any woman ought to come to alone."

"You play the heavy uncle awfully well, Dicky, but it's all right since you and Mr. Pagan are here."

"Yes, but you didn't know that when you came. Why did you come, anyway?"

"Well, you see, Mr. Pagan's account of this inn was so terribly enthralling that I simply had to come."

"Yes, but why alone?" persisted Baron.

"Because I came on the spur of the moment, and in any case Cecil would not have been interested. He was called away to Gerardmer, and I went with him, intending to return to Munster to-morrow. But Gerardmer was too terribly dull, all Rolls Royce and pretty ladies—the sort of place I loathe. And so I started back this morning, and then on the way it occurred to me to spend the night here. Griffin and I consulted the map and found that we could get the car within half a mile or so, and—well here I am."

"And where is Griffin?" asked Baron.

"Why, gone back to Munster. He is coming out for me in the morning."

"Well, at least you might have kept Griffin with you."

"Oh no, Dicky!" she exclaimed with mock horror. "People would think that I had eloped with my chauffeur!"

"Not if they saw old Griffin," said Baron. And they all laughed.

"But what are you two doing here?" she asked. "I thought you were going to Colmar."

"We did," answered Baron. "But we soon tired of the flesh pots of Egypt and yearned for the simple life."

"Baron wanted to sit on a mountain top," explained Pagan. "And so we decided to go to the Honneck."

"And we should have done so," put in Baron with a malicious twinkle. "Only Charles did the map work, and according to him we had to stay at least one night in Munster. It was rather curious because we were there last night, and if you had not gone to Gerardmer we should have all met," he added innocently.

"That would have been a pleasant coincidence," remarked Pagan unabashed. "We were going off to the Honneck this morning, but as a matter of fact, it was only when we got to Munster that we realised how close this place was, and we decided then and there to come up and have another look at it."

She nodded her small head and glanced round the long bare, brick-floored room. "I am awfully glad I came. It's so terribly primitive and brutal, like . . . like . . ."

"Hollywood's idea of Russia," suggested Pagan with a smile.

She made a little grimace. "How cynical you are! But, yes, I suppose that is what I mean. I have the quaintest old bedroom you ever saw—a wooden ceiling and a huge old bed."

Pagan nodded. "Is yours the third door along that balcony arrangement or the fourth?"

"The third."

Pagan nodded again. "We were rather interested in those two doors. In fact we would have had a peep behind them if Bertha had not appeared at the crucial moment. We wanted to know whether there were just bedrooms behind them or whether there was a back staircase leading up to this balcony."

"There may be," she said; "because I do not think that the door beyond mine leads to a room—at least not directly. I heard someone walking past my room on that side and it sounded rather like a corridor."

Baron nodded. "We must have a peep in there, Charles."

"And there is another door in my room," continued Clare.

"Leading into the corridor?" asked Pagan.

"No. It is on the other side of the room. It has a key in it but it will not open, because it opens outwards and there is something against the other side."

"The opposite side to the presumed corridor?" asked Pagan. "Is that on the left as you go in?"

Clare nodded.

Pagan turned to Baron. "Your room must be next to hers on that side. But there is no door there. By jove yes, the press! It must be behind that big press."

"That's it," agreed Baron. "You see, Clare, Charles thinks that when they locked . . ."

"Take care," whispered Pagan. "I believe that girl understands more English than we think."

Bertha had come into the room with a fresh course.

"What are you two going to do?" asked Clare when Bertha had retired again.

"We are going to take a stroll across the old battlefield," answered Baron.

"To look for the ghost?" she exclaimed.

"Well, yes, I suppose so. You see, we heard the most amazing yarn down in Munster—all rot of course. We will tell you about that later. Anyway, that's the programme."

"It is a glorious night and it will be terribly thrilling. I shall love it," she asserted.

"But you are not coming too!" protested Pagan.

"Of course I am."

"But really I don't . . . I mean to say, you never know." He turned to Baron for support.

"Why not?" asked Baron. "This Ghost business is all rot."

"But still . . ." persisted Pagan.

"You don't think I am going to stay quietly here—alone in a lonely inn," she said with a mischievous smile. "Dicky wouldn't let me, would you, Dicky?"

Baron grinned and Pagan shrugged his shoulders with a helpless gesture.

"You don't know Clare yet, Charles," said Baron. "If she has made up her mind to come, she will come, and short of physical force nothing you or I can do will stop her."

"All right then," agreed Pagan, smiling at her. "But if I were her brother I'd spank her."

"Charles means well," commented Baron with a grin.

She smiled back at Pagan. "I'm sure he does. And so as soon as we have finished this meal we put on our bonnets and shawls and walk across the battlefield."

Baron nodded. "That's the idea."

The landlord came from the other end of the room and made them a bow. He hoped the meal was to their satisfaction. They assured him it was. "A poem in proteids," Pagan told him.

The landlord smiled gravely and bowed his thanks. "There is but one thing, Messieures, Madame, that I regret," he said. "This inn, being situated as it is." He made a movement with his hands. "It is not practicable for my guests to take a walk after dinner—a thing so good for the digestion and conducive of good sleep."

Pagan glanced at Clare and kicked out at Baron's foot under the table. But he missed it, and Baron blurted cheerfully, "But that is just what we are going to do, Herr Kleber. Up over the battlefield on a fine night—what could be nicer!"

The landlord looked grave and shook his head. "It would be very dangerous, M'sieu," he said. "In the dark, one might slip into an old trench and break one's leg . . . or the roof of an old dug-out might collapse beneath one. Besides, there is much barbed wire and even unexploded bombs and shells. It is too, too dangerous, M'sieu."

Baron laughed. "It is very good of you, Herr Kleber, to be so solicitous about us, but it will not be by any means the first time that Charles Pagan and I have wandered about on a battlefield at night. And besides, we want to see the Ghost," he added recklessly.

Pagan, watching the landlord narrowly, could detect no change of expression on his face, except perhaps a slight flicker of the eyelids. The man smiled at the word ghost.

"M'sieu, who has been a soldier, does not believe the idle tales of the village folk," he said half-chaffingly. And he went on in the same joking tones. "How comes it that I, who live so close, have not seen this apparition!" And then he became serious again, and there was an underlying firmness in his tones that was half a threat despite his respectful words. "But no, M'sieu would be most unwise to go up there. And I as your host could not allow guests who have been so courteous and appreciative of the hospitality of my poor house"—here he bowed gravely to each in turn—"to go where they might come to harm. That indeed would be poor Alsatian hospitality."

Baron was about to continue the discussion, but again Pagan kicked out under the table, and this time his foot found its target.

"I agree with you, Baron, that we ought to be able to look after ourselves," he said. "But personally, I think it would be a very shabby return for all Herr Kleber's thoughtfulness if just for the sake of—well, a lark, we were to go up there and meet with an accident for which Herr Kleber would feel himself responsible. It was quite an amusing idea of yours to go up there to-night, but it really would be much more sensible to leave it till to-morrow. I vote we turn in early and make a day of it to-morrow."

"Right 'o," agreed Baron, taking the cue. "It certainly is very comfortable here. Well, Herr Kleber, we will take your advice." He turned to the others. "How about a Benedictine? Clare? Charles? Three Benedictines, Herr Kleber, please— and perhaps you will have one too."

The landlord bowed his thanks and withdrew.

"What is the great idea, Charles?" asked Baron in a low voice.

"Didn't you twig?" whispered Pagan. "These people understand English a darned sight better than we give them credit for. He must have overheard us talking about going out. That was why he brought up the subject—to put us off it. And he meant to stop us if necessary; that was why I butted in and agreed."

"But hang it, Charles, we are not going to do just what that cove tells us."

"Of course not," agreed Pagan. "But we don't want any trouble if it can be avoided, and it will be much easier to slip out if he thinks we have given up the idea."

Clare nodded agreement. "I think, Dicky, we ought to elect Mr. Pagan our leader in this adventure. Evidently he has the Sherlock Holmes complex."

"Right 'o," agreed Baron. "You propose him then."

"Proposed," from Clare.

"Seconded," from Baron.

"Carried nem. con.," smiled Clare.

"Well, Charles, you are C.O. now," said Baron with a mock salute.

"We will obey you absolutely and follow you to the death," smiled Clare.

Pagan grinned, but there was an undertone of seriousness in his voice as he looked at her and said, "Will you?"

She did not answer.

CHAPTER EIGHT

I

COFFEE was brought to them, at the more comfortable padded bench by the wall, and while they drank it and enjoyed cigarettes, the subject of their intended excursion was not mentioned. Presently, however, Pagan said in a low voice without changing his position, "Don't look round; but Kleber is going out. He put his head out of the kitchen door just now, and he had a hat and coat on. I saw him in that ghastly plush-framed mirror on the wall. We will give him ten minutes: then we'll go." He turned to Clare. "I hope you have some warm clothes and stout shoes. What you have on is simply ravishing, but it's not the regulation kit for a battlefield at night, is it, Baron? So if you really are coming, you ought to change."

Clare rose with a smile. "Captain's orders," she said.

"Now I think we are all ready," said Pagan as she disappeared up the stairs. "The torch is in the pocket of your mack, and the candles are in mine. And the macks are on the pegs over there. All I need now is a pipe." He unrolled his oilskin tobacco pouch and filled his pipe with deliberation. "You know, I'm immensely cheered up since comrade Kleber said his piece. I really believe we are on the track of something."

Baron nodded thoughtfully. "Looks like it," he admitted.

Pagan drew at his pipe and put the burnt match in the ashtray. "But I am not too happy about taking Clare with us," he said doubtfully.

Baron shrugged his shoulders. "You can't prevent it, Charles. She has made up her mind."

Pagan nodded his head gloomily. "But I never can see," he grumbled, "why just because a woman says she has made up her mind, that should be taken as ending the matter."

"I suppose it is because it usually does," suggested Baron sagely.

A few minutes later Clare came down the stairs. She was dressed in a close fitting tweed hat, a long mackintosh and brogue shoes, and she carried a walking-stick.

"We are going to have trouble with Bertha," whispered Pagan as they met at the table. "I was watching her out of the corner of my eye, and she shied like a horse when she saw you coming downstairs all dressed for going out."

He took his mackintosh from the peg and put one arm in the sleeve. Bertha came hesitatingly towards him. There was suppressed agitation in her broad placid face.

"M'sieu is going out?" she faltered.

Pagan turned to her as he struggled with the other arm in the sleeve. "Just a little walk before by-byes," he answered cheerfully. "*Pour encourager des bons rêves*."

She looked at him appealingly. "But you promised my father . . ." she began.

Pagan laughed. "Promised! Come, come, Bertha, that's a grand *mot!* Cannot we poor men change our minds sometimes like *les belles dames?*"

She did not answer, and there was no answering smile on her stubborn face.

Pagan turned to Clare and Baron. "Well, are you ready?" he asked. He moved towards the door, but Bertha was there before him, her back to it, her face white, her bosom heaving.

"You may not pass," she cried.

Pagan shot an eloquent glance at Clare and Baron, but there was only amusement in his face as he stood, hands on hips, surveying her. He shook a finger paternally. "Bertha, you're a dark horse—*un cheval noir*," he cried. "You have a lover outside that door, *n'est ce pas. Cherchez l'homme, eh!* Well, I suppose frauleins will be frauleins." He took a pace forward. "But we are not spoil-sports are we, Baron? And we will not tell pa—honour bright."

Bertha's taut expression did not relax. She flung her arms wide as though she were crucified upon the door. "You shall not pass," she repeated sullenly.

"Admirable, my dear Bertha," said Pagan with the same air of amused tolerance, "But this is not Verdun. Really ..."

"Let Clare have a go," put in Baron. "She is the linguist."

Pagan smiled at Clare. "Ask her, would you, why 'we shall not pass.'"

Clare spoke in her fluent idiomatic French, but Bertha only shook her head and repeated sullenly, "You may not pass."

"But this is preposterous," cried Baron. "Tell her, Clare, that we don't want to have to remove her by force."

Pagan shook his head. "You won't frighten Bertha," he declared.

"We will try, anyway. Tell her, Clare."

Bertha's reply was to call loudly, "Henri, Henri!"

Pagan grinned. "That will be our friend of the black fingernails," he murmured. "And I would rather tackle him than Bertha if it comes to a rough house. But we can't have that. All right, Bertha. Kamarad!" He held his hands high above his head. "You are quite safe. Baron is far too much the little gentleman to lay hands on a lady and I'm far too frightened."

"But dash it all, Charles, she has either got to get out of the way or else tell us why we may not pass," cried Baron angrily.

"I think that is only reasonable," agreed Clare.

"Look here, Bertha, we are jolly well going through that door or else . . ." began Baron.

But Pagan turned on him and snapped, "Shut up."

Baron subsided with bad grace and an eloquent shrug of his shoulders.

"But really, Mr. Pagan, I agree with Dicky that it is ridiculous that the girl should behave like this and give us no reason for it."

Pagan turned to Bertha and his voice and face expressed the same amused tolerance. "You hear, Bertha? They think that you ought to give us some reason. Won't you satisfy our curiosity? I am dying to know what is on the other side of that door."

Bertha changed neither her position nor her expression. She only shook her head.

"If it's a secret, tell me. I can keep it," he said in tones of wheedling raillery. "You people stand further off—Baron. Miss Lindsey, please." He waved his hand imperiously, and they went back in answer to his look. Then he stepped up to Bertha and put his ear close to her mouth. He was obviously playing the fool, but there was gratitude in her frightened eyes in spite of her agitated breathing. She seemed to have confidence in Pagan.

"Oh, please, please, M'sieu," she said in an agonized whisper, "make them take off their coats."

Pagan straightened himself and put a hand over his face in mock shame. "Bertha, Bertha!" he cried in shocked tones. "I would not have thought it of you. But your secret is safe with me."

"What is it?" asked Baron.

"You're too young," retorted Pagan.

"Stop rotting, Charles. What are we going to do?"

Pagan peeled off his mackintosh. "We are going to have another coffee, and then we are going up to bed," he answered as he brought his foot down gently on Baron's toe.

Clare looked rebellious, but Pagan spoke first. "Miss Lindsey," he said with a smile. "In King's Regulations there is a crime called 'dumb insolence'. If I were really your company commander you would be up at orderly room to-morrow charged with that crime."

Clare regarded him for a moment or two in silence, but his eyes did not waver nor did the look of determination that lay behind the smile. Then she grimaced and laid her stick upon the table.

"To the death," Pagan reminded her with a smile.

"At least tell us what that girl said," she retorted.

Pagan shook his head. "Obedience absolute and unquestioned," he reminded her.

Clare regarded him with rebellious eyes. "This very temporary authority seems to have gone to his head," she said coldly.

Baron guffawed, but Pagan merely smiled and bowed. He sat down. "Coffee, Bertha, Coffee bitte," he called.

Bertha, who had remained standing near the door, hesitated a moment, and then she withdrew the key from the lock and hurried to bring the coffee.

Baron grimaced. "Not taking any chances," he said. "What are we going to do, Charles?"

"Drink our coffee . . ."

"Even if we have not ordered it and do not want it?" put in Clare truculently.

Pagan turned to her with a smile. "It is not compulsory," he answered blandly, "but desirable."

Baron grinned. "Well, Charles, we are going to!"

"Drink our coffee or not as the case may be," repeated Pagan, "and then go upstairs."

"And what then? Try to slip out when Bertha is not looking or has gone to bed?"

Pagan nodded. "If we can. Meanwhile we don't talk about it, since she understands English far too well and it's rude to whisper."

They drank their coffee in silence, and then Pagan rose. "We go up now," he said. "You go first, Baron. And take your coat and mine. I will say good night to Bertha."

Baron went up the stairs. Pagan wandered down the room to where Bertha sat, her back towards them, sewing. "*At huit heures to-morrow Bertha, s'il vous plait*," he said. "I'm sorry we gave you a fright. Good night and *bon rêves*."

Bertha looked at him with gratitude in her eyes. "*Bonne nuit, M'sieu*—and thank you."

Clare said Good night from the foot of the stairs, and Baron called, "*Bon soir*, Bertha," from out of sight on the balcony.

Pagan hummed a little tune as he went up the stairs.

"Well?" asked Clare with raised eyebrows as they met outside Baron's door.

"Don't go to bed for half an hour," he whispered, and then he added aloud, "Good night."

"Good night, Clare," said Baron.

"Good night, Dicky. Good night, Mr. Pagan."

II

Baron came in to Pagan's room through the connecting door. "Well, there is one thing I am certain of at any rate," he remarked. "And that is that there is something behind all this. I very much had my doubts at first, but after Bertha's exhibition to-night, I have none—unless she has fallen for you, Charles, and is terrified that you will break your neck in the dark."

133

Pagan slowly unrolled his oilskin tobacco pouch and began to fill his pipe. "She has got the wind up all right," he said. "But not on my account."

Baron lit a cigarette. "What was it she whispered?" he asked casually.

"Them as ax no questions isn't told a lie," Pagan quoted with a grin.

"Anyway, Charles, I think you were a mug to give in so easily."

Pagan shook his head. "A desperate woman doesn't respond to argument—or force either for that matter. And she was desperate. I swear I have never seen a more perfect impersonation of an animal defending its young. Didn't you see the look in her eyes? She was scared stiff; but not for herself."

"For whom then?" asked Baron. "Kleber—her father?"

Pagan shrugged his shoulders. "That remains to be seen."

"What did she whisper, Charles?" asked Baron again.

Pagan laughed. "Why nothing, you old lout. Except to ask me to make you take your coats off; which I did— because I knew that nothing short of brute force, and a good deal of that, would get us through that door."

Baron sat down upon the bed. "There is always the window," he remarked.

Pagan held a match to his pipe. "Yes. That's why I made sure of having our coats up here."

Baron hooked his arm round the huge bedpost. "Do you think there is any chance of her going to bed and giving us a chance to slip out?"

"I doubt it. You know what these peasants are. At the best of times they don't go to bed till after midnight and are up again at four."

Baron wandered restlessly about the room. "Shall I have a peep out and see what is happening?" he asked presently.

"No harm in that," assented Pagan; and just before Baron reached the door, he added, "Bet you twenty francs it's locked."

Baron turned sharply and looked at Pagan, and then he moved quietly to the door and laid a hand upon the handle. "The young bitch!" he exclaimed. "You win, Charles."

Pagan stood up and grinned. "Just what I expected," he remarked. "And I'm rather glad in a way. It means the window now. All along I haven't been too happy about taking Clare on a stunt like this. At least the window settles that question, and I'm glad. She can't go down the rope."

Baron smiled cryptically. "You think so? By the by, Charles, I was very much amused at you treating Clare rough, so to speak. She's not used to that sort of thing."

Pagan took his pipe from his mouth and regarded the glowing bowl thoughtfully. "Um! She took it rather well on the whole, I thought."

"Very well indeed," asserted Baron. "She was half-amused and half-indignant. But, by Jove, Charles, if she hadn't liked you she would have let you have it."

Pagan stood up. "Anyway we must let her know what we are going to do and tell her she need not stay up."

Baron nodded agreement. "Yes, but how? Our bashful Bertha has probably locked my door too—and Clare's."

"That's pretty certain," agreed Pagan. "We shall have to move the press in your room, that's all."

"By Jove, yes, the door. I had forgotten. Well what about it?"

Pagan glanced at the watch on his wrist. "Yes, there's no point in keeping her up. But we must be careful not to make a row."

They went into Baron's room, and inch by inch and without noise swung the heavy press round till it stood almost at right-angles to the wall. Baron rapped softly upon the door that was disclosed behind it. The sound of movement came from the next room, and then Baron put his head close to the jamb and called softly, "Clare, Clare! You can open the door now; we have moved the press. But don't make a noise."

A key grated in the lock and the door swung slowly open. Clare's head came round the edge of the door.

"Come on," grinned Baron. "There's not much room, but you are not fat and forty yet."

Clare squeezed round between the door and the press into the room. She still wore her hat and walking shoes, but had discarded her mackintosh. Pagan pulled up a chair. She sat down and looked from one to the other. "Well?"

"Bertha has locked us in again," explained Baron. "At least she has locked Charles's door and mine, and it's a hundred to one that yours is locked as well."

"I like that girl's spirit," said Clare decisively. "But she badly wants spanking."

"Hear, hear!" agreed Baron. "Well the only way out now is by the window—the way Charles and I went last time. And so Charles has brought you in here to tell you that presently he and I are going down the rope and you . . ." he smiled knowingly at her, "you are to go to bed."

She smiled back at him amusedly and glanced at Pagan.

Pagan said, "I'm sorry, Miss Lindsey, but you see there is no other way."

"You are not sorry at all," she retorted. "You are glad."

Pagan grinned guiltily.

"You think I should be a terrible nuisance."

Pagan shook his head. "No, I don't. I'm not thinking about myself: I'm thinking about you."

"Since you are smoking in your bedroom, Dicky, I suppose I may."

"Sorry!" said Baron, and he offered her his cigarette case.

She took a cigarette and he held a match. She blew a little cloud of smoke upwards.

"Anyway, you are glad I cannot come with you," she continued to Pagan.

Pagan smiled. "Yes, I'm afraid I am."

She looked up at Baron. "He's very callow, isn't he?"

"Very," agreed Baron with a grin.

"What makes him think that I cannot come just because the door is locked?" she asked innocently.

Baron lit a cigarette. "I expect it's the rope, you know," he said confidentially as though Pagan were not within hearing. "Old Charles has early Victorian ideas about women. And a female with vapours in a crinoline would be rather a distressing sight on a rope."

"It would!" agreed Clare.

"But really," protested Pagan, "it is out of the question. You know yourself, Baron, that we didn't find it too easy getting back again and . . ."

"Don't be an ass, Charles," retorted Baron. "I have never seen Clare on a rope, but I'm willing to bet she can shin up one as fast as you or I. She has legs like us, hasn't she?"

"Really, Dicky!" protested Clare.

Baron grinned. "When I say like ours, I mean more ornamental but just as useful."

Pagan shrugged his shoulders with comic hopelessness. He looked at Clare. "You are determined to come?"

"Absolutely," she answered.

"Very well then, put on your coat while Baron and I rig up the rope."

"There is one thing about old Charles," said Baron. "He's not pig-headed: he does know when he's beaten."

"He is quite docile really," said Clare smiling at him.

They took down the bell-pulls and the curtain loops and knotted them together. Baron stood upon a chair and fastened one end to the hook above the window. They put on their mackintoshes and hats. Pagan pulled the torch from his pocket and took a last look round. "Now we are ready," he said. "Out with the light."

CHAPTER NINE

I

THEY turned out the lamps in all three rooms. Baron drew back the curtains and revealed his dark form silhouetted vaguely in the dim rectangle of the window. Pagan threw out the loose end of the rope.

"I go first," he said. "And then Miss Lindsey. Don't get on the rope till I am off it; and be very careful at the bottom. It is a steep slope and a drop that will not bear thinking about." He climbed on to the sill. "Will you be all right?" he asked.

"Quite," she assured him.

"You would not rather be tied and have us lower you?"

"Of course not," she laughed. "What a long time you take!"

He twisted his feet about the rope and lowered himself gently over the sill. Her head came out of the window above him, and as he hung just below the sill with his head thrown back, her face was close above his, so close that in spite of the darkness he could see the sparkle of her eyes.

"Do be careful," he whispered.

She nodded her small head at him. "I will. Promise," she answered.

He slid down, and at the bottom dug a foothold. Then he shook the rope gently. "All right," he called softly.

A dark shadow came over the sill, and Clare's dim form came slowly down the rope. He put an arm round her to steady her. "Don't let go the rope till your feet are firmly in the footholds I have dug," he whispered. "Then put your hands against the wall and lean inwards."

She did as he had said and moved sideways away from the rope. Baron slid down and closed up beside her. "Right 'o, Charles," he whispered. "Go ahead."

"I make the footholds," whispered Pagan to Clare. "And you step into each when I've left it. It's slow work, but we can't afford to make a mistake here. Lean well inwards all the time, and don't look behind you."

He moved off to the right, kicked a foothold, and put a hand back to Clare. "Now then—into the last one I was standing on. Have you got it? Good! Stay there while I make the next one."

Slowly, in this laborious fashion they progressed sideways and reached the end of the wall where the bank and the pailings faced them. Pagan scrambled over. "Wait," he said to Clare. Baron followed him; then they each took one of Clare's hands and bodily they swung her up and over.

"That's all right," whispered Pagan. "We are on the little terrace beside the house. Another fifty yards and we shall be clear—unless Baron kicks over a few tables and chairs as he did last time."

They stole across the terrace and climbed the palings that bordered it. Twenty yards further on they halted.

"Now then, Charles, which way? You remember the lie of the land?"

"Rather," answered Pagan. "There is a choice of two. Either to the right, round the shoulder of the hill and down on to that old road that leads up on the other side past all the dug-outs, or else keep to this side and pass over the saddle by the quarry. That would be straight ahead and then bear off to the right."

"The quarry is the nearest way to the middle of things," said Baron.

"Yes, but it's the roughest going. It is all right once we are over the saddle, but it is pretty badly ploughed up all round the quarry."

"If you are thinking of me," interposed Clare, "don't—unless I have not come up to expectations so far."

"You have been perfectly wonderful," Pagan told her. "Well, Baron, what do you think—the quarry?"

"Yes, I think so."

"Come on then."

They set off up the hill. It was tiring work trudging along in the dark over the rough grass, and on more than one occasion they nearly blundered into outcrops of rock. Distantly from far below them in the valley they heard the shrill whistle of an engine, but around them all was dark and very silent. A chill night breeze penetrated the upturned collars of their mackintoshes.

"There will be a moon later on," said Pagan, "and I wish it would hurry up. I don't want to have to use the torch and advertise our presence to half Alsace."

To the right they were aware of rising ground, a loom of concrete darkness against the obscurity of the night. Pagan peered at the faint line against the sky till his eyes ached. "I think that is the saddle half-right," he said at last. "The ground seems to dip a bit there. But we don't want to turn in too soon or we shall run into a ghastly mess up of wire and holes."

They trudged on another hundred yards, and then Pagan edged cautiously to the right. They seemed to be on a rough track which threaded a maze of shell-holes, and they moved slowly in single file, Clare in the middle. Presently a dim, ghostly light crept down the tortured ground ahead. Behind them a bright silver rim peeped above the hard black outline of a hill that had been invisible.

"The moon at last," exclaimed Pagan. "If we give him a chance to get a bit higher we shall be able to go ahead much faster."

They halted and stood close together watching the moon sail slowly above the hill-top. The chill night breeze blew in their faces.

"It is pretty cool up here," remarked Baron.

"Ay, 'tis a nipping and an eager air," said Pagan. "Forward to the breach."

They turned to find the saddle now bathed in soft silvery light. Tangles of rusty wire stood out black and web-like against the silver sheen of the grass; countless shell-holes were little pools of darkness. Shivered tree trunks stood black and silver edged upon the debris-littered slope to the right; the quarry to the left was dark and menacing, but the concrete pill-box on top shone like liquid aluminium in the moonlight. It was as though the whole immense charnel house and rubbish heap had risen dripping from a phosphorescent sea. Nothing moved: there was no sound.

Clare uttered a little gasp of dismay and clutched Pagan's arm.

"Scene, a blasted heath," he murmured grimly. "When shall we three meet again! In thunder, lightning or in rain." But he was more conscious of the pressure on his arm than of the desolation surrounding him.

Clare let fall her hand. "I did not know it would be like this," she said in an awed voice. "And so silent and still."

Pagan nodded. "I have known it almost as quiet as this in the line even during the war," he answered in a low voice. "Just such nights as this. The moon sailing away up there ... no sound. Beautiful in a way, don't you think?"

"Yes—very," she whispered. "But so ... so terribly desolate and dead." She gazed at it in silence for some moments, and then she spoke in a low voice without turning her head. "So it was like this, Dicky, where—where Roger died."

Baron stirred uncomfortably. "Well, yes—pretty much. Though the country is much flatter up there at St. Quentin, you know."

She nodded. "Yes, I saw it—last year. I thought it very desolate, but they told me it had been tidied up. Now I know what they meant. It was like this once."

"Perhaps you would rather we did not go on," suggested Baron.

"No, no," she answered hurriedly. "It's horrible, but it's fascinating too, and I am glad I have seen it. I used to picture it, you know, all those years ago—particularly at night. Now I—know."

They moved on slowly along the track in single file amid the tangles of wire, the shell-holes, the crumbling, half-filled trenches and the riven tree stumps. Often they stopped to listen, but no sound reached them except the creaking of a shivered branch in the wind or the faint squeak of rats in a mouldering trench. The moon sailed serenely above the hill-tops.

"Like being out on patrol," murmured Baron. "Just the quiet sort of night that always put the wind up me."

"It really was as quiet as this sometimes?" queried Clare.

"Almost," answered Baron. "A Very light would go up, and then you stood stock still—like this." He remained motionless in an absurd attitude. "I've seen some comic looking groups out in no-man's-land at night. But often it would be nearly as quiet as this. A low rumble north or south—distant gunfire, you know, and an occasional crack of a rifle. Then you would hear the round go whimpering down the valley perhaps, or it would ricochet off a bit of wire which would twang like a guitar. But I never liked quiet nights. I had too much imagination, I suppose. My ears used to stick out a mile listening for the guns to open up."

"Horrible!" she said. "Horrible."

They passed safely over the saddle and down to the narrow road on the other side. "Which way?" asked Baron.

"Oh up, I think," answered Pagan. "Up and round back along the top by that track that follows the old fire trench."

It was dark on that narrow road that slanted up the steep flank of the debris-littered ridge. The moon was hidden by the ridge itself, but the shivered poles of the trees on top stood out above them black and stark against the silver radiance of the sky. The deep valley to the right was a pit of inky darkness from which a bare silvery-grey summit rose island-like into the moonlight.

"These are old Bosche dug-outs on the left," remarked Baron to Clare. "Some of 'em still have names painted over the door. Lend me the torch, Charles."

Pagan handed over the torch, and Baron flashed the light upon the concrete wall of a dug-out that stood, half-overgrown with weeds beside the track.

"Would you like to peep inside?" he asked.

Clare nodded. "Yes, terribly."

"Nothing much to see, I'm afraid," he said when they stood inside and the beam of the torch revealed only bare, greeny-grey concrete walls and a heap of earth and rubbish on the floor. "Pretty mouldy now, but this must have been quite snug when it had bunks and things in it."

Clare shivered. "Is this the sort of place you used to live in, Dicky?"

"Well, hardly as palatial as this," he answered. "You see, this is a Bosche dug-out—concrete and all that. I never had the luck to run across this sort of thing on our side of the line, did you, Charles?"

"Never," asserted Pagan emphatically. "A sheet of corrugated iron and a couple of sandbags was more like it."

Clare looked round the cold bare walls. "You call this a good one?" she asked.

"Rather!" said Baron. "This would keep anything out—shells you know."

"And those you had would not?"

"Well, not many of them would keep out a direct hit, would they, Charles? I will show you the kind of thing, if I can find it. There must be some non-concrete shelters here somewhere."

"There are; I remember seeing them," said Pagan. "But unlike ours they had four or five layers of tree-trunks on top."

"Anyway, it will give Clare some idea of the kind of thing," said Baron.

"Yes, but I would be a bit careful where you go," warned Pagan. "Some of these props must be pretty rotten by now."

They left the concrete shelter and trudged on up the narrow road through the gloom. Baron peered constantly at the steep, debris-littered slope to the left for a suitable dug-out to show Clare.

"Anyway we shall have had a nice walk," he remarked, "even if the ghost doesn't function."

"We have," agreed Clare. "And the night is yet young."

"And for all we know," remarked Pagan, "the ghost—especially if he's human—may be in any one of these dug-outs."

"Here, don't you try to put the wind up me, Charles," grinned Baron.

"I'm not," retorted Pagan. "I'm merely trying to put some sense into that head of yours."

Baron suddenly halted and switched on the torch. "This looks like the very thing," he exclaimed.

The beam of light disclosed a narrow opening in the steep bank, half hidden by weeds and fallen earth, and framed by ancient sagging timbers.

"That's the sort of thing, Clare, do you see," exclaimed Baron. "No concrete or girders, but dug out with a spade and revetted with expanding metal or timber. Come along, we will have a look inside."

He bent his head and entered the low narrow passage. Clare followed and Pagan brought up the rear. The side walls were of weed grown earth, revetted here and there with damp and rotten boards. The roof was revetted with sheets of galvanized iron, supported at intervals by sagging timbers and pit props against the side walls.

The passage was about eight feet long, and at the end of it, Baron, who was a few feet ahead of Clare, stepped under a low lintel into the dug-out. "It's concrete," he exclaimed disappointedly as he swung the torch round. "Didn't Jerry ever take a chance!"

Clare stumbled over a mound of fallen earth in the passage and lurched against one of the pit props. Pagan heard the hollow sound of rotten wood cracking and felt a shower of loose earth upon his head and shoulders. He sprang forward, caught Clare beneath the arms, and swept her before him under the low lintel into the dug-out. Behind him a heavy timber cracked with a report like a gun, and the sound was followed immediately by a roar of falling earth, and then silence, absolute silence.

II

For a moment no one spoke. Then Pagan broke the tense stillness with a laugh. "Well, if Brother Bosche had only built the passage of concrete as well as the dug-out, that would not have happened," he said cheerfully.

"That's true," agreed Baron in the same cheerful tones. "He might have finished the job when he was about it. As it is we shall have to do some grubbing with our hands."

He threw the beam of the torch upon the doorway. The collapse of the passage roof had bent downwards one of the roof sheets of galvanized iron and wedged it tightly against the concrete jambs, leaving visible only an inch or two of earth at the bottom. In the dim halo of light above the clear cut beam his eyes met Pagan's eloquently.

Pagan pulled a couple of candles from his pocket. "It is lucky I brought these," he said cheerfully. "I think a light is indicated." He dug the candles into some loose earth on the floor and lighted them.

Clare had not said a word since the catastrophe. She watched the two men in silence. The candlelight revealed the dug-out as rectangular in shape, some twenty feet long by fifteen wide and seven high. The floor was littered with rubbish, and there was a wire netting bunk in one corner covered with frowsy sacking. Half way across the concrete roof there was a crack some two or three inches wide, and from it a trickle of water made a long dark stain down the side wall, and then ran across the floor to a sump pit in one corner. Pagan carelessly raised a candle to the crack, and as the flame flickered in the draught his eyes met Baron's in a meaning look. He put the candle back upon the floor.

"This is rather comic," he remarked. "We come out to catch a ghost, and we have got caught ourselves."

Clare spoke for the first time, and her voice was calm. "That sheet of corrugated iron across the door is rather unfortunate for your grubbing idea, isn't it Dicky?"

Pagan glanced at her quickly. "Well, it won't make it any easier," he admitted.

Clare looked him straight in the eyes. "In fact it makes it impossible?" she suggested.

He did not answer that question. "I think the best idea would be to wait for somebody to dig us out," he said. "We can shout through that crack in the roof."

"And you think somebody would hear?" she asked calmly.

"I can assure you," he laughed, "that when Baron and I lift our voices in song, somebody is bound to hear."

"If anybody is there," she added quietly.

"Well, not at night," he admitted. "But in the morning old Baron and I will lift the roof off! There are any number of people up here in the daytime salving wood and stuff," he fibbed cheerfully.

She did not press the question. She glanced at Baron and then said lightly, "Well, what do we do now?"

"If we had only brought a pack of cards we might have played dummy bridge," suggested Pagan cheerfully.

"Anyway we might sit down," said Baron.

They removed the frowsy sacking from the wire netting bunk and tested it. It seemed sound, and they sat down.

"Reminds one of old days, Charles, somewhere in France," said Baron.

Pagan nodded. "It does." He turned to Clare. "This must be rather thrilling to you. Do you know, I was most frightfully thrilled the first time I slept in a dug-out," he went on conversationally. "It was in a bit of the line near Fricourt that we had just taken over from the French. I had a little cubby hole dug in the side of a communicating trench about twenty yards from its junction with the fire trench. There was a bunk like this and a couple of sheets of galvanized iron and four sandbags on top." He pulled out his pipe and filled it. "But the bane of my life was a trench catapult that was in the neighbourhood. One of ours: not Jerry's. A trench catapult, you know was a contrivance that might well have formed part of Caesar's field artillery. It was just a large edition of a schoolboy's catapult—a contraption of wood and iron, and the motive force was supplied by springs wound back by a handle and released by a trigger. A grenade placed on the instrument, was, when the trigger was pressed, propelled or not, as the case might be, in the direction of the enemy's lines. I say was or was not, because instead of describing a graceful curve and alighting in the German trench, the bomb frequently dropped on the floor of the pit in which the catapult was mounted." He struck a match and puffed at his pipe. "This eccentricity of the mediaeval weapon left open only two courses to its minions: either to bolt for their lives and leave the catapult to be blown to pieces, or to pick up the bomb and hurl it out of the pit. They were stout fellows those catapultists, I will say that for them, and the absurd affection they bore their primitive weapon was equalled I think, only by my hatred of the damned thing. Anyway they invariably flung the bomb out of the pit. This no doubt was in accordance with the best traditions of the army, King's Regulations and all that, but when a man flings away a bomb that may at any moment explode and blow him to small bits, he is none too particular as to the direction in which it goes."

"I should think not!" exclaimed Clare.

"That catapult pit was behind the fire trench and close to the communicating trench in which my cubby hole lay. To their honour, be it said, they seldom flung the bomb into the fire trench, but it frequently landed in the doorway of my dug-out, and bursting bombs are much alike be they of alleged friendly or enemy origin. As I have said, my roof consisted only of a couple of sheets of galvanized iron thinly covered with earth from which a torn piece of iron protruded at one corner. Every scrap of flying metal in the neighbourhood rendezvoused on this piece, which was as full of holes as a sieve; and the violent impact of metal upon galvanized iron doesn't help one to sleep."

"That was all Charles thought about—sleep," commented Baron.

Pagan ignored the interruption. "I remonstrated with those catapultists. They were reasonable fellows and answered me with fair words. But stray bombs continued to detonate in the immediate neighbourhood of my dug-out; and so one dark night when the catapultists were snoring in their dug-out I took a sandbag full of detonated bombs to that pit and left them there under the catapult to fulfil their destiny."

"But how terribly immoral!" smiled Clare.

"Not half as immoral as their language in the morning," retorted Pagan.

A long pause followed. Clare's eyes strayed round the cold grey concrete walls of the dug-out, lit by the two candle flames. Pagan glanced covertly at his wrist watch. Baron shifted uncomfortably on the bunk. "Um yes, pity we didn't bring cards," he murmured. "Nothing much we could play here."

"Except hop-scotch," said Pagan eyeing the dusty floor.

"Hop-scotch!" exclaimed Baron. "By Jove, Charles, do you remember that game of hop-scotch we had on the Bray–Corbie road back in '16?"

Pagan nodded and signalled with his eyes for Baron to continue.

Baron cleared his throat. "That was rather amusing," he went on. "We were out on a tactical scheme, a rearguard as a matter of fact, and the chap who was supposed to be chasing us, a poisonous cove called Groucher, was slow off the mark. Anyway there we sat on the top of the ridge between the Ancre and the Somme and waited and yawned, and yawned and waited. Charles went to sleep I believe: he usually did. Anyway he woke up at last and being a resourceful cove, suggested a game of hop-scotch. I had never played this refined game before—nor have I since for that matter. Anyway, Charles showed us how to play—that is me and poor old G. B., Bretherton, who went west in '18.

"Well, there we were in a most exciting part of the game with sous all over the road and marks scraped in the dust. Suddenly along comes a car with a flag fluttering over the radiator—the Divisional General! G. B., who was one of the coolest coves I've ever met, managed to wipe out most of the marks on the road as he sprang to attention, and between the three of us we managed to cover most of the sous with our feet. But the A. D. C. spotted one, which of course Charles pocketed, though it wasn't his, and then I was thrown off my guard by the General asking some silly question or other. It was about whether one of my men could see the section he was keeping touch with, I believe. Anyway, I being full of military zeal and all that, took him along to prove to him what a clever fellow I was and what a fool he was, and left three or four sous lying on the road where I had been standing. Of course the A. D. C. being a perfect little gent., picked them up, and that fellow Charles there pockets them and with a face like wood remarks loudly to the A. D. C. that I must have a hole in my pocket. Meantime I have to talk seriously to the General and say, 'Yes sir, yes sir, three bags full.'"

"And that is how you won the war, Dicky, is it!" smiled Clare.

Pagan knocked out his pipe and nodded gratefully at Baron. "I once won a tarpaulin in rather comic circumstances," he said. "It was when that disgusting fellow Hubbard went on leave and left me in charge of B. Company. We were bivouacking in a little hollow at the time, wedged in with a couple of million other troops, and we badly wanted a tarpaulin for the men. The town major, a disgusting little tick, had a tarpaulin, but would he part with it! Not he.

"Well, one day Melford, back at headquarters, sent up to know whether we would like to have the battalion water cart. I said, 'Yes.' But the fool of a Quartermaster sent it up full, so that the poor wretched horse had to pull that heavy weight up the steep hill to the Bray-Corbie road and then trek to our camp. During the night the C. Q. M. S. woke me up to say that the wretched horse was ill—and no wonder. Well, we gave the poor beast some pills and trotted it up and down for a bit, and then it lay down and died there in the middle of sleeping thousands.

"The C. Q. M. S. said we should have to get it out of the way and bury it. I said, 'No. Leave it where it is. It hasn't got a mark on it and no one will know whose it is.'

"In the morning there was the deuce of a fuss. The town-major running round like a dog with four tails, because, you see, he is the fellow who is responsible for the general cleanliness of the camp, and of course a dead horse is an abomination. The difficulty was to get somebody to bury it, because although the town-major is responsible for the camp he is neither fish, flesh nor good red herring and has no power to detail men from other units in the camp, and his own staff usually consists of an ancient batman with one eye and a game leg. Anyway, the sun rose higher and higher, and still our poor old horse lay out there bang in the middle of the camp.

"Just after midday the A. P. M. came up and dropped into my hut for a chat. Of course he was livid about that horse, and thirsting for the town-major's blood. Just then the town-major came along, and the A. P. M. gave it him good and proper. The town-major said he couldn't get a fatigue party and all that, and the A. P. M. cursed him hot and strong and ended up with, 'Here, Pagan's a good chap; he'll give you a fatigue party if you ask him nicely.' I said I would be charmed to do so, but unfortunately all my men were employed on most important work for Corps, etc., etc. Then I suddenly became magnanimous. 'Look here,' I said. 'You've got a tarpaulin that I badly want. If you let me have that tarpaulin, I will stretch a point and let you have a fatigue party.' The town-major hesitated, but the A. P. M. chipped in with, 'Give him his old tarpaulin or you will have to dig a hole with your toothpick and bury the horse with your own hands.'

"And so the town-major thanked me warmly, the A. P. M. said I was an obliging chap, and we got the tarpaulin and buried our own horse."

Baron laughed. "That was a good bit of work, Charles. You see, Clare," he explained, "there was not enough stuff to go round, and what there was, was tied up with all sorts of dam silly red tape. The men whose officers were not smart enough to get things by hook or by crook went without, and that made all the difference between a happy and a grousing battalion. So you see, old Charles isn't really such a scoundrel as he would like you to believe."

She looked at him with her head on one side. "He is not really the criminal type," she smiled.

Pagan bowed. "A mere amateur, I am afraid," he murmured. He glanced again at his wrist watch and stood up. "Really the most sensible thing would be to go to sleep," he said with a smile at Clare. "I assure you that those wire netting bunks can be quite comfortable, and—well, early to bed and early to rise, you know!"

She looked in silence from one to the other. Baron lit a cigarette nonchalantly. "I think so too," he agreed. "And if Clare wants to preserve that schoolgirl complexion!"

She looked back again at Pagan. "If you wish it," she said.

"Well, it's really the only sensible thing to do, don't you think?"

"What are you going to do?" she asked.

"I am going to smoke another pipe, if you don't object, and then I shall probably go to by-byes too," he answered easily. "That is if old Baron doesn't snore too loudly." He began taking off his mackintosh. "We will make you so comfortable on that bunk that you will think that you are sleeping at the Ritz."

"It is no good taking that off," she said firmly, "because I refuse to have it."

"But it will not be too warm, you know," he protested.

"All the more reason why you should keep your coat," she retorted. "Yes, I mean it," she went on in answer to his look. "Really. I go to sleep on that funny bed without your coat or not at all."

He shrugged his shoulders with a look of comic resignation. "Well, we will have to make you a pillow anyway," he said. He dragged a small white muffler from the pocket of his coat, took his own soft hat and Baron's, and rolled them up into a loose ball. "That is the best I can do for you—a poor thing but mine own." He arranged the improvised pillow at the head of the bunk. "Now then, say your prayers," he smiled. "God bless Uncle Charles and make me a good girl, and then it's shut eyes."

She pulled off her hat and shook out her shingled hair. Then she slipped on to the bunk and laid her head upon the pillow.

"All right?" he asked.

"Splendid."

"Good. Change your mind and have my coat over your feet," he pressed earnestly.

She shook her head emphatically and smiled up at him. "Good night, Uncle Charles," she murmured.

He picked up the little tweed hat from the floor and placed it on the foot of the bunk. "Good night, my child," he answered soberly.

Baron lifted the two candles from their beds in the mound of earth. He blew out one of them and carried the other to the end of the dug-out and placed it on the floor behind a heap of debris so that the bunk and its occupant were in shadow. He and Pagan sat down on the floor side by side with their backs against the wall.

CHAPTER TEN

I

Pagan slowly refilled his pipe and lighted it from the candle. Baron also pulled out his pipe and lighted it. Neither spoke. The single candle beside them threw grotesque shadows of their heads and shoulders upon the wall. The pile of rubbish behind which it stood threw the remainder of the dug-out into shadow. The bunk at the far end was dimly discernible. Clare's gentle regular breathing was just audible in the intense stillness.

Baron took his pipe from his mouth and blew a little cloud of smoke upwards. "Bad show, Charles," he whispered at last.

Pagan nodded and gloomily regarded the glowing bowl of his pipe. "About as bad as it could be," he agreed. Silence settled down again, and then he nodded towards the other end of the dug-out. "She asleep, do you think?"

Baron listened for a moment to the soft regular breathing. "Sounds like it," he answered.

Pagan heaved a weary sigh. "Thank God she's got guts," he murmured.

Baron stared with knit brows at the bent sheet of corrugated iron that so effectively sealed the narrow entrance. He looked away and glanced up at the crack in the roof. "I suppose one ought to be thankful for small mercies," he murmured. "There is air at any rate."

Pagan puffed jerkily at his pipe and stared before him with knit brows. "We got her into this mess, Baron, and it is up to us to leave no stone unturned to get her out of it," he said at last.

Baron nodded with a wry smile. "I'm sufficiently interested personally not to leave even a grain of sand unturned," he answered drily.

Pagan scrambled noiselessly to his feet and prowled silently about the dug-out. He paused at the foot of the bunk and looked down at Clare who lay curled up with closed eyes, her head pillowed on one hand. He peeled off his mackintosh and laid it gently over her feet. Baron started to take off his coat also, but Pagan stopped him. "No good both being cold," he whispered. "But if you like we will take it in turns to wear it."

They wandered back to the other end of the dug-out and examined the narrow doorway. By silent agreement, they placed their shoulders against the sheet of iron and heaved, but without result. They grimaced at one another and tried again. Pagan shook his head, and they gave it up.

Baron sat down again in the old place on the floor, but Pagan continued to prowl. He halted by the half choked sump-pit, and gazed at it thoughtfully. It was about eighteen inches in diameter, and the tiny stream of water from the crack in the roof found its way across the floor and disappeared over the rim among the debris as a narrow dark stain.

Pagan stared at it and rubbed the back of his neck. Then he went down on one knee and pulled out a mouldy bit of sacking, some pieces of rotten wood and a handful or two of earth. The circular concrete rim of the floor was revealed and below it a few inches of the damp earth wall of the pit. Below that the pit was choked with more rubbish.

Baron stole up beside Pagan. "What is the idea, Charles?"

"I don't believe this is an ordinary sump-pit," said Pagan. "That trickle of water isn't much to write home about, I know, but it must have been going on for some time, and if the pit had no outlet I believe the rubbish and muck would be a good deal damper than it is. You see, the dug-out is cut into a steepish slope and they would only have to put a bit of a turn on this pit to give it an outlet lower down the bank. Anyway, it's worth finding out."

"I don't see why," answered Baron. "We are not rats— worse luck!"

Pagan was too busy scooping rubbish out of the pit to reply. Colourless fragments of mouldering clothing, one or two rusty tins, a mildewed leather pouch, a rusted rifle bolt and several handfuls of earth came out and were piled on the floor of the dug-out. At a depth of some two and a half feet the pit took a sudden turn and sloped towards the outer wall of the dug-out. Pagan lay on his stomach with his arms in the pit, and he twisted his head and looked triumphantly at Baron.

Baron nodded. "Yes, it's got an outlet all right," he murmured. "But what is the good of that to us? It's choked up with earth and stuff, and we are not ferrets anyway."

"I can get my shoulders in; it's worth trying," retorted Pagan.

"But my dear old idiot," protested Baron aghast, "this drain may be twenty yards long, and even if it were clear of rubbish the whole damn thing would probably come in on top of you."

"That's my funeral," retorted Pagan stubbornly.

"That's exactly what it would be," agreed Baron drily.

"Well, what else do you suggest?" demanded Pagan.

Baron shrugged his shoulders and glanced helplessly around the dug-out.

"You know as well as I do," went on Pagan testily, "that as far as shouting is concerned we shall still be doing it this time next week."

Baron had no reply to make, and Pagan turned again to his laborious task of removing handfuls of earth and rubbish from the drain. His right arm was now hidden to the elbow in the sloping part, and his head and trunk hung almost from the hips in the narrow pit. He laboriously brought up another handful and deposited it upon the floor. Then he took off his coat and waist-coat and lay down again. "Hang on to my feet, will you, as I work in," he said.

"Of course if you like committing suicide!" protested Baron.

"Like it!" retorted Pagan irritably. "I dislike the whole job intensely. But what else can we do: tell me that!" He took up the torch and put his arms into the hole. "Lay hold. The muck seems looser now and I am going to try to push it out in front of me."

"If you do, you will push the roof in on top of you," warned Baron. "And once you are in that sloping part I shall never be able to pull you out, even though I have got hold of your legs."

"I sincerely hope you won't have to try," retorted Pagan grimly. "Lay hold."

His head and shoulders disappeared again into the pit. His body hung vertically downwards from the hips. Inch by inch it went further in, till Baron had to kneel on the edge with a leg under either arm. Slowly the legs went down till only the shoes protruded above the level of the floor. Inch by inch they too went down. Baron had to lie upon his chest with his arms in the pit and his hands grasping the ankles.

"For God's sake chuck it, Charles," he whispered loudly. "You will get stuck in there."

There was no reply, but the feet sank an inch or two lower from time to time.

At last only a pair of shoes and ankles were visible at the bottom of the straight part of the pit. Baron crouched upon the brink and cursed softly beneath his breath.

Inch by inch the ankles disappeared from view, and then the shoes.

Baron strained his ears to catch the slight sounds of movement which came from the drain. He could hear the watch ticking upon his wrist and the faint breathing of Clare on the bunk at the other end of the dug-out. The seconds dragged by slowly like hours. The dug-out was damp and chilly, but perspiration dripped from his forehead. He was not a religious man, but he prayed.

Pagan lay full length in the drain. There was barely an inch to spare on either side of his body, and progress was possible only by digging his fingers into the ground and dragging his body forward till the slight bending of his elbows caused them to touch the sides of the drain and make it necessary to repeat the process.

He was not a little relieved therefore, when his right hand, with which he was pushing before him the rubbish and loose earth which obstructed the drain, encountered grass and weeds; but another five minutes elapsed before his head emerged from the hole and the chill night breeze blew upon his grimy, dripping forehead. A foot or two below him, beyond the weeds that fringed the hole, lay that narrow road up which they had come. In the darkness beyond it swam the moonlit hill-top across the valley.

For the moment he was content to lie there with the cool breeze fanning his grimy perspiring face. The strain of the last few minutes had taken its toll: he felt weak and shaky.

Footsteps sounded suddenly close at hand, and he turned his head to see a dark figure approaching down the road. Instinctively he lay still. It crossed his mind that it would indeed be ironical if the "thing" had chosen this moment to make its appearance. But as the figure passed within a few feet of him, he recognised the squat form of the innkeeper.

His first impulse was to call to Kleber and enlist his help in digging out the dug-out entrance; but the seconds passed, the footsteps rang out more faintly, and Pagan made no sound.

When the scrape of footsteps had died away completely, he dragged his body out into the night. He rose to his knees and called softly up the drain. An anxious voice answered distantly, "Hullo Charles; are you all right?"

"Yes, I'm out," he answered. "You stay there with Clare and I will soon dig you out, too."

He switched on the torch and climbed the short track that led to the dug-out. The weed-grown entrance with its sagging timbers seemed unchanged, but a foot or so within the passage the beam of light revealed a mound of earth reaching from floor to ceiling. He climbed further up the bank and searched among the debris for something with which he might dig. The chill night breeze dried the sweat upon his face and neck and the damp patches on his earth-stained shirt. He shivered as he poked about with the torch among the weeds, but he found something more suited to his purpose than he had dared to hope—a rusty pick head, one end pointed, the other flattened.

He needed now only a handle, and he was not long in finding a small stake that would serve the purpose. His teeth were chattering, and he was glad to get back to the passage and restore his circulation with violent exercise. He put the torch in his trouser pocket and dug in the dark.

He worked hard and he was forced to rest at intervals; and it was during one of these rests, as he stood leaning upon the improvised handle of his pick, that he heard a footstep on the road below. His hand went to his pocket for the torch. Was this Kleber again or the "thing" at last, he asked himself.

The footsteps died upon the road. A dim figure was coming up the short track towards him. He transferred the torch to his left hand and gripped the handle of the pick. Then he switched on the light.

In the blinding beam of light a dishevelled, shirt-sleeved figure flung a hand across his face and halted. Then a voice cried, "Put that damn thing out, Charles."

Pagan lowered the beam. "Oh, it's you," he exclaimed in relief. "What on earth are you doing!"

"Coming up to give you a hand," answered Baron.

"Idiot!" returned Pagan. "You might have got stuck in that drain."

"I realized that quite vividly as I was coming through it," answered Baron drily. "But I told myself that if you could get through when it was partially blocked, I could after you had cleared it out. But I wouldn't do it again for a fortune."

"There was no point in it," persisted Baron.

"Except that the two of us will do the digging in half the time."

"Yes, and if she wakes up in there and finds us gone, she will be frightened to death," objected Pagan.

"Not she," declared Baron easily. "I believe she realized the mess we were in just as well as we did, and she wasn't frightened."

"Well I was, anyway," confessed Pagan. "Scared stiff!"

"So was I," admitted Baron.

"Well, there you are! And you go and leave her alone."

"I have left her a note," retorted Baron, "and if she wakes up she will know what is happening."

"Good! Well, let's get down to it."

Baron found a board that could be made to do duty for a spade, and with it he shovelled away the earth which Pagan dug out with the pick.

"Reminds one of those blasted cable trenches we used to dig at night, Charles," murmured Baron.

Pagan nodded. "But no gas shells now, thank Gawd!"

They worked hard with few pauses for rest, but even so more than an hour went by before Pagan's pick rang dully upon the sheet of galvanized iron. A further five minutes sufficed to clear away the earth which still covered it; and then they dropped their implements and, putting their hands under the bottom edge of the sheet, they bent it upwards.

II

The one guttering candle gave the dug-out a depressing air of gloom and space. The little mound of earth behind which the candle stood threw a monstrous shadow upon the opposite wall. Clare was seated bare-headed upon the edge of the bunk. She smiled at the two dirty dishevelled figures that came through the low doorway, but her face was pale.

"Hullo, there you are!" cried Baron cheerfully.

She nodded her small head a little wearily. "And, as Uncle Charles would say, for this relief, much thanks," she smiled.

"Sorry we made such a row and woke you up," apologized Pagan.

She stood up. "I was not really asleep," she confessed. "The horrid thought that I was buried alive kept me awake."

Baron threw a glance that said, "I told you so," at Pagan. "Then you did know how serious it was," he said.

She nodded her head. "It was rather obvious wasn't it?" she said with a wan little smile. "Although you and Uncle Charles were such conscientious optimists about the shouting."

Pagan took his handkerchief from his coat pocket and rubbed some of the sweat and dirt from his face. "And yet you lay down when I suggested it, and never made a sound afterwards! Nothing much wrong with your nerves."

"It seemed the only thing to do, and it would allow you to act as though I were not there. You see," she added with an elfish smile, "I knew that your Victorian ideas would not allow me to be useful. I dozed off and on, but I knew you were up to something."

"We were—or at least old Charles was," agreed Baron heartily. "And thanks to him we are out of a very constricted corner indeed." He took her by the arm. "Come and have a look at the rabbit hole he went down."

She shook her head and shuddered. "I have seen it. I saw your coats and the rubbish round it and I guessed." She sat down abruptly on the bunk. Baron was beside her in a moment. She looked up at him with a wan little smile. "I am all right, Dicky; but I very nearly was Victorian then," she said ruefully.

Pagan picked up his mackintosh from the bunk and took a packet of chocolate from the pocket. "Time for tiffin," he remarked and handed it round. He put on his coat and they sat on the bunk and munched chocolate. "Feeling better?" he asked.

She nodded with her mouth full.

He surveyed his grimy fingers that held the chocolate by the silver paper. "Pale hands, pink tipped like lotus buds that float." He turned to Clare. "Now I'm perfectly certain you have never eaten chocolate before sitting between two grimy chimney sweeps."

She shook her tousled head. "Never," she said. "And I rather like it."

"Chocolate or us?" he asked. "But it must be us, and in that case I shall not have to put into execution my bright idea of holding my handkerchief in that trickle of water and rubbing it on my face."

"But I don't like it as much as all that," she cried.

Pagan grimaced. She took a small mirror from her bag and handed it to him with an expressive gesture. He glanced at it and started back in mock alarm. "Oh that this too, too solid flesh would melt," he groaned. "Is this the face that launched a thousand ships?"

"*Beached* a thousand ships, Charles—judging by the amount of mud on it," corrected Baron.

Pagan handed back the glass.

"Well?" she queried.

"Beauty is only skin deep," he grinned.

"Yours is fathoms deep," she retorted, "—in dirt. Give me your handkerchief."

He handed it to her and she moistened it at the trickle of water on the wall. "Come now," she cried imperiously. "Dicky will hold the torch."

He rose obediently with comic resignation. "I go and it is done," he quoted whimsically; "the belle invites me. Hear it not, Baron; for it is a knell that summons me to Heaven."

She dabbed his face with the damp handkerchief as he stood submissive before her. "Now, Dicky; your turn."

Pagan unrolled his tobacco pouch and filled his pipe with a leisurely air while Baron's face was being rubbed. Then he took his wrist watch from his pocket and re-strapped it upon his wrist. "Now that we are all swept and garnished; how about getting back!" he suggested. He turned to Clare. "Are you fit?"

"Quite."

"Good." He put on his mackintosh. Clare picked up her hat and pulled it on her head. Baron switched on the torch.

"Ready?" asked Pagan. "Right 'o then; walk march. I will lock up." He extinguished the candle with his foot and followed the other two down the passage.

III

It was dark on the road, and the air was cold with the penetrating chilliness that comes before dawn. They marched along abreast, Clare in the middle, their chins sunk in the upturned collars of their mackintoshes.

"Tired?" asked Baron at last.

Clare nodded her head. "Um—my legs are." She slipped her hand through Baron's arm.

Pagan on her left marched along for a pace or two in silence. Then he asked whimsically, "Only the right leg tired?"

She glanced up at him and smiled. And then her left arm came through his.

They tramped on in silence down the road, past the track which led up over the saddle by which they had come. The moon had set and the morning was dark and cold and very still. Above them on the crest the stark trees were no longer distinguishable against the western sky. Eastwards dull grey streaks were beginning to appear above the dark line of hills. They reached the southern end of the ridge and turned off round the grassy shoulder, wading knee deep through the wreathing mist.

Pagan was aware that the hand upon his arm had grown heavier during the last twenty minutes. "Nearly home now," he cried. "Home with the milk!" He swept a hand towards the brightening streaks of grey in the eastern sky. "See! Night's candles are burnt out and jocund dawn stands tiptoe on the misty mountain tops."

Baron was for marching up to the front door of the inn and knocking up Kleber, but Pagan objected that there was no point in advertising their adventure, or possibly annoying Kleber and giving him the opportunity of saying "I told you so." "And besides," he concluded, "I haven't by any means given up my intention of finding out what that fellow is up to."

It was now light enough for objects to be seen at some distance, and they approached the inn warily; but the building stood silent and with curtains drawn, a little forlorn looking in the cold dawn light. They crossed the little terrace unseen, climbed the palings beyond, and passed from foothold to foothold along the steep slope at the foot of the wall; Pagan the while keeping a protective hand upon Clare's arm.

The red knotted rope, swaying slightly in the breeze, looked forlornly tawdry in the cold grey light, like paper caps or coloured streamers on the morning after a party. Baron went up first, and he went slowly, for he was tired, and he had to struggle to drag himself over the sill. Pagan put a small loop in the end of the rope for Clare, who he insisted was too tired to climb; then he too went up and was helped through the window by Baron. Clare put her foot in the loop and was hauled slowly upward.

"Well here we are all present and correct," said Pagan as they stood together in the shadowy room. He glanced at the luminous watch upon his wrist. "Just over two hours to go before the beauteous Bertha calls us to the troubles of another day! Bed, I think, what? And I hope you will really sleep this time," he added to Clare.

"I am sure I shall," she answered. "Good night—or rather good morning."

She passed through the door into her own room. The two men swung back the press into position, dismantled the rope and put everything back into its proper place. Pagan took a final glance round before passing through the connecting door to his own room. He smothered a yawn. "All quiet on the western front it seems," he murmured. "And so to bed."

CHAPTER ELEVEN

I

To Pagan it seemed but a moment after he had closed his eyes that he opened them again to find Bertha in the room with a can of hot water. He got out of bed reluctantly. And Baron, too, when he came through the connecting door, in his pyjamas, yawning and rubbing his eyes, looked tousled and heavy-eyed. "No rest for the wicked," he growled. "And my shirt is about the most disgusting thing you ever saw."

"Have a look at mine then, and you will feel better," Pagan advised.

They succeeded in brushing most of the dried earth from their trousers, but their shirts, and particularly the shoulders could not be cleaned in this way. Fortunately they had each brought a clean collar.

"Well, what the eye doesn't see, the heart doesn't grieve for," philosophized Pagan as he put on his coat over the soiled shirt. "We may be full of dead men's bones, but at least outwardly the sepulchre is whited."

"The sepulchre will feel better when it has some coffee and rolls inside it," Baron remarked.

But Clare came down the stairs looking as neat and clean and fresh as a flower. Baron regarded her with amused envy.

"Behold, the weaker sex, Charles! There she is after a night out, looking as fresh as a daisy, and positively flaunting her freshness in our teeth!"

Pagan nodded his head gloomily. "If ladies be but young and fair they have the gift to know it," he quoted sadly.

"You poor dears," cried Clare sympathetically. "What is it, do you think—liver?"

Pagan took the cup of coffee she handed him. "Worse than that," he affirmed. "There was a time when after one hour's sleep in forty-eight I arose like a giant refreshed with wine or a young unicorn full of—er—the unicorn equivalent of beans." He shook his head with mock sadness. "You see this sunken eye; this palsied hand! If you have tears prepare to shed them now. I am growing old!"

Clare laughed, but the expression of her eyes was almost tender. "Old!" she exclaimed. "Why, by the time you are seventy you will just be beginning to grow up."

Griffin arrived soon after they had finished breakfast and took them back to Munster in the car. They parted on the big balustraded landing of the hotel. "Well, that's the end of one chapter," said Baron. "And now bath for me."

"Me too," agreed Clare.

"And I am going to finish that beauty sleep Bertha so prematurely interrupted," declared Pagan.

Pagan slept till half-past-three. He bathed, dressed and felt again, in his own words, fit for treasons, stratagems and spoils.

Downstairs he found the hotel almost deserted. He passed through the French doors on to the terrace and leaned upon the stone balustrade. Before him stretched the garden in which gravel paths meandered between bushes, flower-beds and trees. Beyond it rose the green mountain side, its lower slopes dotted with cherry trees and two or three homesteads.

Presently among the bushes in the garden he caught sight of Clare walking slowly towards the hotel. He watched her for a moment, and then turned back indoors. Three rooms gave on to the terrace by French doors: the long dining-room and two small drawing-rooms. Both the smaller rooms were unoccupied at the moment, and he went into one of these and ordered tea.

Clare came slowly along the sunny terrace. He saw her reflected in the glass of the open door. She looked in at the other small room, and then passed slowly the six long windows of the dining-room beneath the gay striped awning. A moment later she stood upon the threshold of the room in which he sat.

"Hullo, there you are—Rip Van Winkle," she drawled.

"Hullo," said Pagan. "I've ordered tea for two."

She came slowly into the room. "For two! You and Dicky?"

He shook his head. "No—you and me. And I have managed to get crumpets—in summer and in France. What do you think of that! I hope you like them."

She sat down. "I adore them," she said with a smile.

"Good."

She pulled off her hat and smoothed her shingled hair. "Sugar?" she asked.

"Two please," said Pagan.

As she poured tea into her own cup she looked up at him with a grave little smile. "It sounds rather silly and ridiculously inadequate to say 'thank you for saving my life last night,' but—well, what else can I do!" she asked whimsically.

He laughed. "Don't do anything," he advised. "It was the least I could do after having dragged you into it."

"Dragged!" she echoed.

"Well, I didn't stop you as I ought to have done," he explained. "A battlefield was no place to take a girl at night."

She put down her cup. "But believe me I am very glad I went," she said earnestly. "Particularly at night. To you, no doubt, it was a familiar enough sight; but to me it was—a revelation." She knit her brows and stared at the tea tray. "Before, I had only a vague picture: now—I know."

Pagan nodded and stirred his teacup thoughtfully. "Um, pretty ghastly mess, I agree," he murmured. He toyed with the handle of the spoon for a moment or two, and then without looking up asked gently, "But in the circumstances are you sure it was either wise or—desirable to have that knowledge?"

She shot a swift glance at him and gave an almost imperceptible shrug of her shoulders. "Perhaps not," she admitted at last. She stirred her cup thoughtfully. "Then you know about—Roger?" she said quietly.

Pagan nodded. "Baron told me." He examined the tips of his fingers. "And may I say—how sorry I am?"

"Thank you," she answered simply. There was silence for a moment. Then she looked at him suddenly, and there was a challenge in her eyes. "You think my attitude is morbid?"

He met her eyes frankly. "It would be impertinent for me—" he began.

She shook her head a trifle impatiently. "Not if I ask you; and I do ask you—you think it morbid?"

He regarded his teacup for a moment. "No," he answered slowly. "I don't think reverence for a—a sacred memory is morbid—any more than I think reverence for holy things is morbid."

She glanced at him gratefully and then down at her lap. "It was very sweet of you to say that," she murmured.

"But one must keep one's sense of proportion," he added gently.

She looked out at the sun-washed terrace. "Then you think I am in danger of losing mine?" she asked.

He made a little French movement of his hands. "Who am I to judge . . .!"

"But you think: tell me what you think. I—value your opinion."

He acknowledged the compliment with a little inclination of his head. "It does not distress you to talk about him?" he queried.

She shook her head.

Pagan put down his cup. "I never met Vigers," he began. "I wish I had."

"You would have liked him," she said.

"I am sure of that."

"And he would have liked you."

"Thank you," he said. "I am glad that you think that." He picked up the teaspoon and stirred his cup absent-mindedly. "I never met him, but from his army record and the accounts of his friends, I know he was a very fine and gallant fellow. He would, I am sure, like everyone else, myself included, find your loyalty admirable. But—I speak bluntly but, believe me, not unsympathetically."

She nodded her head. "I am sure of that. Please go on."

"But I don't think that any decent fellow, and least of all such a splendid man as Vigers must have been, would expect or wish his—his betrothed to renounce her just and natural fulfilment because it was denied to him. We have only one earthly life, and when it is finished it is finished. What we miss here, we miss for good and all. In the next we cannot carry on where we left off. They neither marry nor are given in marriage."

She stared in silence at the sunlit garden.

"I am sorry," he said gently. "But you asked me. You are not angry?"

She shook her head without looking at him. He took his cup again from the table. A long silence followed, and then suddenly she turned her head again towards him; and he saw that her mood had changed. "Did Dicky tell you that I had sworn to remain single to the end of my days?" she asked.

Pagan put down the cup. "Well, not quite that," he protested.

She took his cup and refilled it. "But words to that effect?" she suggested.

"Well he did say that you had turned down any number of good fellows," he admitted.

She nodded her head slowly and handed him his cup. "Perhaps it was because I did not like any of them well enough," she said with a smile.

Pagan made an expressive gesture with his hands. "In that case I solemnly foreswear, abjure and utterly recant all that I have said previously," he smiled. He raised his cup and looked at her across the top of it with sudden seriousness. "But, if somebody does come along," he said slowly, "are you quite sure that you will give yourself a fair chance of liking him well enough?"

She glanced at him quickly and then looked thoughtfully away.

A sudden shadow darkened the doorway and Baron's voice broke the silence. "Oh, there you are. And hogging it too—as usual!" He came slowly into the room. "Crumpets, by gosh!" he exclaimed. "Trust old Charles!"

"Here you leave those alone," cried Pagan. "If you want any, you jolly well order some for yourself."

"I will," declared Baron making for the bell with fierce determination. "It's the pore what 'elps the pore—every time."

"And it's the Barons what helps themselves—every time," asserted Pagan grimly with his hands held protectingly above the crumpets.

II

"The great advantage of a boiled shirt," remarked Pagan that night at dinner, "is that it shows the dirt."

Baron ruefully regarded the big smear of cigarette ash which he had just made across his shirt front. "It does," he agreed. "And I wish you had had one on last night when you crawled through that damned drain," he added viciously.

Pagan drank his coffee and smiled tolerantly. "Why so bitter?"

"You are so damned sympathetic, aren't you!" growled Baron.

"I am merely trying to keep a stiff upper lip in the face of another's adversity," retorted Pagan with dignity.

Baron snorted and gulped down his benedictine.

"I miss the little Baronial ray of sunshine," remarked Pagan blandly.

"Confound you, Charles," exploded Baron. "Why can't you shut up? You know I'm damned bad tempered to-night."

"Strange!" murmured Pagan sweetly. "I'm feeling particularly cheerful."

"No wonder," retorted Baron. "You have been hogging it in bed half the day while I have had only one hour's sleep since the night before last."

Pagan nodded his head and hummed the tune which the dance orchestra was playing in the next room. "Then you don't feel like going up to Bertha's pub again to-night, I suppose?" he asked suddenly.

"Good Lord, no!" exclaimed Baron. "I thought we all had enough of that last night. It was hardly a successful bit of detecting from any point of view, was it!" he added caustically.

"Not as successful as it might have been," conceded Pagan. He swung round in his chair and leaned his elbows on the table. "But look here, Old Baron, I'm damned keen to get to the bottom of this. Kleber roams about that old battlefield at night, and I want to find out why."

"How do you know he does?" demanded Baron. "He went out last night certainly, but we don't know where he went to."

"He went to the battlefield, I tell you," said Pagan. "And I know he did because I saw him. He walked down that road past me when I was in the drain. I was having a breather and only my head was sticking out. He didn't see me, but I saw him all right."

"You are a funny fellow, Charles," said Baron. "If I had been lying in that confounded drain and somebody had come along, I should have sung out for help at the top of my voice."

Pagan held a match to his cigarette. "As a matter of fact I did think of it," he confessed, "but on second thoughts it seemed better not to. I knew I should be able to dig you out all right, and it seemed a pity to let Kleber know I had seen him. I was dead keen on finding out what he was up to."

"When I was in that drain," remarked Baron dryly, "the only thing I was dead keen on was getting out of it. However. . . . So friend Kleber was strolling down that road in the middle of the night, was he! That's intriguing certainly."

"It must have been pretty late," said Pagan. "After midnight, I should think. He may go out again to-night, and I thought that if we went up there later on this evening and hung about outside the inn, we might find out where he goes."

Baron laughed and shook his head. "Not to-night, Old Charles, thank you! To-morrow perhaps, but not to-night. I'm as sleepy as an owl. I'm going to bed." He glanced at his watch. "And pretty soon at that. You go and dance with Clare; I'm off to by-byes *toute suite*."

Pagan found Clare and her brother having coffee in the lounge. "Are we going to dance?" he asked.

She looked up at him and nodded. "Not more than two though. I am getting so sleepy."

He looked at her severely. "Do you mean to tell me that you have not had a sleep since you came back this morning!" he scolded.

She shook her head with comic docility. "Please, I had half an hour after lunch," she answered.

"It seems that I am the only one who has any sense," he said virtuously.

He took her empty cup, and she rose to her feet. "My dancing is on a par with my other attainments," he said as they walked into the other room. "So you must be charitable."

They glided round the room in silence. Pagan had no desire to break it; and she seemed content. The cheerful rhythm of the music suited his mood, and he was very conscious of her hand upon his shoulder and the gentle pressure of her body against his. When the music stopped he led her to a settee in a corner of the lounge. "Come let us sit upon this mossy bank and tell sad stories of the death of kings," he laughed.

She regarded him critically. "At the worst of times you are not a lugubrious person," she told him. "But to-night you positively ooze cheerfulness. I felt it all the time we were dancing. Have you come into a fortune?"

"No—not yet," he answered smiling cryptically.

"Is one then allowed to ask the cause of this insuppressible glee?" she said. "Or is it too secret?"

He looked at her with a whimsical smile. "Oh no. It concerns you. But if I told you, you probably would not like it." He spoke lightly, but there was an undercurrent of seriousness in his voice.

"Now of course you have thoroughly aroused my feminine curiosity," she smiled.

"No doubt," he said with a thoughtfully appraising look. "But all the same I am not sure that it would be wise to tell you."

"I am simply dying to know," she coaxed.

He did not answer for a moment. He tucked the white silk handkerchief down into the pocket of his dinner jacket with rather elaborate care; then suddenly he looked up. "It concerns your—memory," he said soberly.

She turned a serious and puzzled face towards him. "My memory," she echoed.

He nodded his head emphatically. "Yes. I have been bothered about it."

She watched him in silence, waiting for him to continue.

"You remember what we—or rather what I said this afternoon?" he asked presently.

She nodded her small head.

He clasped his hands about one knee and went on with his eyes fixed upon the opposite wall of the room. "Well, it seemed to me that if somebody else did come along, he would not stand much of a chance. He would not be able to compete with—the memory. And that seemed a pity, both from your point of view and from his." He turned his head and glanced at her with appraising eyes. "You are not liking it," he asserted.

"I don't know yet," she said. "Go on."

"At your own risk," he warned her. "Well, as I was saying, I thought that he would never stand a chance. But I don't think that now, because I see that the two things are different. The one affection does not necessarily preclude the other. They can carry on side by side. As a—as a man, for example, might reverence the saints and yet love his wife. The two things don't clash a bit really. They are on different planes—this somebody else and the memory."

He glanced at her again. Her face betrayed only thoughtful attention. He went on slowly and solemnly. "I see that now, and I am sure that you too will see it—in time. That is why I am glad." He paused and took a breath. "I am glad because I know that time"—he looked at her and added soberly, "time—is on my side."

Their eyes met, and the expression in hers was indefinable. "On—your side," she repeated slowly. The tone was half questioning.

He nodded his head solemnly. "Does that sound conceited?" he asked. "I am not really conceited—least of all at this moment. I think you know that."

She nodded her head. "I know that," she repeated earnestly. Then she looked up at him. "But you mean—?"

He nodded his head again and met her eyes. "Yes."

There was a long silence. The sound of voices and laughter mingled with the rhythm of a fox trot came from the dance room. When at last she spoke, it was in a low voice without looking at him. "I wish you had not said all this. I enjoyed that dance so much. Now you make it very difficult for me." Suddenly she turned and looked at him. Her face was serious but kind. "You would like me to be frank with you, wouldn't you. Even though it—hurt a little." She put out a hand and touched his arm, and her eyes were very kind. "Though, believe me, there is no one I would less willingly hurt."

He patted her hand gently. "Go on. I can take one straight between the eyes if necessary."

She looked away again, and when she spoke her voice was low and distressed. "Don't you think, don't you think," she asked gently, "that you are mistaking gratitude and admiration for . . . for love?"

Slowly she turned her head and looked at him. He smiled into her distressed eyes. He shook his head slowly from side to side without speaking. "No," he said at last. "I think that *you* are mistaking love for . . . gratitude and admiration."

A startled expression leapt into her eyes for a moment and was gone again. Then she turned her head away. "Let us dance," she said at last in a composed voice.

They glided again round the floor. Neither spoke. He steered her skilfully among the other dancers, and she responded to the slight pressure of his guiding arms as unerringly as though one mind only controlled their two rhythmically gliding bodies. He knew that she was thinking and that she was not angry with him, and he was content.

"That must be the last," she said when the music slowed and ceased on a long drawn note. "I am getting so sleepy."

They walked in silence side by side to the big entrance hall and across it to the foot of the broad staircase. She turned with a little smile. "I enjoyed the dance."

His hand rested upon the polished balustrade; she was two steps above him.

"If," he asked gently, "if—what I said proved to be true, would you—would you be—sorry?"

She halted with one foot raised upon the next stair and turned her head slowly towards him.

"Would you?" he persisted.

She looked down into his eager face, and her eyes were motherly and thoughtful.

"Would you?" he whispered.

The shake of her head was almost imperceptible. "I think I should be—glad," she answered softly.

His radiant smile brought the colour to her cheeks.

"Good night—Clare," he whispered.

"Good night—Charles," she answered softly. Then she turned and went quickly up the stairs.

CHAPTER TWELVE

PAGAN was in an expansive mood as he strolled back across the foyer. He had slept all the morning and he was feeling very wide awake. He stood for a moment in the doorway of the dance room watching with abstracted eyes the couples gliding by; then he walked back to the lounge. He found young Cecil in a big arm-chair in a corner of the room and they had a liqueur together. Clare had told her brother something of the strange behaviour of Kleber and Bertha, and he was disposed to be dogmatic on the subject.

"The wild man of the woods story is obviously tosh," he said as he lighted a long cheroot. "Baron is much nearer the mark. I was talking to a man on my way back from Gerardmer to-day. He is manager of one of those linen factories near Longermer. And he said that there was a lot of unrest among the lower orders. Many of the workmen think they would be better off under German rule; and apparently the religious question is mixed up with it too. And so what with one thing and another, he said he would not be surprised if before very long there was a dust up. And then, I suppose, the French would trot out their machine guns and mop them up. And a good job too, I say."

"You bloodthirsty young ruffian!" laughed Pagan. "Ever seen a machine gun at work?"

"Only on the pictures," grinned Cecil.

Pagan nodded. "I know; and the belt jams conveniently whenever the hero comes on the scene," he laughed. "But it does look as though some sort of trouble is brewing. I have heard it from two or three sources."

"And that fellow Kleber is in it for certain," said Cecil.

Pagan nodded thoughtfully. "I shouldn't wonder. Anyway, I have made up my mind to find out what he is up to." He glanced at his watch. "I have half a mind to pay an unofficial visit to his pub to-night. You are not game, I suppose?"

Cecil put down his glass. "Rather late, isn't it?"

Pagan grinned. "It would not take long in that car of yours," he suggested.

Cecil shook his head. "No, I'm not really interested; but if you want to go, Griffin can run you up."

"Thanks very much," said Pagan. "But I don't like to drag your man out this time of night."

"Oh, he will be tickled to death. There is a battlefield nearby, isn't there. He loves battlefields. He will talk for hours about it if you let him—which I don't. How he had his knapsack full of eggs or something and what the S. O. S., or the X. Y. Z., or whatever it is, said to him. But you understand his jargon and it might interest you. We will dig him out if you like. He is always down at that café by the station at this hour."

Pagan fetched a coat, and they walked down to the little open air café. They found Griffin seated on an iron chair under a tree, in the branches of which little red, green and yellow electric bulbs were entwined. On the little iron table before him stood a tall glass a quarter full of beer, and the upper three quarters of the glass were ringed at almost mathematically regular intervals with wreaths of white foam. Between his teeth was a half-smoked cigar with the band on. Opposite him sat the patron wearing a dark blue beret.

As Pagan and Cecil came unnoticed within earshot, Griffin removed his cigar and asked oratorically, "What did she say! San fairy anne; that's wot she said." The patron raised an interrogative eyebrow. Griffin took a pull at his glass and wiped his mouth with the back of his hand. "An' it didn't," he added cryptically.

Pagan grinned. "Seems a pity to interrupt these tender reminiscences," he said. But Cecil had no such delicate feelings in the matter; and ten minutes later Pagan was seated beside Griffin in the car which was leaving the outskirts of Munster behind it.

The evening air blew coldly as the car throbbed steadily upwards. The two bright cones from the headlights threw into shadowed relief the inequalities of the road ahead. Below them in the darkness twinkled the lights of Munster. Griffin handled the wheel with careless skill and rounded the steep hairpin bends in faultless style and with silent gears.

In a little over twenty minutes the car throbbed over the crest and glided to rest in the col. Pagan clambered out and examined his wrist watch in the glare of the headlights. "Don't stay longer than an hour, Griffin," he said.

Griffin coughed. "Well, sir, I was 'oping you'd let me come with you. I'm 'ot stuff on night patrols."

Pagan hesitated. "Right 'o," he said at last. "Come along then."

The soft purr of the engine died away; the headlights faded out. Griffin climbed out of the car and slammed the door. "You see, sir," he said as they set off up the grassy side of the col, "I'd like to see this 'ere ghost, never havin' properly seen one afore."

"Who said anything about ghosts?" demanded Pagan.

"Well, sir, it was like this; the Frenchies in Munster was chewing the rag about it, and then I 'eard Mr. Cecil and Miss Clare talking about what you done last night, and well, do you see, sir?"

"You put two and two together," supplied Pagan.

"That's right, sir," agreed Griffin cheerfully. "Not that I altogether holds with ghosts myself," he added. "What do you say, sir?"

"I don't know that I 'hold' with them either," answered Pagan. "But there is something queer up here, I know, because—well, I saw a figure that was not quite ordinary."

"How do you mean, sir?"

"It's rather difficult to say," answered Pagan. "Your friend at the café thinks it is a sort of ape man," he added half seriously.

"I shouldn't be surprised, sir," answered Griffin cheerfully. "I've seen lots o' them."

Pagan laughed. "So have I; the sort you mean. I don't agree with him, but he really means a sort of wild man—half ape, half man."

"Lord, sir!" exclaimed Griffin. "What, one of them chaps like what I saw on the fair at Lewes! Covered all over with hair, he was and a tanner a time to look at him."

"Yes, that's the idea, more or less," laughed Pagan. "So now you know what we are up against. But seriously," he added, "there is something queer, and I don't want to drag you into this against your will."

"And what would you do alone, sir, if this monkey chap jumped out on you all of a sudden?" asked Griffin scornfully.

"That would be rather awkward, wouldn't it!" agreed Pagan. "But you need not worry about me, I can look after myself all right. So if you would rather push off, don't hesitate to say so."

Griffin tramped onward for a moment or two in silence; then he said, "If it's worth a tanner to see a monkey man in a fair, I reckon it's worth a walk over a mountain to see one for nix."

There was no moon, but the clear starlight showed up the dark roof and the chimneys of the inn as they turned down the track in the hollow beyond the col. They approached the clump of buildings warily. Narrow panels of yellow light escaped from the edges of the lower windows, and the white palings in front glimmered faintly in the starlight.

"What do we do now, sir?" asked Griffin as they halted in the gloom by the wall of an outbuilding. "Drore picks and shovels from the R. E.s!"

Pagan chuckled. "And then wait a couple of hours for a sapper lance corporal to turn up and show us where to dig, what! I see you have played that amusing game. No, I think the only thing we can do is to hang about for a bit in the hope that Kleber—that's the innkeeper—comes out. He often goes out at night, and I would very much like to know where he goes to."

They waited there in the lee of the wall and talked in whispers of those other nights, years ago, when they had trudged through the mud of Picardy towards the soaring Very lights or dug for hours beneath the stars on some weed-grown hill side to the intermittent accompaniment of staccato machine-gun bursts and occasional salvoes of gas shells. No sound came from the inn. Overhead, the great sky-sign of the stars revolved slowly.

Pagan had just made up his mind to send Griffin back when the silence was broken by the banging of a door. The sound came from the side of the inn, and was probably made by that door under the covered way which he and Baron had discovered during their exploration of the premises.

He whispered to Griffin to be quiet, and they stood there motionless, flat against the gable wall of the barn. Beyond the wall they could see the dim line of the fence which extended from it along the front of the house, broken some ten yards distant by the open gate which gave access to the barn and outbuildings.

Presently came the sound of heavy footsteps crossing the yard. The sounds grew nearer, and then almost died away as the approaching feet encountered the soft ground near the fence. A moment later a dark figure passed through the open gate.

The light was dim, but Pagan recognised the figure as that of Kleber; he was carrying what seemed to be a basket. He plodded slowly up the track through the hollow.

"Is he the one, sir?" whispered Griffin.

Pagan nodded. "Yes—we are in luck. Come on. I am very interested to see what he is up to."

They left the shelter of the wall and followed cautiously after Kleber's dim figure. Presently the hollow flattened out, and away to the right could be seen against the night sky the dim line of the ridge with its crest of stark dead trees. The dim figure ahead followed the track for some distance, and then suddenly diverged from it half right and began to ascend the grassy slope diagonally towards the ridge.

"Looks as though he is making for the saddle by the quarry," whispered Pagan. "Look here, Griffin, it is no good dragging you any further. We are getting further and further away from the car. You go back. There is a road on the other side of the ridge; I can come back by that."

Griffin was disposed to argue. "If there's a road, sir, I'll fetch the car and bring it round," he whispered.

"You couldn't get very far up it," objected Pagan. "It runs across the old battlefield and it's all cluttered up with branches of trees and bits of corrugated iron."

"Then I'll bring it up as far as I can and walk the rest," persisted Griffin.

Pagan gave in. "Right 'o then," he agreed. "But don't come up further than the saddle—you can't miss it: it makes quite a notch in the ridge on your left. Got a map?"

"In the car."

"Good. Look here, you need not go back the way we came. Cut across to the left; march on those two stars. Got 'em? Good. They will lead you down and then up, and when you hit the road over the col turn left down it. You will be bound to strike the car. Cheery 'o. And if you don't come across me on the road over here, don't wait more than half an hour."

Griffin went noiselessly down hill and soon disappeared in the gloom. Pagan quickened his steps and soon came again within sight of the dim figure ahead. It led him, as he had anticipated, to the saddle, and for a moment he thought the old quarry was the goal; but the figure passed on and down the far side of the saddle.

Here Pagan had to move very cautiously indeed, for the narrow track was littered with fragments of wood and debris, and he dared not use his torch. Several times he lost sight of Kleber altogether, but on each occasion that he did so the snapping of a twig or some other sound enabled him to pick up the trail again.

The track he was following was not that which he and Baron had taken on their morning exploration leading directly down from the saddle to the road, but one which diverged to the left and descended diagonally along the steep flank of the ridge. It threaded a forest of short splintered stumps with here and there a tall stark trunk like a lightning struck telegraph pole.

Suddenly the dim form ahead wavered and disappeared. Pagan stopped immediately to listen, and presently he was rewarded by the sounds of movement higher up the slope.

Evidently Kleber had left the track and was climbing the steep slope to the left. Pagan moved on again till he reached the point at which he judged Kleber must have left the track. He looked for some smaller path leading upwards but could find none.

All sounds of movement had now ceased, but Kleber could not be more than fifty yards away. Possibly he suspected that he was being followed and had stopped to listen. Pagan, therefore, stood still and listened.

For more than five minutes this game of waiting and listening continued. No sound disturbed the silence of the night except the faint and intermittent skurryings and gnawings of rats and other rodents. Pagan decided to go on again. But he could find no trace of a path leading upwards. He placed his hat on the track as a guide and went back twenty yards and searched every inch of the bank up to it; and then he searched for twenty yards or more beyond it. But no trace could he find of the path by which Kleber must have ascended: everywhere the way was barred by riven tree stumps, tall weeds, wire and brambles.

Kleber could not be very far away, that was certain. The noise of his progress had continued only for a minute or two after his dim form had disappeared from the track. He was up there somewhere among the shattered tree stumps on the steep bank above, either listening and waiting or in one of the many dug-outs with which this ridge was tunnelled like a rabbit warren.

Pagan crawled up the bank among some tall weeds and settled down to wait. He was rather pleased with the way in which he had followed Kleber across this difficult country; he was quite sure that no sound had betrayed his presence. It was unlikely, therefore, that Kleber had halted to listen. He had gone into a dug-out.

Pagan would have given much to know what was going on in that dug-out, but he knew that for the moment any attempt to find it was out of the question. Impetuosity could only ruin whatever chance remained of finding out the reason of Kleber's wanderings. In any case he could find this track again and this very spot if he marked it. In the full light of day a careful search within a radius of fifty yards might reveal something.

He pulled out his pipe, but he put it back half filled into his pocket without lighting it. The smell of tobacco carried far at night, and Kleber was no fool for all his stolid appearance.

The time passed slowly. The night air was chilly, and Pagan sat with the collar of his coat turned up about his ears. Though it was dark where he sat on the shadowed hillside, across the valley a hill-top rose into the moonlight like a snowy peak, just as he had seen it on the previous evening when he had thrust his head from the drain. He could not be very far from the scene of last night's adventure. Perhaps thirty yards below him was the road, and that old dug-out and drain could not be more than two hundred yards down it.

Suddenly he raised his head and listened. Sounds of movement had begun again on the dark hillside above him. This must be Kleber returning.

Pagan decided to remain where he was and lie still. The weeds hardly covered him, but they made a dark background against which it was very unlikely he would be noticed in the dim deceptive light of the stars.

The sounds of movement drew nearer, and he noted that Kleber seemed to be making a good deal more noise in descending the slope than he had done in going up it. And then the reason of this increase in sound became apparent, for suddenly Kleber spoke. He was not alone.

CHAPTER THIRTEEN

I

PAGAN strained his ears to locate exactly the direction from which the sounds were coming; for he realized that if his rather inadequate hiding place were upon the near side of that mysterious path down which Kleber and his companion were moving, they would come out upon the track somewhere away to his left and, assuming Kleber to be returning by the way he had come, would walk up it right past him; whereas if his hiding place were beyond the path, they would come out upon the track somewhere away to the right and walk away from him.

As the sounds grew nearer he located them definitely as coming from the left, and he turned his head and strained his eyes in that direction. Suddenly he was aware of a vague form, dimly discernible as a moving patch of darkness, in the gloom a few yards away. A moment later another vague form appeared beside it; and the two moved slowly towards him up the track, looming larger and less vague with every step. He hoped they would speak, but they came on in silence in single file, for the track was narrow.

Pagan lay motionless among the weeds, calculating the chances of his being seen. In any case it was too late now to move. Movement and sound were the two things that would betray his presence: without them he was comparatively safe. He lay with muscles taut and his breath coming lightly between parted lips.

The two figures came on slowly. They passed within a foot or two of where he lay among the weeds; and he saw them silhouetted from the hips upwards against the night sky across the valley. The broader and shorter figure in front wearing a hat was undoubtedly Kleber. The tall, powerful figure that came behind was bare-headed, and the dim silhouette of its head against the sky startled Pagan and set his heart pounding against his ribs. It was no human profile that he saw, but an irregular concave line.

The two figures passed slowly up the track and were lost in the darkness, but the sounds of their progress continued. These ceased suddenly, and the murmur of voices came again. Then the voices ceased and the sound of movement began again, growing fainter as it passed into the distance.

Pagan decided to follow. He raised himself upon one elbow, and he was drawing up his legs as a preliminary to thrusting them out upon the track when fresh sounds struck him motionless again. The sounds came from the same direction as before. They were sounds of footsteps upon the track, footsteps coming nearer. He lowered his elbow and dropped back to the more comfortable prone position. This could mean but one thing; Kleber had gone and that other figure was returning.

The sounds came gradually nearer. Pagan's brain was working actively. Should he let the figure pass and then track it to its lair among this labyrinth of old dug-outs and trenches or should he confront it boldly and settle once and for all whether it were man or beast? That it might prove dangerous had to be considered, but an old war maxim ran in his head: the best form of defence is to attack.

The footsteps sounded very near now. Pagan prepared for action. He rose noiselessly upon one knee and transferred the torch to his left hand. A dim figure had emerged from the darkness and was coming slowly down the path towards him. It came closer—five yards, three yards, two.

Pagan rose quickly to his feet and switched on the torch. "Halt!" he cried in French; and then added, "My God!"

The figure had halted, and the bright wavering circle of light from the torch in Pagan's uncertain hand revealed a rough tweed coat and neat collar and tie about a strong tanned human neck. But the face above was hardly human. There appeared to be no eyes. There was no nose; only a dark cavity. And the mouth was a slit through which white teeth glimmered like those of a snarling beast. All the rest was shapeless, livid corrugated flesh like purplish crepe rubber, and by contrast the neatly brushed fair hair above, added if possible to the ghastly affect. There was a long silence.

Pagan's voice shook as he cried at last harshly, "Who are you?" He spoke in English under the sudden stress of emotion.

Some twitchings of two spots of naked flesh made it apparent that the creature had eyes after all, but they had been fast closed against the blinding glare. They opened slowly, and Pagan was startled to see how sparkling and blue they were, set in that dull livid, shapeless mass of flesh. They were keen, intelligent and above all, sad eyes that went far to restore his shaken confidence.

He pulled himself together and lowered the beam of light so as to lessen the glare. "Who are you and what are you up to?" he demanded again.

Then the creature spoke. "Who am I!" it echoed irritably. "What the hell has that to do with you? It seems much more to the point to ask who are you and what you are up to—unless it's highway robbery!"

To Pagan's surprise the language was English and the voice well-bred, thought a trifle indistinct, due no doubt to the twisted mouth. There was silence for a moment, and then the creature made as though to pass on down the track. But Pagan stood his ground.

"Who are you?" he repeated doggedly.

The creature halted again. Its blue eyes peered at Pagan's shadowed face as though it were trying to make up its mind about him. "Why should I answer you?" it retorted at last.

Pagan shrugged his shoulders. "Because, because you..." he began; and then a lifelong habit asserted itself, "because you come in such a questionable shape."

The other made a sound that might have been a laugh or a sigh, and a long silence followed. He looked away across the valley at the moonlit hill-top and then back again at Pagan. "Well I will answer your question," he said at last. "Though I do not admit your right to ask it. Who am I? I am a fellow who, as you see, got a little damaged in the late war. And as for what I am doing here, well . . ." He paused and then continued with tragic nonchalance, "I prefer to live up here where there are no women and children to frighten."

For some moments they stood there in silence facing one another in the gloom above the pool of light spilled upon the path by the torch in Pagan's lowered hand.

When at last he spoke his voice was low and gentle. "I am afraid I have made rather an ass of myself, sir," he said uncomfortably. "I'm sorry. I had no intention of barging in on your private affairs like this. I had no idea, I am awfully sorry."

"No matter. After all, how could you possibly have known!" answered the other in a more friendly tone. "Though your manner was a bit brusque, wasn't it! I suppose you had heard tales of something queer up here and wanted to see for yourself. Yes, they call this the haunted battlefield, you know," he went on with a half laugh. "And now you have seen the ghost!"

"Alas poor ghost," murmured Pagan under his breath.

The other fumbled in his pocket and produced a pipe which he put into his twisted mouth. "Possibly you are one of the people Kleber was telling me stayed at his inn last night," he said.

Pagan nodded. "As a matter of fact it was his rather curious behaviour that led me to play the part of Paul Pry and brought me up here again to-night. That is my only excuse, such as it is; and . . . well, I'm most awfully sorry."

The other nodded. "Kleber is not very subtle, I'm afraid. But don't let it worry you. I can see that you are not the sort of fellow to go shouting it from the housetops." And then after a slight pause, he added, "I never thought to talk to one of my own kind again, and I find it rather good after all these years."

Pagan nodded his head sympathetically. "Do you talk to no one then except Kleber?" he asked.

"Only Kleber," repeated the other. "He is a good fellow but he has his limitations as a conversationalist."

"But how long is it . . ." began Pagan. And then he stopped and added hastily, "There I go asking questions again. I'm sorry."

The other made a sound that might have been a laugh. "Don't apologise," he said. "You have no idea how good it sounds to hear English again. It's a long, long time now since I heard another Englishman speak it—not since that crump spoiled my beauty." He laughed softly without bitterness. The trace of embarrassment which had at first characterized his manner seemed to be passing. "You would hardly believe it," he went on. "And I can say it now without being suspected of vanity, but I was considered rather a handsome fellow in my time."

Pagan nodded in embarrassed silence.

"Let's see, how many years now is it since the great fracas?" went on the other. "I suppose you came in for that?"

"I did," said Pagan.

"What division were you?"

Pagan told him. He nodded and went on reminiscently, "Oh yes. I ran across them on the Somme in 'sixteen; they were coming out from Trones wood: we were going in."

"Sticky spot that," commented Pagan.

"It was," agreed the other. He was silent for a moment and then he said diffidently, "I say, I hope it doesn't bore you to talk about those old times."

"Not a bit," returned Pagan. "I like it."

"So do I," confessed the other. "Only I don't often get the chance nowadays," he added simply.

Pagan directed the light of his torch upon the bank beside the track. "Suppose we sit down, then," he suggested.

"If you are not in a hurry," said the man. "But now that you have run me to earth, I was going to suggest that you came along to my quarters and had a powwow."

"I would like to," answered Pagan. "But I don't want to pry into your affairs," he added.

The other dismissed the remark with a wave of his hand. "We will go then, shall we? They are not luxurious, you know, but there is a pew at any rate."

He led the way for a few yards down the track, and then halted. "If you lend me your torch, I will show you the way."

Pagan handed over the torch, and his companion directed the beam on to a large clump of brambles. There was a small gap in the middle of the clump, and the man stepped from the track over the intervening brambles into it. Then he went down an invisible step so that only that part of his body above the waist was visible. He held the torch so that Pagan could see.

"Step across," he said. "But not too far or you will fall in. There is a ledge here about a foot wide."

Pagan stepped across as directed and found himself standing upon the brink of a narrow, half-filled trench.

"Now follow me and keep your head down," said his companion. He bent low and disappeared beneath the brambles.

Pagan stepped into the shallow trench and followed, with head bent low, into the deeper part beneath the brambles. Presently it was possible to walk upright. The trench zigzagged up the hill, and was evidently an old communicating trench. Weeds and brambles grew right across the top in many places, and occasionally tangles of wire showed above against the sky.

The guide halted at last where the trench was roofed with two sheets of galvanized iron covered with weed-grown earth. He stooped and went through a low dug-out entrance in the side of the trench, and held the torch behind him so that the beam was directed upon the floor. Pagan followed along a short low passage to a curtain of sacking which the guide held aside. A yard beyond it, the beam of the torch shone upon a rough wooden door.

"A door in a dug-out is a refinement of luxury I have not met before," commented Pagan.

"It is a post-war addition of my own," explained the other. He pushed it open, disclosing a light beyond.

Pagan passed through into what was evidently a dug-out, though it was like no dug-out he had seen before.

Not a square inch of earth showed anywhere. All the walls were covered with creosoted planks, and on two walls the planks themselves were hidden behind dark green curtains of some thick rough material. The floor also was boarded and was in part covered with a worn green carpet. The planks forming the roof were creosoted a dark brown, but the two great timbers which stretched from side to side and carried the great weight of the earth above were beautifully carved along the edges with the old Norman dog-tooth pattern and painted a rich red, green, white, gold and black.

The furniture consisted of a rough bookcase containing a number of books, the greater part of which were paper covered Tauchnitz editions. A worn French, green plush arm-chair was placed beside a small deal table on which stood an oil lamp and a tin of tobacco. There was a smaller wicker chair beside the bookcase. A larger and more solid table on the other side of the dug-out contained some tools, such as chisels and gouges, some pots of paint, and a small block of wood, the upper part of which had been roughly carved to the shape of an Alsatian head-dress. Upon a shelf behind the table stood some more pots of paint and a beautifully carved and coloured model of an Alsatian cabin with a stork's nest on the chimney.

"That is not your handiwork, is it!" exclaimed Pagan admiringly. He kept his eyes from the man's dreadful face which seemed to draw them like a magnet.

"Yes, that is one of my efforts," answered the man. "And this is another on the way," he added with his hand on the half carved block of wood. "This is how I get my living. Kleber disposes of them for me to the shops. Tourists buy them, you know."

"I bought one myself," Pagan told him. "I don't buy travel souvenirs as a rule, but I pride myself that I know a good piece of work when I see it."

"Thanks," said the other. "Sit down, won't you. I will put some coffee on; I'm afraid that is the best I can do in the way of a drink."

"There is nothing I should like better, if it isn't an awful fag," said Pagan. He glanced at his watch. "But I must not stay long."

The owner of this strange home went behind the curtain that screened the end of the dug-out and returned with a primus stove and a kettle. Pagan unbuttoned his coat.

"Oh do take that off," said the other. "I'm afraid my manners have gone to pot living alone." He hung the coat on a nail behind the door and went back to the stove. But his eyes wandered wistfully over Pagan's black bow and dinner jacket.

"It's a long time since I wore a boiled shirt," he murmured as he poured methylated spirit into the collar of the stove. "Reminds one of old times." He struck a match and lighted the spirit. "Did you ever see *Romance?* he asked suddenly.

Pagan nodded. "I think everybody did; Doris Keane in *Romance* was one of the seven wonders of the war."

The stranger began to pump the stove. "What is she in now?" he asked.

"Nothing as far as I know; I haven't heard of her for years," answered Pagan.

The other nodded his head. "Of course it is a long time ago now. I suppose all the old shows have gone — *Chu-Chin-Chow, Zig Zag, To-night's the Night . . . Vanity Fair?*"

"All gone, I'm afraid," answered Pagan gently.

The stove was roaring well now and the man sat down in the wicker chair. "I saw *Chu-Chin-Chow* seven times," he said reminiscently. "Three times on one leave! And *To-night's the Night* four times. Do you remember that song, 'Any old night is a wonderful night if you're there with a wonderful girl?' It was too," he added half to himself.

Pagan nodded. "Happy days," he murmured.

There was silence for a moment or two, and then the stranger asked almost conventionally, "Any good shows on in Town now?"

"No—not like the old ones," said Pagan. "At any rate they don't seem as good as the old ones seemed."

The other filled his pipe thoughtfully. "I'm rather glad of that," he said slowly. Silence settled down again.

Pagan looked appreciatively round the dug-out. "You have made yourself very comfortable here," he said.

"I'm glad you like it. I'm rather proud of it."

"You have every reason to be," Pagan told him. "This is an old Bosche dug-out, I suppose," he added.

The other nodded. "Yes—all this side of the ridge was German."

"But did you get your . . . your Blighty one down in this part of the world?" asked Pagan.

The man rose and began to make the coffee. "Oh no," he answered. "This part of the line was always in the French area. I don't think we ever had any troops down here. I 'copped my packet' as Tommy says, much further North." He poured the coffee into two plain white cups of thick china, one of which he handed to Pagan. From behind the curtain he produced a box of sugar cubes.

"I expect you are wondering how I got down here."

Pagan stirred his coffee. "I don't want to pry," he said; "but, well, naturally I am rather curious."

The other nodded his head slowly. "It was rather curious." Either by accident or design he sat where the direct light of the lamp did not fall upon him, and his head was turned so the full horror of his face was not visible. "If it would interest you."

"It would very much," Pagan told him.

II

The man took the tobacco tin from the table and filled his pipe. "It was during the big Bosche attack in the spring of eighteen. I don't know whether you were in that?"

Pagan shook his head. "No, we missed it. We were just north of Arras at the time; we came in for it later on. But we heard the racket down south."

"We just caught it," said the other. "We had been in only a couple of days when it came. Misty weather; couldn't see a damned thing. All the telephone cables were cut during the first half-hour of the barrage and nobody knew what was happening. I had a frightful lot of casualties in my Company and I couldn't get in touch with Battalion. Heavy machine gunning going on behind us too. Then the crump came along that got me, and I suppose my fellows thought I was done for. Anyway I was too smashed up to remember that or what happened for some time afterwards. But I suppose what did happen was the Bosche pushed our fellows back and found me." He sucked at his pipe. "You know what things are like during a push, and it must have been the merest fluke that they didn't leave me there to make an end of it. Anyway, for some reason or other they didn't; they brought me back to a hospital. And there again I was lucky—or unlucky." He regarded the glowing bowl of his pipe and went on. "As you may imagine, the doctors had their hands pretty full at that time and they might reasonably have put on one side one who, like myself, was an enemy and a pretty hopeless case. Undoubtedly they would have done so, only the fellow in charge happened to be an enthusiast on his job—the worse a case was the better he liked it—and the moment I was brought in, he lost interest in all the rest. Here was something that would really test his skill, he thought, and, well, I became his pet case.

"Some of these German doctors are much cleverer than ours, I think; anyway, this fellow pulled me through. It was a million to one chance apparently, and he brought it off. But there were limits even to his skill; and the construction of a human face was one of them."

He struck a match and held it to his pipe. "I lay in bed for weeks covered in dressings. And most of that time I cursed that fellow's skill that kept me alive when I ought to have been dead. I knew he had no interest in me personally: it was just his damned professional pride. He wanted to be able to exhibit me as a trophy of his skill.

"He was kind enough though, you know. He offered to try to get into touch with my people for me. I knew they thought I was dead, and as it was still very much touch and go whether I lived, I said no. And besides, I knew he would never make a job of my face. It was all covered in dressings and I had not seen a glass, but I knew. I asked him about it once; but he hedged. Then I asked Kleber, and he told me the truth."

"Kleber!" exclaimed Pagan.

The other nodded. "Yes; that was where I first met Kleber. He was a hospital orderly; and he was very good to me. The Germans did not treat their enemy wounded badly, you know, but they were short of things themselves at that time, and when there was not enough to go round, it was only natural that their own wounded came first. Kleber got me lots of little comforts that I should have missed otherwise."

"Stout fellow," murmured Pagan.

"He was an Alsatian, conscripted of course into the German army; but he hated war, and he had no great love either for French or German. His one idea was to get it over and get back to his farm here in the Vosges. He often used to talk to me about it. He didn't get on too well with the other orderlies; as an Alsatian he was rather suspect, and he was glad to talk to me. He used to sneak in at odd times with any little delicacy he could get hold of and then talk about his home and his wife and daughter. They were on the German side of the line, living down at Turkheim and making a living by selling stuff to the troops back in rest. His little farm and estaminet were of course on the French side, just over the ridge here. His wife became ill and died during the time that I was in that hospital, and he never forgave the authorities for refusing him leave to go to see her."

"Rotten trick," commented Pagan. "We always gave our fellows leave."

The other nodded. "Well, after a bit I began to sit up and take notice. I was still all swathed in bandages, but I used to sit in a chair outside in the sun and take little walks occasionally. Kleber nearly always went with me. By this time he looked upon me as a friend, and I knew all his personal history. He told me all the news that came from the official communiqués and that drifted back from the line, and we discussed it together, more like a couple of retired chess players watching a tournament than two enemies in the middle of a war. The allies were just beginning their last series of offensives then, and our one subject of discussion was whether they would be able to break through and win the war that year. Kleber thought they would; Germany was on its last legs, he believed. I was not so sanguine. Next year perhaps when the Americans really got going, I said."

He tapped his pipe out into the lid of a tin. "Well, you know what happened. You were in it yourself, I expect. We were in a little backwater away among the woods, but day by day the news came rolling in—Bapaume retaken, the Hindenburg Line crossed; we knew then we were getting near the end.

"Then Kleber came in one morning with a serious face and whispered to me to meet him in a quiet spot in the grounds. I did so, and we sat down beneath the trees and he told me the news. There had been a revolution in Germany it was rumoured, the Kaiser had abdicated and an armistice was being asked for. Anyway, the hospital was to pack up and go back. Then Kleber unfolded his plan and asked my opinion of it.

"If he went back with the hospital to Germany it would mean weeks of delay before army red tape could demobilize him, quite apart from any complications that might arise if, as was said, a revolution really had broken out. He had no interest in a German revolution; he wanted only to get back to his home. The war was over; therefore he proposed to demobilize himself. He was nearer home there than he would be in Leipzig or Munich. He proposed to leave that night and tramp southwards to Alsace; he had only to follow the trench line which would bring him within a mile of his home.

"We discussed the idea, and it seemed to me to be a good scheme. Then I put forward my own idea. 'Look here,' I said, 'take me with you. I have no more use for Germany and revolutions than you have. My people think I'm dead, and with a face like mine I had much better remain dead as far as they are concerned. You can find me a job of work on your farm.'

"We argued a bit, but he agreed in the end, for he was glad to have my company. We agreed that night was the best time to clear out; but the patients were always shut in after dusk, and so it was arranged that I should pretend to go for a stroll in the grounds during the afternoon and make for a hiding place he knew of about a mile away. It was unlikely that any great fuss would be made over my disappearance, as discipline had largely gone to pot during the few previous days. Anyway, I was to lie close, and he would join me after dark with as much food and kit as he could collect.

"It all worked well. I strolled out in the afternoon, and as soon as I was out of view from the window of the hospital, made straight for the hiding place, which I found without difficulty. I had on the old trench coat in which I had been captured, and the pockets were stuffed with my few belongings and what little money I had. Soon after dark Kleber arrived. He carried a pack full of food and a couple of blankets. Apparently in the general disorganization my disappearance had not even been noticed.

"We had no map, but that didn't worry Kleber. The trench line, he said, led to his house; and we started off then and there.

"Have you seen much of the line—up and down, I mean?"

"A good bit," answered Pagan. "The Salient, La Bassée, Vimy Ridge, and most of the Somme."

The other nodded. "But only bits, I expect; not continuously. Did you ever think of that great deserted highway of no-man's-land running from the Channel to the Alps?"

Pagan nodded. "Yes—often."

"Well, Kleber and I marched down most of it—every inch of it from St. Quentin to the Vosges. The Chemin des

Dames, the Argonne, Verdun—we saw it all—by night. It was one of the queerest experiences I ever had, tramping along night after night through no-man's-land. And not a sound. And we came across some queer things too.

"We marched always at night and lay up during the day in some old dug-out. Kleber managed to exchange his uniform for civilian clothes, and sometimes he went to cottages and bought or begged food to eke our scanty supplies. We had a little paraffin stove and we cooked on that. I don't know how long it took us to get here, for I lost count of the days. I was not yet properly fit, and we had to move by easy stages.

"I shall never forget Kleber's joy when at last we reached the hills. He didn't say much, but he kept striding ahead and then pulling up short when he remembered my weak condition. Anyway, it was several days after that before we arrived. I remember that night particularly. It was moonlight and we came along the top of the ridge here from the north. Kleber had not told me we were so close, but I had noticed that he seemed more impatient than usual. He kept on stopping and peering down to the right, and then he would grunt and move on again. Suddenly he turned off half right and led the way down the grassy slope on the other side of the ridge—you probably know it, though there wasn't much grass there then. He said the going would be easier than on top. I was pretty tired and did not pay much attention. I know we crossed a hollow and then climbed another steepish slope. On top he seized me by the arm and pointed.

"As I said, it was moonlight, and below us was a shallow hollow that seemed to run straight off the mountain to a deep valley south of us. I could see a line of high hills beyond. But at the bottom of the hollow, where it ran off the mountain so to speak, was a dark building with the moonlight shining through the skeleton rafters of its smashed roof. It was towards this that Kleber was pointing.

"'That's my home,' he said in a quiet voice. I didn't know what to say, for I knew he was thinking of that smashed roof, and for all I knew the whole building was just a gutted shell like all the others in the forward area. You know what their sticks and houses are to these peasants; you've seen them farther north, I expect, risking their lives to bring out a mattress or a broken chair. It's their very life blood. He must have known that a building as close to the line as that could hardly escape damage, but I suppose he had always pictured his home in its peaceful setting as he had known it, so that he never connected it with the gaping ruins he had seen in other parts of the line.

"But he didn't rave and curse. 'That's my home,' he said quite quietly and then led the way down towards it.

"When we got close to it I was glad to see that the damage seemed to be confined to the roof: the walls looked sound enough. He climbed in through a broken window and told me to wait while he got a light. I heard him moving across the floor inside, and then I heard another sound which seemed to come from another room. Someone else was there too, and I started to climb through the window, for I knew that Kleber was in the mood for murder just then.

I heard him growl angrily and swing open a door, and I saw a dull patch of light appear at the end of the room. Then there followed an ominous silence broken only by a sort of panting, shuffling noise.

"I scrambled through the window as quickly as I could, but before I was half way across the room, I heard Kleber's voice again and it didn't sound a bit angry. And then I heard a woman's voice. Kleber called me, and I just had time to pull the collar of my trench coat across my face before the door opened and Kleber came out with his arm round a girl. Of course it was Bertha, his daughter.

"You know what these peasant women are for grit, you've seen 'em farther north. Directly the last shot was fired, she'd packed her traps in a sack, flung it over her shoulder and tramped straight back to her home. She had been there about four days then and she had already started repairing the roof with odds and ends of stuff that was lying about. And . . . well, that's how I came to be here."

Pagan relighted his pipe. "You didn't work on the farm then, as you suggested."

The other shook his head. "At first I helped Kleber to get things going—house watertight and all that. At that time, of course, the place was deserted. Munster was flat and the people were only just beginning to come back. Nobody ever came up here, and I could wander about much as I liked. Both Kleber and Bertha wanted me to remain in the house, but it wasn't playing the game. I don't belong to the family. And besides I'm an independent sort of fellow. I found this dug-out and rigged it up; and then I hit upon the idea of making these gadgets for the shops. So now I have my own house, such as it is, and earn my own living such as it is. That is much more satisfactory. And no one could want better or more loyal friends than Kleber and Bertha."

"I am sure of that," agreed Pagan. "And you are content?"

The other tapped out his pipe. "Yes—why not? I will not pretend that I'm not bored at times. But I have no worries and I am my own master." He indicated the dug-out with a wave of his hand. "I have my home—such as it is, my books, my simple work. And I have enough to live upon in my own little way. Yes, I am content—even happy."

When Pagan rose to go, he asked, "Is there anything I can do for you?"

The tall lonely man shook his head.

"Sure?"

"Sure."

Pagan produced a small pocket diary from his coat; he pulled out the thin pencil and wrote. Then he tore out the page. "There is my name and the hotel I am staying at in Munster," he said. "Also my English address. If at any time I can be of any use, don't hesitate to write. Promise?"

The other glanced at the paper, folded it up and put it in his pocket. "I promise," he said. "And thanks very, very much."

He led Pagan back down the old trench, up through the brambles on to the track, and thence down to the road. The moon swam high above the ridge, and the white shivered tree stumps glimmered eerily like watchful ghosts in the cold greenish light.

"Please don't bother to come any further," said Pagan.

They shook hands and said good night. Pagan set off at a smart pace down the road. He turned after some twenty paces and waved his hand to the tall figure standing motionless against the rising background of the ridge, and a hand was waved in reply. When next he turned his head the figure was gone and only the white splintered trunks stood forlornly in the moonlight.

III

He expected he would have to walk back, but some half a mile down the road where it swept round the big grassy hummock at the end of the ridge before descending in loops to the valley, he came upon the car. A dark silent figure was distinguishable in the front seat under the cover. It stirred as he came up. "I'm afraid I have been a very long time," said Pagan. "But I told you not to wait."

Griffin smothered a yawn and climbed stiffly from the car. "That's all right, sir. I've slept like a top."

Pagan got in, the headlights blazed out, and the car glided from the grass on to the road. The keen night wind hit them as they slid swiftly round the grassy hummock and began to descend the steep zigzags to the valley.

Griffin lay back with one hand lightly on the wheel. "Well, sir, did you find out what that fellow was up to?"

"Yes," answered Pagan after a pause. "But he was not up to any harm. I'm sorry now I poked my nose in." He considered a moment. "As a matter of fact it is nothing more than a relation of his who was terribly smashed up in the war. He is not a pretty sight and does not want people to see him—poor devil."

"Poor blighter!" murmured Griffin sympathetically.

"I shall have to tell Mr. Baron," went on Pagan, "or he might come poking round up here himself; but apart from that, I think it would be better, Griffin, if you and I forgot all about to-night."

Griffin nodded his head understandingly. "That's right, sir. We've just been for a ride round in the moonlight, I've been to sleep and that's all I know."

"Good man," said Pagan.

CHAPTER FOURTEEN

I

Pagan came down rather late for breakfast in the morning. In the sunny room leading to the terrace he found Clare and Baron having coffee and croissants. Upon their little table was a third cup, empty, and a becrumbed plate.

"That is the remains of Cecil's feast," said Clare. "He is off to earn the daily bread."

"Then I will take his chair if I may," said Pagan.

Baron put a generously buttered piece of roll into his mouth and mumbled, "Yes, do. All nice and hot from the cow."

Pagan sat down, and a waiter took away Cecil's dirty cup and brought some coffee.

"Very solemn this morning!" remarked Clare as she poured out the coffee.

He smiled at her. "I am still an optimist!" he said in a low voice.

"Late hours and a languishing liver," diagnosed Baron, who had not heard the other remark. "What happened last night, Charles? I hear that you and Griffin went off detecting."

"Yes," added Clare. "I was surprised when Cecil said this morning that you had been up there again last night. You are a very persistent person, are you not!" she ended with a smile.

"Too persistent in this case, I'm afraid," answered Pagan solemnly. "I wish now I had not meddled with the affair at all!"

Baron put down his cup. "Then you did find out something, Charles."

Pagan nodded.

"Well then, come along, out with it. I'm quite mildly interested, you know, and of course Clare, being a female woman, is simply dying to hear; aren't you?"

"Simply dying," agreed Clare.

"Well then, out with it," repeated Baron as Pagan hesitated. "Were you right or was I? Does Kleber keep a pre-historic man on his mountain top or is he a dangerous Bolshie from Moskowvitch?"

Pagan stirred his coffee thoughtfully and shook his head. "Kleber is a jolly good fellow," he answered slowly. He glanced round the little room and went on when he saw that except for themselves it was deserted. "And his activities are quite harmless; but as we suspected there is a connection between him and the apparition."

"You don't mean to tell me, Charles," mumbled Baron with his mouth full of buttered croissant, "that you have seen the apparition."

Pagan nodded. "Not only seen him but spoken to him."

Baron put down his cup with a bang and looked round eloquently at Clare; then he looked back at Pagan. "Well, go on, curse you!" he cried. "Can't you see we're all agog?"

"He is a friend of Kleber's," explained Pagan. "A poor fellow who was frightfully smashed up during the war—no face left at all."

"Well I'm dashed!" exclaimed Baron. "So that's it!"

"And he is English," added Pagan.

"English! But look here, Charles," began Baron.

"Don't you think, Dicky," put in Clare quietly, "that it would be better if we let—" she hesitated a second—"let Charles tell us what happened."

Baron nodded. "Right 'o. You go ahead, Charles; you have the Speaker's eye."

Pagan related his adventures of the previous evening.

"Poor devil!" exclaimed Baron when he had finished.

"Poor, poor fellow," murmured Clare.

"Griffin knows," said Pagan. "I had to tell him something, and I thought it better to tell him the truth. But I told him to keep it to himself. I hope he will."

"He ought to be pretty safe in a case like this," said Baron. "There are not many things the gentle Griffin respects but war derelicts are certainly one of them."

"Is there nothing we can do for that poor man?" asked Clare with troubled eyes.

"I asked him that," said Pagan; "and he said no. But I would like to do something for him."

Baron nodded his head. "Poor devil!" he repeated. "But he ought to have gone back to his people, you know," he added thoughtfully. "After all, there must be quite a number of fellows who have done so, and their people are probably only too glad to have them, crippled as they are."

"But he is thinking of his people, Dicky," said Clare gently. "He is trying to spare them."

"I know," said Baron. "But do you think his people would worry about the deformity. Don't you think they would be only too glad to know that he was alive?"

"In the case of an ordinary cripple—yes," said Pagan. "But think of this fellow's face."

"Is it very terrible?" asked Clare in a low voice.

"Frightful. Horrible. I'm not squeamish, but it gave me the creeps. And I could hardly keep my eyes off it: it had a sort of horrible fascination. However much one's relations might care for one, after all they are only human, and they couldn't stand that. Don't you agree?" He turned to Clare.

She held her spoon upright in her cup and regarded it with a little frown of concentration on her forehead. "I don't know," she answered slowly. "I am trying to think. He is the same person, of course, however different his face may be. And one can get used to anything—almost. Mere plainness, of course, does not matter; but real ugliness, hideousness . . ."

"Ghastliness, nightmare horror all day and every day," supplemented Pagan.

"I—I don't know whether he is right or not," she went on in an awed voice. "Perhaps he has chosen the kindest course."

"He might wear a mask," suggested Baron. "They make some wonderful things nowadays."

"And would you have the mask as like his original face as possible?" asked Pagan. "Think of it, an expressionless travesty of the face one once knew—always grinning or always solemn. Personally I think that would get on my nerves so much that I would rather have the straightforward horror."

Baron nodded his head gloomily. "And of course if the mask were not like his original face, one would always feel it was someone else."

"And besides, he is a sensitive fellow," went on Pagan. "He was good-looking once. He told me so himself half-jokingly. But it was true: I could see it for myself. Back view he was as fine and well proportioned a man as one could wish to see."

"Poor chap!" repeated Baron.

"Poor, poor fellow," repeated Clare. "Was he married, I wonder?"

"I don't know," answered Pagan. "I don't think so. But from something he said, I fancy there was a girl."

"Poor, poor girl," she murmured.

Baron offered her his cigarette case. "Um! I suppose that makes a difference. You think that he is right then, Charles?"

Pagan held a match to Clare's cigarette. "Well, honestly, isn't it the kindest thing? To his people he has been dead now ten years and more; they had one sharp blow instead of years of wearing hammering."

Baron nodded his head. "Kindest to them, yes. But what about the poor devil himself. Do you think he regrets his decision? Is he content?"

Pagan shrugged his shoulders helplessly. "He says he is. Though he admitted he is bored at times."

"Poor fellow, he must be," murmured Clare.

"Good lord, yes, he must get tired of everlasting work, reading, reading, work," exclaimed Baron. "And he has nothing else, you say, not even a wireless."

"By Jove, that's an idea!" exclaimed Pagan.

"What is?" asked Baron.

"Why wireless. If I got him a wireless it might liven things up a bit. He could listen to plays and when they put on those old musical comedy programmes he would hear some of those old tunes he likes so much."

"Yes, that certainly is an idea," agreed Baron.

"You do not think it might bring back old times too vividly," suggested Clare thoughtfully. "We do not want to make things harder for him."

Pagan considered a moment. "It might," he said doubtfully. "But surely he would get more pleasure than sadness out of it in the long run. He would not feel quite such an outcast, and he would hear his own language. It was jolly pathetic the way he listened to me talking English."

"Poor devil!" murmured Baron again. "Well, old Charles, I will go halves with you. But remember I'm a poor man."

"And please include me," said Clare.

"Thanks awfully, both of you," said Pagan. "We will go and see what the local Harrods can do in the way of wireless, shall we."

II

It was arranged that Pagan should take the set up to the inn and ask Kleber to deliver it to the lonely Englishman. After much consideration he had with great care written a note which he hoped would overcome any reluctance which this obviously sensitive man might feel about accepting the gift. It was a short but exceedingly tactful composition in which the fact that they were brother officers was gently stressed. Clare's eyes were suspiciously misty as she handed him back the rough draft. "It is the kindest note I have ever read," she said.

"Old Charles isn't much to look at, but he has a kind heart when you get to know him," agreed Baron cheerfully.

"Yes, he certainly improves upon acquaintance," said Clare. Her tone was light but the eyes that smiled into his were very kind.

The late afternoon sunlight was gilding the wooded hill sides across the valley when Pagan knocked at the door of the inn. It was opened by Bertha, and he knew at once by the expression in her eyes that she had heard something of his adventure of the previous night. He stepped into the long brick-floored room and dumped his heavy parcel upon a table. "*Bon jour*, Bertha," he cried. "Is Herr Kleber in?"

She shook her head half sullenly while her eyes remained fixed upon his face. "No, M'sieu. He ees abroad."

Pagan ordered a drink, and when she had brought it, he untied the knots of the parcel with slow deliberation. She watched him in silence as he removed the wrappers one by one, and only when the polished wood case of the set was disclosed, did her eyes flutter from it half-questioningly to his. He lifted the set clear of the wrappings and placed it on a table by itself. Then he sat down and drank from his glass.

"Bertha," he said presently, "you are angry with me for what happened last night."

She did not reply, but watched him with resentful eyes.

"I am angry with myself now; I wish I had taken your advice," he went on. "But don't be afraid. I have no intention of pushing myself in again, or of making him unhappy or trying to take him away. My wish is the same as yours—to make him happy."

Still she was silent, but her eyes were less resentful and suspicious.

"You were right to stop us from going out the other night, and we are so glad to know that he has such loyal friends in you and your father. And we want to thank you for all your kindness to a fellow countryman of ours. We can never do anything for him such as you have done; but we should like to do something. And so we have bought this wireless set, and we want you to give it to him. Will you?"

She did not answer, but her eyes travelled from him to the set and back again.

"You see," went on Pagan, "he will be able to hear music when he is working. And when he is lonely he can turn it on and hear people talking and singing. Will you give it to him for us, Bertha?"

She did not reply, and for a moment he thought that she was going to refuse. Then suddenly her eyes filled, and two large tears ran down her broad cheeks. "*Vous êtes très, très gentil, M'sieu,*" she murmured. "Oh, M'sieu, it will make him so happy." She dabbed her cheek with a handkerchief, and went on quickly, "When you arrived that night I had fear. You were English and I think that perhaps you know the *pauvre M'sieu* and you take him away. I had fear very much that you take him away, an' I say you not take him away."

Pagan nodded his head understandingly. "We are not going to take him away from you, Bertha," he said gently. "We only want to make him happy. And I want you to give him this set, will you? If I gave it to him myself I should have to push in again; and I don't want to do that. And then he might not take it from me; he might be too proud and sensitive, you understand? But you will know how to persuade him." He handed her the note. "I have written this little note to him asking him to accept it, but it is really you that I am relying upon. Will you do it?"

She nodded her head and bit her lip in an effort to keep back the tears that seemed inclined to flow again. He took her by the elbow and led her to the table on which the set stood.

"I will show you how to work it, and then you will be able to show him."

She watched with a childlike concentration of attention upon her face as he switched on and manipulated the dials; and when the syncopated strains of a dance band grew suddenly and filled the long room, she put her hands upon her hips and listened attentively with her head on one side. Then her eye caught his, and she broke into a frank delighted smile that transfigured her homely face and made it almost beautiful. "It will make him so happy, M'sieu," she murmured.

"You will have to get the batteries renewed for him," said Pagan when he was satisfied that she understood how to manipulate the set. "There isn't a spare one at present, but they promised to have one ready for me to-morrow, and I will send it up."

Bertha went to the little bar in the corner of the room. From its recesses she produced a bottle which she dusted with a solemn care that showed that it was no ordinary bottle. Then without speaking she brought two glasses to the table and reverently filled them with golden liquid from the bottle. She raised her glass and regarded him gravely across the top. "*Votre santé, M'sieu*," she said, with a gracious inclination of her head.

Pagan thanked her and raised his own glass. "To your heart's desire, Bertha," he said and drank. She bowed her head quickly in acknowledgement, but not before he had seen the wave of colour which momentarily flooded her brown healthy cheeks.

CHAPTER FIFTEEN

THE hot midday sun beat down upon the irregular pavé of the Place du Marche in Munster. On the hot pavements the gay striped awning of the Café de la Cigogne threw hard edged shadows like water spilled on sand. The rows of trees on the opposite side of the square stood dusty and listless against the dazzling white walls and blistered shutters of the buildings behind them, and every projecting stick and twig of the big stork's nest perched on top of a pyramidical roof above the trees was etched black and clear cut upon the cloudless blue sky.

Pagan, in the shadow of the awning, drained his iced bock and put the glass down on the little table before him. He passed his handkerchief across his moist forehead. "Beware the noonday devil!" he murmured. "By the way, what *is* the noonday devil?"

Baron shook his head. "I have no idea, Charles," he answered languidly. "But he would need to be a hardy little devil to function in this square." He leisurely turned his head so that through the glass of the side screens he could see the brown sandstone tower of the florid Lutheran church that seemed to flame in the sunlight at the top of the square. At the lower end of the square the rustic whitewashed walls and slender lead spire of the Catholic church rose against the green background of hills.

Pagan grunted and pulled out his pipe. They sat in lethargic silence for some moments. Pagan tilted back his chair and idly snapped his fingers to an Alsatian dog that was sniffing among the little tables.

Presently Baron murmured, "There's friend Kleber."

Pagan turned his head and idly watched the square form of the innkeeper coming along the pavement towards them.

"*Bon jour!*" cried Baron as Kleber drew level. The man turned his head and then stepped under the awning towards them.

"Have a drink," invited Pagan.

Kleber thanked them and asked to be excused as he was in a hurry. He pulled a letter from his pocket and held it out. It was for M'sieu Pagan. He was on his way to the hotel to deliver it, but perhaps M'sieu Pagan would be good enough to accept it now and so save him the remainder of the journey. Then he raised his hat, said good day and passed on.

Pagan tore open the envelope.

"From that poor devil with the smashed face, I suppose," murmured Baron.

"Yes—thanking us for the wireless set," answered Pagan still reading.

"Is he pleased with it?" asked Baron.

Pagan turned over the letter and then passed it to Baron. "Seems to be. Signs himself 'yours very gratefully, R. V.'"

Baron withdrew his hands from his pockets and took the note.

Pagan pulled out his pouch and began filling his pipe. A long silence ensued. "He seems quite pleased, doesn't he?" said Pagan at last as he fumbled in his pocket for a match.

"Yes," answered Baron in a voice that was strangely quiet. "And he signs himself R. V.—the initials of Roger Vigers."

Pagan, his pipe in one hand and the other in the act of withdrawing a matchbox from his pocket, became suddenly motionless like a wax figure. Then he slowly turned his head and looked at Baron. Baron appeared to be staring at the note which he held in his hand, but there was a frown of concentration upon his forehead, and his eyes were in reality fixed upon the sunlit pavement beyond the shadow of the awning.

"But, my dear chap, you don't think . . ." began Pagan at last.

"No, I don't think, I know," answered Baron quietly.

Pagan allowed the matchbox to drop back into his pocket. "The same initials, yes," he began. "But just a coincidence surely. There is no . . ."

"It is not merely the initials," interrupted Baron. "Though they do add the final touch." He tapped the note with his hand. "This is Vigers' own handwriting."

Pagan carried the unlighted pipe slowly to his mouth. "Are you sure?"

"My dear Charles, I've seen Vigers' writing on orders and things hundreds of times—too often, anyway, not to recognise it now."

Silence settled down again. With knit brows Pagan regarded the high perched stork's nest that looked so hard and brittle in the harsh sunlight. "Clare," he said at last, "how will she take this?"

"Thank God, she doesn't know!" said Baron.

Pagan removed his pipe again and rubbed his forehead thoughtfully. "But she will have to."

Baron raised his head sharply. "Why has she to? What good will it do?"

Pagan rubbed the back of his neck. "But she must be told. Hang it all we can't . . ."

"Look here, Charles," interrupted Baron, "we have got to think this out from every point of view; from hers, Roger's and yours. What effect it would have upon her, God only knows—or upon him. She is happy now, and so is he in his way. I wish to God we had never poked our noses into this."

"So do I," murmured Pagan fervently.

Baron stared at the sunny pavement with knit brows for some moments. "We have hung together for a good long time, old Charles, you and I," he said at last without looking up. "And we have been through some pretty bloody times together too, and . . . well, I ask you as man to man are you serious about Clare? You know what I mean."

Pagan took the cold pipe from his mouth and regarded the unlighted tobacco in the bowl. "More serious than I have ever been about anything in my life, Dicky," he answered at last.

Baron nodded. "I thought so." He pulled out his own pipe and remained staring at the pavement. "I know

Clare pretty well, Charles. She doesn't spread herself over people—particularly men, but . . . well, she's taken things from you that I would have sworn she wouldn't take from any man on earth. I warned you that I was convinced that she would never marry, and . . . well, I'm beginning to change my opinion now." He stuck his pipe in his mouth and unrolled his pouch. "I would give anything to see her happy and married and all that. I'm damned fond of Clare, you know, in a brotherly way, and . . . well, I can stick you better than I can stick most blighters, so you can imagine that I have been rather bucked with the way things seemed to be turning out."

He put his pipe in his pouch and began to fill it jerkily. He went on rather diffidently: "I don't know how far you have got, Charles. I don't know whether you have come to any understanding with her."

Pagan shook his head.

"You don't mind my saying this, old Charles, do you? But . . . as a . . . well a naturally rather interested observer, my diagnosis of the situation at the moment between you and Clare is that it has reached a critical stage. Personally I think that Clare is damned fond of you and doesn't know it. Now if she hears that poor old Roger is alive it might, it might, I say, have the effect of making her realize that she is more fond of you than she thought: on the other hand it might not. Anyway, she'd feel that she wasn't free, and it would certainly finish your chances for the present— and perhaps for good." He turned his head and looked at Pagan. "Why not leave it alone then?"

Pagan was gazing miserably at the sunlit pavement. He seemed to rouse himself with an effort. "But don't you see, Dicky," he said at last in a tired voice, "that that is just why I cannot leave it alone? I'm too interested in it personally. Suppose I did say nothing and suppose my luck was in, could I honestly take her, knowing that I had won her by what after all would be a pretty mean trick? And what would she think of me if ever she found out! And think of that poor devil Vigers himself—one of us, knocked out in the war. I'm not a sentimental cove, Dicky, but damn it all there is some sort of camaraderie among us who went through it. God help us if there isn't."

Baron took his unlighted pipe from his mouth with deliberation. "I see all that, Charles, but if you don't mind my saying so, I think you are a being little sentimental. I remember during the war how some people at home were horrified when they heard that a man would take, let us say, the boots of his best friend who had just been killed and wear them. They thought it callous. But you and I know better.

"God knows I'm not callous about poor old Roger. He is the finest fellow I ever met, bar none except perhaps old G. B. And the six months we were together he was my best friend. And as you know, six months in the line is worth twenty years with a man in civilian life. So no one can accuse me of being unduly prejudiced in your favour. But much as I love old Roger, we must face the facts without sentiment. The two of you went into the war. You were lucky; Roger wasn't. It was the luck of the game. He will never be any good any more; you will. You may say it isn't fair. Perhaps not. Anyway you took the risk. He lost; you won. It is the way the cards were played. And it's no good trying to put the clock back now. I suppose all of us who came through have asked ourselves sometime or other why we had the luck. We don't know. There seemed to be no rhyme or reason about it. You were one of those who had the luck; Roger wasn't. It's no good trying to reverse it now. The justice of it doesn't enter in to it; that's no concern of ours: it's on the shoulders of the power that arranges these things. We can only accept the fact. Poor old Roger had his innings and went out. He can't expect to have a second; and he knows it—that's why he is up there. Your innings is still going on, admittedly, if you like, not because you are a better bat, but you can't retire in favour of a fellow who has already been in. You can only bless your luck and carry on. It's not callousness: it's the luck of the game."

Pagan raised his head wearily and thrust his hands into his pockets. "You argue damn well," he said almost irritably. "But you are only making out a case. I *know* what is the only decent thing to do, and what's more you would do the same yourself if you were in my place, wouldn't you? Now, honestly, wouldn't you?"

"What I would do, does not affect the question," retorted Baron. "Maybe I can see what ought to be done better than you can. If I were in your place, the personal element would come in and possibly spoil my judgment. And just because I am not in your place, I am able to judge better than you can."

Pagan shook his head slowly. "I put it to you again, Dicky: would it be playing the game? Answer me that."

Baron did not reply for a moment. He pulled out a box of matches and lighted his pipe. "It seems to me, Charles," he said at last, "that you are thinking too much about yourself and too little about other people."

Pagan uttered a mirthless laugh. "I like that!" he exclaimed. "If I were thinking only of myself I would go ahead and say nothing. Do you think it amuses me to chuck away the only thing I have ever really wanted in my life!"

"You are thinking of yourself, Charles," repeated Baron. "You say, 'Is it sporting' without stopping to consider whether doing what is sporting is really going to make Vigers happy or unhappy. Is it sporting? That is the important question because Charles Pagan is a sportsman and he must not do anything that would lower his sportmanship in his own eyes or in those of other people. It does not matter if being a sport hurts someone else."

"Hang it all, I . . ." began Pagan, but Baron went on imperturbably.

"You say, 'What would Clare think of me if she ever found out.' It is her opinion of Charles Pagan that matters: not her happiness. Far better that she should be made miserable for the rest of her life than that she should think Charles Pagan unsporting. That's damned selfishness and damned cruelty."

"Cruelty!" exclaimed Pagan.

"Well, isn't it? To walk up to a girl and say 'Here's this fellow you thought was dead, the fellow you've loved all these years, whose memory you almost worshipped, that fine handsome soldier Captain Roger Vigers, V. C., look at him now—look at his face.'

Pagan stirred uncomfortably in his chair.

"Isn't that cruelty?" demanded Baron.

"Who but a fool would do it like that!" protested Pagan, but his voice had lost its ring of confidence.

"That is what it amounts to, however it's done," retorted Baron. "And think what it means to her, Charles. First of all, there is the shock. Then the reopening of all the old wounds that these long years have nearly healed. That sad but pleasant memory of hers destroyed and this, this ghastly reality put in its place.

"And then what is she going to do? Well, there are only two courses open, aren't there? Either to stick to the original contract and marry him . . . but that is out of the question. She couldn't do it. You see that. Why you shied like a horse just now when I mentioned it. But supposing she did; do you think that they would be happy? Apart from his disfigurement, do you think that Vigers can be the same man that he was all those years ago? That ghastly disfigurement must have affected his character as well as his body. And anyway he hasn't stood still all these years; neither has she. You and I are not the same as we were fifteen years ago, and neither are they. But do you think that their two lines of development have converged since 1918? I don't.

"But take the other course. She is terribly, terribly sorry for him, but she cannot bring herself to marry him. What then? Isn't the picture of that terribly disfigured man going to be with her for the rest of her life? That and the picture of what he once was? And isn't the thought of him up there in his dug-out going to take the edge off every enjoyment? Do you think she would ever be really happy again? Wouldn't it be cruelty to force her to make a choice?"

Pagan nodded his head miserably.

"And how about Vigers? He is content now in his way, but I would be prepared to swear that it has taken him some years of careful self-discipline to reach that state of content. All those years of effort and self-denial would be chucked on the muck heap. All the old hopelessness, misery and longing would be let loose again. He could never go back to his dug-out again and be content. What is left of his life would be wrecked.

"That is why he is living up there—because he knows all this. He is not doing it for the fun of it; he is doing it for her. He does not want her to know. Any time during the last fifteen years he could have let her know if he had wanted to. But he hasn't. You talk about it being unsporting to Clare not to let her know. I think it would be damned unsporting to Vigers to tell. It would be directly contrary to what are obviously his wishes and it would be to destroy deliberately all his years of patience and self-sacrifice.

"He has made his choice. He is able to judge for himself. What is more, he has the right to judge for himself, and you haven't the right to butt in and reverse his judgment. He has thought it all out. He must know damn well that a woman like Clare can't go about without somebody wanting to marry her. And if I know old Roger at all, he wants her to marry. He is thinking of her; he wants her to be happy. And you, Charles, haven't the right to stop his efforts to make her happy. Supposing you were Vigers. Supposing you had done what he has done. Supposing you had deliberately chosen that life in order that the girl you loved should never know your tragedy and be made miserable by it; what would you say if some clumsy conscientious fool butted in and spoilt it all?"

Pagan nodded his head slowly without speaking. "I suppose you are right, Dicky," he said at last. "But it seems so callous and dirty somehow, to leave him up there."

"But it is the only decent thing to do; isn't it now—honestly?"

"I suppose it is," answered Pagan.

A long silence ensued. To Pagan the harsh, garish sunshine seemed irritating and cruel. "You will go and see him?" he asked at last.

Baron thought for a moment, and then he shook his head. "No, I don't think so. I would like to, but I think it would be kinder not to. It might bring back old times rather vividly, and it would be bound to bring up the subject of Clare. I should probably have to tell lies; I mean I couldn't tell him she was here in Munster and that the other night she was within half a mile of him. The whole thing would be too unsettling and unfair to him. It would not do any good, and would only make things more difficult for him. As it is he does not know I am here, and had he really wanted to get in touch with me he could have done so any time during all these years. I can always send little comforts to him by way of Kleber from time to time. I don't suppose he makes much of a living out of those carvings."

Pagan shook his head. "They are too well done to be a commercial success," he agreed. "But didn't you say he had some money—oh, but of course as he is officially dead, he can't touch that."

Baron nodded. "Yes, but I think I told you that he left all he had to Clare. And don't you see, that is another complication. Obviously he wants her to have it, but if she knew he was alive she would give it back; and it would complicate that difficult choice of hers too, wouldn't it? She would feel she was bound to him in a way. The more we look at this thing, Charles, the more certain it becomes that we have got to keep quiet. It's all a horrible mess up."

Pagan nodded his head slowly. "It is," he agreed with a sigh.

CHAPTER SIXTEEN

I

BEFORE the dessert stage was reached that evening at dinner, the orchestra in the big chandelier-hung room adjoining the restaurant began to beat out the plaintive rhythm of a fox trot; and here and there among the tables spoons beat time above pink and yellow ices and the light glinted upon sheeny shingled heads that swayed unconsciously to the compelling rhythm. One by one the tables emptied, and the solitary couple gliding over the polished parquet in the adjoining room were soon joined by many others.

Out of doors the stars were beginning to shimmer in the dusk above the mountains: indoors the lights flooded down upon the bright frocks of the dancers and were reflected from the polished brown panelling of the walls. There were three long windows from floor to ceiling, each covered by heavy blue plush curtains with a gold braided pelmet across the top. Young Cecil stood by the centre one, talking with a bored proprietary air to a striking-looking girl to whom he had paid marked but peculiarly off-hand attention ever since her arrival in the hotel that morning.

She had sleek, short flaxen hair, brushed back like a boy's, and she wore a scarlet frock.

Before Pagan's eyes, however, as he glided beneath the brilliant crystal electroliers with Clare in his arms, there floated persistently the picture of Vigers, disfigured and forlorn in his bizarre dug-out on the mountain. Clare gave a little low peal of amusement as she glided past her brother and his colourful companion.

"Cecil is deliciously young, isn't he!" she laughed. "He is terribly attracted by that pretty little scarlet minx. He has been following her round ever since she arrived, but neither she nor we are supposed to know. Hence his bored look of male superiority and his off-hand cave-man manner."

Pagan nodded. "Yes, he is rather like a young eastern potentate chatting with one of his female slaves."

"It is really rather clever of him if he only knew it," smiled Clare. "Girls at that age sometimes find that sort of treatment attractive."

"Only at that age?" asked Pagan innocently.

She tilted her head and cocked an eye at him suspiciously. "At twenty a girl takes a man, more or less at his own valuation," she retorted. "At thirty she makes her own valuation of him."

"I see," answered Pagan with a whimsical smile. "And of course that valuation is never as high as his!"

She shook her head cheerfully. "No; not in nine hundred and ninety-nine cases out of a thousand, though in the thousandth usually for no apparent reason, it is far higher."

"And then?" he asked.

She shrugged her pretty shoulders. "Then she marries him or else makes a fool of herself."

He laughed. "Then women, after they have reached years of discretion, are not really illogical—only once in a thousand times!"

She nodded her head. "Um-m."

"Now I understand the meaning of divine illogically," he smiled. "That thousandth time."

The music slowed to an end, and they walked into the cooler lounge and sat upon a sofa by the great staircase.

"You have been very solemn all the evening," she said presently.

"Have I?" he answered.

She nodded. "I have been solemn too, inside," she said. "I cannot get the thought of that poor lonely, disfigured man out of my head."

"Nor can I," he admitted.

She sipped the little cup of coffee that had been brought to her. "I am so glad he seemed pleased with our little present."

"He seemed very pleased," answered Pagan. "Which reminds me that I must not forget to send up the spare battery when it arrives."

"It came just before dinner," she told him. "And I asked Griffin to take it up to Kleber."

"Oh did you; thanks very much," he said.

"Poor lonely man," she murmured softly.

Pagan stirred his coffee absently and regarded the slowly revolving spoon with a frown. "Do you," he asked without looking up, "do you think he is right in the course he has chosen?"

"You mean—to cut himself off from the world for the sake of others?"

Pagan nodded.

She stared at her cup with a little frown of concentration. "It is rather splendid, don't you think?"

He did not answer, and she glanced at him quickly. "You do not admire that kind of self-sacrifice?" There was a tinge of disappointment in her tone.

He answered without looking up. "On the contrary, I should like to think that I would have the grit to do the same if I were in his place."

She stared at her foot in silence. "I think you would," she said slowly at last.

He thanked her with a far-away little smile. "You think then that he has chosen rightly, both from his own point of view and from that of his friends?" he persisted presently.

"You mean of course chiefly—the girl?"

He nodded his head. "Yes." And then he added in a low voice, "Suppose you were in her place."

She tilted her cup and regarded the dregs at the bottom. "It is always so much easier to decide theoretically what is best," she murmured. "The personal element complicates things terribly, don't you think?"

"It does," he agreed solemnly. "But still, tell me: I would like to know—if you were in her place?"

Clare stared at her cup with a little frown of concentration. "Of course," she said reflectively, "she does not know he is alive, and the early bitterness of her grief must have worn off a little. But if I were in her place and I were given the choice of having him alive and so ghastly disfigured or just—dead; I—I don't know." She cupped her chin in her hand and frowned at the little pointed toe of her shoe. "I—I almost think I would have him dead and at peace."

Pagan nodded his head slowly. "And . . . and supposing the girl suddenly discovered he was alive—what then?"

"Yes: I have been thinking of that all the time," she answered slowly.

"What then?" repeated Pagan solemnly after a pause.

She smoothed her frock upon her knee absently. "In a novel of course one would marry him and try to compensate him for his infirmity. But, in real life I—I wonder." She gazed again at her shoe. "Is his poor face very horrible?" she asked in a low voice.

Pagan nodded his head slowly. "Terrible."

She nodded her head sadly. "We say it is not the face that we love," she went on almost as though she were talking to herself. "And that is true: it is not the face, but the whole man. And yet how much of the whole man the face really is! All the little tricks of eye and expression. Without those it is hardly the same person, is it? Without arms or without legs it is the same person that we loved before, even dearer now perhaps because of the pathetic helplessness; but without the dear face. . . . And yet it is the same person really—inside. It must be—unless such a terrible change affects not only the outside, but the whole man. It might; I believe it would in a case like this where a man has lived for years alone with his thoughts."

"That was what Baron said," murmured Pagan.

She nodded. "I wonder. Our characters certainly affect our faces, but it does not follow necessarily that the opposite is true. Poor man!"

"Poor girl," murmured Pagan gently.

"Yes, poor girl," she repeated. "I wonder what she would do. She might love him so much that she would see only the man that she had known and not the poor wretch that he had become. Pray heaven that she would. Otherwise it would be terrible for her and for him. Pray heaven that she may never have to make the choice."

"Amen," said Pagan.

They sat in silence for some moments, occupied with their own thoughts.

Presently Pagan passed a hand wearily across his forehead. "It's all wrong," he burst out suddenly. "It's all wrong. He should be either dead or else alive and well and married to her. It's all so hopelessly unfair.

"Other men will want to marry her—and although he, poor fellow, is out of the running, he at least has had the satisfaction of knowing that she loved him. Whereas the other fellow, if he knew, would feel a skunk to push his claim." He thrust his hands into his pockets and frowned at the little crumpled red cigar band in the big palm pot beside him. "Why is it that life is so complicated?" he complained. "Why is there never a straightforward issue? Why are there always nagging details that dull the edge of enjoyment? We ourselves complicate it too. We hesitate and delay among tabus and inhibitions as though life went on for ever and the sun always shone." He looked up at the ceiling and quoted with a sigh of exasperation. "Thus is the native hue of resolution sicklied o'er with the pale cast of thought. Why can't we go straight for what we want and enjoy it without regret and without remorse?" he demanded savagely. "Surely the war is not so old that we have forgotten that we can count only upon this very moment. What is not said now may be forever left unsaid." He pulled his hands from his pockets and turned impulsively towards her. His face was puckered with the intensity of his feelings. "I love you, Clare," he murmured earnestly, "I love you, dear. Say, 'I love you, Charles, and one day soon if life still goes on I will be your wife'—or else say, 'I can never love you,' and let me go away and take what else there is left to me in life."

There came a long silence. In the dance room the orchestra was throbbing another fox trot.

She raised her eyes to his slowly. "Charles, dear," she said gently, "you said you were content to wait—you said that time was on your side. Why are you different to-night?"

He raised his head defiantly as though he were awaiting the attack of unseen foes, but his eyes were fixed abstractedly upon the curtained doorway past which the dancers were gliding. "Do you remember that atmosphere of the old war years when it seemed that a shadow stood always just behind one? That atmosphere of constant flux and uncertainty!"

She nodded her head and murmured in a low voice, "I remember."

"I feel it to-night. I feel as I felt then—that the future must take care of itself. It is too uncertain. There may be no to-morrow, but there is to-day. Eat, drink and be merry; to-morrow we die, who knows! I'm greedy of life; I am greedy of the moment. This moment—the only moment we know for certain we shall ever have." He turned his head and looked at her. His face seemed lean and drawn, but his eyes were very bright and alive. "Just say, 'I love you.' It shall not bind you beyond the moment. To-morrow you shall go your way if you wish. To-morrow shall take care of itself. But then whatever it brings, joy or sorrow, life or death, I shall have had this moment. Say it; oh say it—if you can with truth."

For a few moments she drew little patterns on her knee with her fingers. Then she raised her head and looked at him in silence. "Charles, dear," she began at last, and stopped abruptly.

A shadow moved across her light-coloured frock and Baron's voice broke in cheerfully.

"Hullo, here you are!" he cried. "I say, isn't there an awful frowst in here to-night! Come out and get some fresh air. We might all go down to the little café by the station and have some coffee. What do you say?"

Pagan stirred and looked up. "We have just had some," he murmured at last.

Baron threw a contemptuous glance at the two tiny cups on the glass-topped table beside them. "Oh yes, but that amount wouldn't damp a thirsty canary," he retorted. "Coffee in tall glasses, I mean, *comme ça.*"

II

They sauntered out into the night. It was dark beneath the trees of the avenue except where the electric road lights threw up the overhanging foliage in sharp cardboard relief like stage scenery. Ahead of them twinkled the little coloured lights of the outdoor café, and high up in the night sky, upon the invisible mountain side, lights twinkled here and there.

They passed through the open gate in the white palings which separated the café from the road. A wizened old man in a greasy blue beret moved slowly among the tables fiddling Tosselli's Serenade. The lights from the coloured lamps among the leaves above revealed the absorbed expression of his face with bizarre changing patches of colour, and glinted upon his swiftly gliding bow. At a larger table beneath the spreading branches of two huge old gnarled trunks some half dozen youths, lavishly decked in tricolour ribbons, were celebrating with wine and song their calling up to perform the customary military service.

Baron led the way to some vacant seats under a tree. A child in a long pink pinafore removed an empty glass from the table, swabbed away a circular liquid stain and brought them coffee in tall glasses. Baron produced his cigarette case and offered it to Clare. It contained only two cigarettes, and she hesitated and looked at Pagan.

"Charles always sucks a foul pipe," said Baron. "And I am going to get some more presently." He held a match to her cigarette and lighted his own. Then he took a drink from his glass and rose. "If you are going to get some cigarettes, will you buy me some too?" asked Clare.

"Any particular brand?" he asked.

"The yellow packets please."

"Those French things?"

She nodded.

"Depraved taste!" he remarked and strolled towards the species of coffee stall where the patron presided over the boxes of cigars, cigarettes, picture postcards and liqueurs.

Pagan pulled out his pipe and filled it slowly. Clare sipped her coffee and looked at the old man who was now fiddling at the young conscripts' table. "He plays awfully well," she said.

Pagan returned the pouch to his pocket. "He does; better than many a fellow who is drawing a huge salary in a dance band."

Silence dropped like a curtain between them. A car glided up by the white palings and stopped. Pagan recognized it as Cecil's. Griffin got out, and, with his hands in flaps of his breeches like an ostler, swaggered into the café. He met Baron returning with the cigarettes, and clicking his heels, greeted him with a quivering military salute.

"Friend Griffin, apparently, has sampled the local bock," commented Pagan.

"He is given that way in moderation," murmured Clare.

His voice, indeed, which carried clearly to where they sat, rather confirmed the impression. It seemed slightly more eager and hurried than the occasion demanded; and Baron's voice in contrast sounded very quiet and unhurried.

"I took that there accumulator up to the histameny, sir," said Griffin eagerly.

"Oh did you; thanks very much, Griffin," answered Baron.

"Yes, I give it to the old Fritz myself, sir; but I left Mr. Cecil's flashlamp there on the table."

"Oh never mind," said Baron. "I expect Mr. Cecil will forgive you. You can fetch it some other time."

"But I did fetch it, sir; I went back," went on Griffin hurriedly and excitedly, "and as I came up to the door, someone at the side of the house sings out, 'Good night, Kleber,' and it was the Captain's voice, sir—Captain Vigers.' Don't you see, sir, that this here . . ." His high pitched eager voice suddenly sank and became inaudible. Baron had half turned his head for a fraction of a second and his elbow was bent as though his hand were raised towards his mouth.

Pagan stole a glance at Clare. Her face was very pale, and so still was she that she might have been mistaken for a wax figure were it not for the fluttering rise and fall of the lapels of her cloak. To Pagan, time seemed suddenly to have suspended its beat; but he was conscious that the sweet toned violin was still whispering the serenade. Five seconds had gone by, no more; yet they had seemed like hours. He must say something. He raised his head. "Yes, friend Griffin has done himself very well indeed," he found himself saying. But his voice sounded to him foolish and trivial.

She remained silent, and the gentle sound of the fiddle seemed a fitting background.

Baron had parted from Griffin and was coming back to them. He sauntered up with studied nonchalance, but he must have noticed the extraordinary immobility of Clare, for he shot a swift glance from her to Pagan. He put the yellow packet of cigarettes on the table. "There are your pernicious gaspers," he said cheerfully and sat down.

She took them mechanically without speaking. Pagan made another effort. "We thought Griffin seemed a little elevated to-night," he said.

Baron took the hint. He nodded. "Yes; in the parlance of the vulgar, I think he had 'had a couple'."

Clare spoke at last. "Dicky." Her low, unhurried voice had a peculiarly clear-cut quality. "Dicky, is it true—what Griffin said?"

Baron avoided her eyes. "My dear Clare!" he laughed. "Griffin in his cups has a more wonderful imagination than he has when sober—which is saying a good deal."

She turned from him as one turns from a babbling child. She looked at Pagan and laid a hand upon his arm. "You will not lie to me. Is it true?"

He raised his eyes and looked at her mutely. Her hand dropped from his sleeve.

"I knew it—I felt it," she murmured.

The eyes of the two men met miserably. The wizened fiddler approached their table, stood fiddling for a moment and then passed on.

Clare suddenly raised her head. Her eyes were wild, and her voice had an unfamiliar ring of harshness. "You knew all the time and you did not tell me," she cried. She swung round on Pagan almost scornfully. "I suppose one could not expect *him* to tell me; but you, Dicky, you might have told me."

Baron did not flinch before her anger. He raised his head slowly and met her wild angry eyes. "Clare dear, we did not know till this afternoon," he answered gently. "Charles' first impulse was to tell you—to play the game, he said; but I persuaded him not to."

Her haggard eyes came back to Pagan. "I am glad you wanted to play the game," she cried.

"We talked it all over, Baron and I," said Pagan miserably, "and we both agreed that it would—be kinder not to."

She turned the little packet of cigarettes over and over and over in her lap. Suddenly she shot out her hands impulsively and touched Pagan's arm and Baron's. Her voice had lost its strange harshness. "I am sorry," she said gently. "I know you did what you thought was best for me. You are both very kind. You must forgive me; it has been a shock." And then suddenly she covered her face with her hands.

Baron stumbled quickly round the table. He put one hand gently on her shoulder and with the other grasped her wrists. "Clare, Clare," he murmured soothingly.

She felt and found the hand that held her wrist and pressed it against her face. "Oh, Dicky, Dicky," she cried shudderingly. "Beautiful, handsome Roger, all horribly maimed."

Pagan looked on in silent misery.

Presently she put down her hands and raised her head.

Pagan stumbled to his feet. "Let me get you something," he said. "A cognac."

She shook her head and looked at him with a wan smile. "Thank you—but I am all right, really."

"Sure?" asked Baron looking down at her.

"Yes—really."

Baron picked up the packet of cigarettes which had fallen upon the ground. She thanked him with a tired little smile and put them in her bag. Then she pulled the high collar of her cloak about her throat. "Would you mind very much if we went back now," she asked. "I—I would . . ."

"Of course," agreed Pagan.

They walked slowly back up the long avenue to the hotel, Clare in the middle silent but with head erect, Pagan and Baron in embarrassed sympathetic silence on either side. Behind them the coloured lights of the café disappeared behind the intervening trees, and the quavering skirl of the violin sank to a distant murmur. Slowly they mounted the hotel steps and passed into the foyer. In the light of the warm-shaded lamps her face seemed less pale. She halted at the foot of the broad staircase and turned to them with a sad little smile.

"I think I will go to bed now," she said. "You have been very sweet to me, both of you." She smiled at them a little unsteadily. "Thank you." She placed her hand upon the broad polished balustrade. "Good night."

"Good night," murmured Baron. Pagan looked at her in mute misery.

She mounted a step and paused. She turned her head and smiled at them bravely, and then she went slowly up the stairs.

When she had disappeared from view round the broad sweep of the staircase, the eyes of the two men met in an eloquent look. Baron pursed up his lips and nodded his head gloomily. Pagan stared abstractedly at the tall palm in its tub of hammered brass.

"And what is going to happen now!" he murmured at last.

"God only knows," answered Baron, "but I would like to wring that damned fool Griffin's neck," he added with sudden vehemence.

CHAPTER SEVENTEEN

I

BRIGHT sunlight streamed through the long open windows of the dining-room as Baron and Pagan sat at breakfast the next morning, and on the green mountain side across the valley the dark red roofs of the scattered homesteads glowed brightly in the cheerful light. The coffee and rolls and cool fresh butter were excellent, but it was not a cheerful meal. Baron ate in gloom silence, and Pagan's customary cheery word to the waiter was absent.

"What do you think is going to happen?" asked Pagan after a long silence.

Baron put down his cup and scowled at his plate. "You mean, what will Clare do?"

Pagan nodded.

Baron shrugged his shoulders helplessly. "Lord only knows, I don't. What can she do? She will be miserable whatever she does. There isn't anything to do except forget all about it, which of course she can't do." He dabbed some butter viciously on to a piece of roll. "I'd like to wring that fool Griffin's flaming neck."

Pagan stared out at the sunlit garden. "Can't we do anything?" he asked doubtfully.

Baron shook his head. "No, we can't do anything; it is out of our hands now. We can only sit back and look on. Nice cheery little holiday for all of us, isn't it!"

Pagan stared at his cup in silence. "What *do* you think she will do?" he said again.

Baron made a movement of impatience. "My dear Charles," he said irritably, "there is only one sensible thing to do; we know that. And if she does it she will be miserable because she has done it. And who knows what a woman will ever do, anyway?"

Clare, when she appeared, was pale, and looked as though she had slept but little, but about her there was an air of quiet dignity and determination that had been lacking the previous evening.

"Dicky," she said, "will you do something for me?"

"Of course," agreed Baron readily.

"I want you to go and tell Roger that I am here."

Baron's eyes met Pagan's gloomily. "Is that necessary?" he asked gruffly, after a pause.

"Please, Dicky!"

He shrugged his shoulders helplessly.

"And I want you to make arrangements for me to meet him."

Baron gave way to a gesture of impatience. "But really, Clare, don't you think . . ." he began.

"Please, Dicky, will you do what I ask?"

Baron relapsed into gloomy silence. She went on in a calm and almost toneless voice. "At first I had thought of going to his dug-out, but I think it would be better not to. The best plan, I think, would be to meet at Kleber's inn. The sooner the better—to-day if possible."

Baron scowled at his plate. "That's all very well," he cried at last with obvious restraint, "but you ought not to rush into this on the spur of the moment. You ought to think the whole thing out from every point of view."

She turned to him wearily. "What do you imagine I have been doing all night?" she asked with a mirthless little laugh. Then her voice softened again. "But you will do this for me, Dicky?"

He thrust his hands deep into his pockets and nodded gloomily.

"Thank you," she said simply. "I know it is horrid for you, Dicky, but—I cannot ask Charles."

"Oh no, no," protested Baron. "Certainly I will go."

"Thank you. Griffin will take you up."

Baron rose to his feet. "I think I will go and see about it now."

Pagan followed him from the room. "Would you like me to come with you?" he asked.

"Oh no, old Charles. I am going now. She is all keyed up and wants to get it over. I am going at once. Though heaven only knows how it's all going to end. But she has made up her mind, and you and I might just as well try to stop Niagara." He took a couple of paces forward and then turned back. "But I am damned sorry for you, old Charles . . . and Clare . . . and poor old Roger."

II

Baron returned soon after midday and flung himself wearily into a chair in Pagan's room. "I have fixed it up, Charles," he said. "He will be at the inn at five o'clock. It was pretty ghastly. He didn't want to do it at first, but I persuaded him—much against my better judgment. Poor devil, he asked if I thought he had better put something over his face, and I had to say yes." Baron turned his head and looked at Pagan with strained eyes. "I say, Charles, he is a ghastly sight!" He turned his head again and stared at the carpet. "And if only you had seen him as he used to be when I knew him."

Pagan rang the bell. "You had better have a drink," he said.

Baron roused himself from his brown study and looked up with a rather haggard smile. "Thanks, old Charles, I knew there was something I wanted."

"I found it a bit trying," said Pagan, "and he was not even a fellow I knew."

Baron nodded his head solemnly. "It was damned uncanny," he murmured, "talking to a fellow one had believed dead for years. He was—sort of—flummoxed, and I—I wasn't too happy. Found it a bit difficult to strike the right note you know. Didn't want to overdo the cheerfulness business—nor the other thing. We were both a bit worked up, but we managed to get through the business all right— kept it matter of fact. Nice weather, jolly little place you've got up here, sort of thing. One or two awkward pauses though. Bit of a strain."

III

The car came round for them at four o'clock, and Clare came down a few moments later. Except for a certain strained immobility of expression she looked her usual self, but Pagan noted that the colour in her face was for once artificial.

"Will you come too, Charles?" she asked.

"If you want me to," he answered quietly.

"I would like it, if it wouldn't be too much of an ordeal."

"I will come," he said.

Cecil was driving. But just before they entered the car, Baron took Clare aside. He spoke with embarrassed awkwardness. "It is only fair to tell you this," he said. "Charles told us that—that he was very badly knocked about. And no doubt you have formed your own picture of him—as I had."

She nodded with pathetic half-frightened eyes.

Baron looked at the ground and shifted uncomfortably on his feet. "I have seen him now, and—well, he is worse than I imagined. It is only fair to tell you this. You see, it is bound to be a—a big shock."

She nodded her head. "I had realized that," she answered in a hushed voice; and then she smiled bravely but a trifle unsteadily. "That is why I am all made up. He must not notice any—any weakness."

The car left the town behind and climbed the steep mountain side in the golden afternoon sunshine. Pagan sat in front with Cecil: Clare was behind with Baron. Hardly a word was said till the car climbed over the bare grassy crest and halted in the col. Then it was Cecil who spoke. "Fine view," he remarked, glancing at the magnificent panorama of mountains, woods, and valleys that stretched around them. Then he switched off the engine and opened the door.

Baron leant forward with his elbows on the back of the front seat. "That track to the right," he said, "leads over into the next hollow where the inn is. I don't know whether you could take the car along it."

Cecil thought he could. He pulled his foot inside again and started the engine. The car bumped gently off the road and slowly climbed the uneven grassy track. It glided more swiftly over the flat grassy top of the dividing shoulder, and bumped gently down into the hollow not fifty yards from the inn.

Baron climbed out. "Charles and I will go on ahead," he said to Clare. "You come along presently."

He and Pagan walked towards the inn down that now familiar track, which they traversed first in the darkness of that rainy, windy night less than a fortnight ago; and as he passed through the gate in the whitewashed fence Pagan wished devoutly that his map-reading on that night had been as faulty as Baron had chaffingly suggested it was.

Baron knocked at the door. It was opened by Bertha. Without a word she held it wide for them to pass, but she looked at Pagan with reproachful eyes which he found hard to meet, and he noticed that she had been crying.

The long, brick-floored room, which had looked so cheerful that first night he entered it, now seemed gloomy and neglected. Yet the red-brick floor was clean and smelt of soap; the empty, clean scrubbed tables with their chairs pushed close to them stood in neat alignment around the walls. The sunlight, streaming through the coarse bleached muslin curtains, drove low misty wedges of light across one side of the room and made the walls and intervening spaces seem dark by contrast. The drowsy buzzing of a blue-bottle on one of the windows was the only sound that broke the country stillness.

Vigers sat silent and alone by a table at the far end of the room. The lower part of his face was covered by a coloured handkerchief, and above it his blue eyes seemed strangely watchful. He rose slowly to his feet as the two men came in and stood with one hand resting upon the table beside him. Bertha stood in tragic silence by the door.

"Hullo, Roger," cried Baron cheerfully. "Here we are. You have met Charles Pagan already, I think."

Vigers' answer came slowly. His voice appeared to be under studied control and it was muffled by the handkerchief over his face. "It is very nice of you and Pagan to come."

"Not a bit," answered Baron. There followed an embarrassed silence for a moment or two; and then he asked quietly, "Well—shall I—shall I fetch her, Roger?"

Vigers made a slight inclination of his head. Baron turned towards the door, but before he could reach it, Clare appeared on the threshold. She came slowly into the room and glanced enquiringly at Baron. He looked at her and then turned his head slowly towards Vigers standing motionless at the far end. She followed the direction of his eyes and then halted.

"Roger!" Her voice was low, but clear and un-shaking.

Vigers neither moved nor spoke. He stood with his hand still resting on the table, his head slightly averted, his shoulders a little bent, his whole body motionless.

Clare moved slowly forward again. She covered half the distance separating him from her. Then she stopped. Her voice was very low, but had again that peculiarly clear cut quality.

"Roger—Roger, take—the handkerchief away."

Silence followed. Only the blue-bottle buzzed intermittently upon the window. The motes revolved gently in the long oblique shafts of sunshine. Slowly Vigers raised his hand. The handkerchief dropped.

Seconds passed, seconds ticked out softly by a clock made audible in another room by the deathly stillness. Then a shoe scraped on the brick floor, and Clare moved swiftly forward. His unblinking blue eyes watched her approach as though fascinated.

"Roger," she murmured and went close up to him. She put her arms about his neck and kissed his mutilated face.

He stood a moment with his hands hanging stupidly at his sides; then he sank upon the chair and deep sobs broke the silence.

Baron turned a strained face towards Pagan. Together they stole quickly out into the sunshine.

They walked slowly and in silence along the front of the inn and sat down at one of the little iron tables on the side terrace. Pagan pulled out his pipe and filled it mechanically. He threw the burnt match over the blistered white palings and watched it fall and come finally to rest on the mountain side fifty feet or so below. Across the valley the grassy mountain tops glowed greeny-gold in the late afternoon sunlight. Far below he could see the toy-like, clustered roofs of Munster.

"What did Vigers get his V. C. for?" he asked suddenly.

Baron, who was filling his pipe with great deliberation, stuck it in his mouth and felt in his pockets for matches. "Scuppering a machine-gun nest, I believe," he answered absently. "It was before I joined the battalion."

Pagan leant forward with his elbows on his knees and nodded. He took his pipe from his mouth and regarded the glowing bowl. "Well, whatever it was," he said slowly, "I would be willing to make a bet that it wasn't a braver act than that we have just seen—in there." He made a motion of his head towards the inn.

Baron nodded his head solemnly. "It's about the finest thing I have ever seen," he agreed.

Cecil sauntered up and sat down. "I do not see why we should not have a drink," he suggested.

Baron looked up absently. "Not a bad idea," he murmured in a far away voice. "We shall have to get hold of Bertha, though."

Pagan jumped up. "I will see if I can find her," he said. He was glad to have something to do. He went along the front of the inn and round to the other side where the outbuildings projected from it. The door under the covered way was open, and he put his head inside and called. Bertha answered. She took the order in silence and put the three glasses on a tray.

"I will take them out," said Pagan.

She looked up at him with sad eyes. "M'sieu, will she take him away?"

Pagan put down the tray which he had lifted an inch or two from the table. "I don't know, Bertha," he answered slowly.

"She will be kind to him, M'sieu?"

Pagan nodded his head slowly. "Yes, Bertha, you may be sure of that."

"She is very beautiful," said Bertha.

"Yes." Pagan put his hands again on the tray.

"Does she love him, M'sieu?"

"She was his fiancée, Bertha."

She looked at him with sad, sympathetic eyes. "And what will you do, M'sieu?"

"I do?" echoed Pagan. He gave an involuntary shrug of his shoulders, and then he smiled at her kindly. "It is, what shall *we* do, Bertha; for we are both in the same boat. I expect we shall smile and carry on, eh! Come." He pushed one of the glasses towards her. "The other day I drank with you; now you must drink with me." He took up one of the glasses.

She did not take the glass; she looked at him with grave eyes. "What shall we drink to, M'sieu?" she asked. "It would not be practicable to drink to your toast of the other day."

"No," agreed Pagan, "but we can drink together nevertheless." He raised his glass. "Long life and happiness to those we love, Bertha."

With her grave eyes still fixed on his she raised her glass and clinked it against his.

Cecil sat alone at the table on the terrace when Pagan returned.

"Where is Baron?" asked Pagan.

Cecil took a glass from the tray and drank from it. "Talking to Clare and Roger," he answered.

A moment later Baron returned. "So you found Bertha, did you!" he remarked as he took up his glass. "Well, cheery 'o." He took a gulp and set the glass down. "Clare may be staying up here for dinner," he announced. "So why don't you and Cecil clear off back. I told Clare I was going to send you back. Don't you think it is the most sensible thing, Charles?"

"Is there nothing we can do?" asked Pagan.

"No, really nothing, old Charles. I would cut along if I were you. If you like to keep to the road, we can pick you up in the car if we overtake you."

"What are you going to do?" asked Pagan.

"I told Clare I would bring her back. Don't bother about me; you get along."

Pagan rose. "Walking is something to do, at any rate," he sighed. "Well, Cecil, what about it?"

Cecil rose languidly from his chair. "It is all downhill, anyway," he yawned.

IV

Baron was not back to dinner that evening, and Pagan ate the meal alone. Young Cecil also was alone at his table at the other end of the room, but he hurried the meal and rose quickly to follow the fair-haired, scarlet-frocked girl into the dance room. Pagan had coffee in the lounge and smoked a cigarette. He felt curiously remote from the other visitors, and their presence jarred upon his taut nerves. He went out into the garden and smoked his pipe. Down the long avenue he could see the twinkling coloured lights of the little café. He walked restlessly towards it and then changed his mind and came back. Baron had not yet returned. He could only wait with what patience he could muster. He went upstairs and prowled restlessly round his room.

Soon after nine o'clock Baron came in and dropped into the chintz-covered easy chair. His face looked tired and drawn in the shadowed light of the stand lamp on the little table by the bed.

"Well, it's all settled," he said wearily.

Pagan sat on the broad window ledge with his back to the dark blue curtains. He nodded his head without speaking.

"The engagement is to stand."

Pagan nodded his head again without speaking.

Baron threw back his head with a restless movement and went on in the same weary chafing tones.

"Vigers is to wear a mask. Young Cecil, apparently, knows of a man in Strasbourg who does that sort of thing, and he is going in to-morrow to bring him out to the inn." He put his hands on the arms of the chair and turned his head and looked at Pagan with troubled eyes. "It is going to be modelled from an old photograph of Vigers!" He turned his head again and stared at the carpet. "Pretty ghastly, isn't it! I hope to God Clare has the guts to stick it. It would break old Roger's heart if anything went wrong."

Pagan sat with clasped hands and his forearms resting on his knees. He raised his hands still clasped and removed his pipe. "She will stick it," he affirmed. "You can't doubt that she has the guts after what you saw this afternoon."

Baron sat for some moments in gloomy silence, and then he rose wearily and walked across the room to the tiled alcove. "I'm as thirsty as a fish," he said. He took a glass from the rack and filled it with water at the silvered tap over the wash basin. He drank and turned glass in hand. "This is damned hard luck on you, old Charles."

Pagan slowly shrugged his shoulders. "I won't pretend I'm not hard hit," he said at last. "I am—damned hard." He took his pipe from his mouth and regarded the stem critically. "But I am not sure it isn't all for the best. I'm not a particularly humble cove, Dicky, as you know, but—well, even I if had been lucky, I'm not sure, after what we saw this afternoon, that a fellow like me could live up to a girl like that."

"Oh rot," retorted Baron. He emptied the glass into the basin and walked slowly back across the room. "I expect you will be wanting to get away from here now, Charles. It is a bit awkward, I know."

Pagan thrust his hands into his pockets. "It isn't too easy," he admitted.

Baron nodded. "I quite agree, but I feel that I ought to be on hand just until things are more or less in running order. You see, Clare has only Cecil. She is going with him to Strasbourg to-morrow to bring this mask fellow out to the inn, but once he has seen Vigers and got on to the job, it ought to be more or less plain sailing, I take it. So, unless any fresh difficulties crop up, I think we might reasonably go the day after to-morrow. In fact I told Clare to-night that we should be off then."

Pagan nodded and knocked out his pipe. "Frankly I shall not be sorry to leave Munster," he said.

"Neither shall I," agreed Baron emphatically. He dropped again into the easy chair, thrust his legs out before him and scowled at the carpet. "What gets me," he complained, "is that I cannot see where it's all going to end." He continued to stare gloomily at the carpet. Then he went on as though talking to himself. "Years ago, during the war, I remember thinking to myself that if I came through, how wonderful it would be after it was all over to go and stay with Roger and Clare, and perhaps play with their kids. I think I was almost as keen on Roger marrying Clare as I myself was on marrying Helen. I loved old Roger. And then he was killed—as we thought." He drew in his legs and rested his elbows on his knees. "I ought to be overjoyed to find that he is still alive: but I am not. Somehow it does not seem to me that he is really. Of course I know he is, but it still seems to me that the old Roger died—when we thought

270

he did. This poor devil without a face doesn't seem to me to be the Roger I knew in the old days. His elder brother perhaps, but not the old Roger I knew. I wonder whether she feels that." He sat for a moment in moody silence, and then he took the map from beside the lamp on the little table and unfolded it.

"Well, old Charles, where shall we go when we leave here?"

Pagan wrenched his mind back to the workaday world. "Somewhere cheerful, don't you think? Do you know, I find these hills and pine woods and particularly Munster a little depressing."

"Depressing! Lord, depressing isn't the word for it."

"How about one of those old fortified villages at the foot of the valleys," suggested Pagan. "They looked sunny and cheerful and had vineyards all round them."

"Right. Which one?" said Baron.

Pagan came and leant over the map. "What is the name of that one we passed on the way up—near Kaysersburg? It had walls all round it and a moat covered with flowers and grass, and there was an avenue of trees leading over a stone bridge."

"Yes, I liked the look of that one," agreed Baron. He consulted the map. "Yes, this must be it—Kientzeim. Shall we trek all the way; what do you think?"

Pagan looked over his shoulder. "No; I suggest we train down the valley to Turkheim—that was the place with the old gate tower with the stork's nest on top—have lunch there and then take this track over the hill to Kientzeim."

Baron nodded agreement. "Good." He glanced at his wrist-watch and rose with a yawn. "And now I'm going to bed. I don't want another day like this for a very long time to come."

"Neither do I," murmured Pagan.

CHAPTER EIGHTEEN

PAGAN saw nothing of Clare on the following day. She had already left in the car for Strasbourg when he came down to breakfast and he was having coffee at the little café by the station when she returned to the hotel late in the evening. Baron, however, saw her for a few moments and learnt that all had gone well. The mask was to be ready in a few days and then Vigers was to move down to Munster. Nothing, therefore, need delay their proposed departure for Kientzeim on the morrow.

They breakfasted early, packed their few belongings, and then went into the town to buy a few things which they needed. Cecil was in the lounge when they returned. Clare, he said, had gone with Griffin up to the inn, but she would be back to lunch.

Baron looked enquiringly at Pagan as they went up the stairs. "I suppose this means taking an afternoon train," he said.

"I don't know," mused Pagan. "I don't see why we should not go this morning as arranged. She is awfully busy, and anyway she doesn't want me hanging round sighing like a furnace to say good-bye. We can leave a note wishing her all happiness, and we can ask Cecil to say good-bye for us.

If she wants anything, she knows where to find us. It is hardly our party now."

"I quite agree," said Baron. "I was only thinking of you; I thought perhaps you might want to—well . . ."

Pagan shook his head. "This may be my funeral, Baron, but I am not going to be morbid about it."

Baron thrust his arm through Pagan's, "I am glad you are taking it like this, old Charles."

Pagan shrugged his shoulders. "There is no other way to take it. I doubt whether I ever had much of a chance, but whether I had or not, I am not going to whine about it." He stared thoughtfully at the carpet for a moment. "At least it is something to have known a girl like that," he murmured half to himself. Then he looked up and said with a smile, though there was an undercurrent of seriousness in his tone, "And so, like the old Roman johnnies, I say, Hail and Farewell."

Half an hour later the train moved slowly out of the station down the valley, and the outlying buildings of the town slid by, one by one and disappeared. High up on the bare mountain dome, the lone ragged tree showed black and diminutive against the clouds. Pagan watched it thoughtfully. At that distance he was unable to make out the inn. He pulled out his pipe and filled it with care.

"Well, there goes Munster," he said at last. He rolled up his pouch and returned it to his pocket. "And do you know, Baron," he went on slowly, "I think we had better forget we went there, and try to enjoy what remains of our holiday."

Baron nodded agreement. "I think so too, old Charles. We will make a fresh start. It's a topping day for it. We will have the most gorgeous lunch that Turkheim can produce, and then if we are still mobile after it, we will totter over the hill through the vineyards to Kientzeim."

The train rumbled on down the valley. The sombre pine woods and grey ragged outcrops of bare rock gave place to dark green broad-leaved woods and cherry orchards. Lush green water meadows formed the valley floor, through which meandered the stream and the straight, white, tree-shaded road.

Presently the hotels of Trois Epis came into view, peeping white and red-roofed among the trees on the hill top to the left. Beyond them the line of hill ran gently downwards, and the trees gave place to sunny terraced vineyards.

Here at its mouth the valley broadened; it was, perhaps, threequarters of a mile in width. The enclosing mountains, shrunk now to the stature of hills, swept outwards in two low, sunny headlands, and between them flowed the vineyards in a broad green flood to the wide Alsatian plain. On either side, against these terraced headlands, the green vines lapping round their walls and towers, nestled two tiny towns like fishing harbours on a river estuary.

The little railway had thus far hugged the southern hill slope, but now it curved across the valley through the horse-high vines towards the tiny town of Turkheim, nestling at the foot of the terraced northern headland. But the railway, small though it was, did not enter the town;

nor did unsightly buildings straggle out to meet it. The old protecting walls, pierced now though they were by window casements, and the moat though dry and bush-grown stayed the houses from straying out and the railway from straying in.

The train approached the walls no nearer than a hundred yards and set down its passengers at a tidy rural platform on the tree-shaded bank of a stream.

Pagan dumped his pack on the platform and watched the little train go puffing out towards the open plain. Then he turned and surveyed approvingly the little town across the stream.

"Nice old sleepy little place," commented Baron.

Pagan nodded. "By the waters of Turkheim we sat down, yea we slept," he murmured.

"I thought you confined your gross misquotations to Shakespeare, Charles," protested Baron.

"A Pagan can quote scripture for his purpose," retorted Pagan.

They crossed the little bridge towards the town. Flags and streamers fluttered on the further bank among the trees upon the strip of grassland, some fifty yards in width, that ran between the town walls and the river. Booths were set beside the road, and wide umbrellas sheltered from the sun large baskets of foodstuffs and the fat loquacious countrywomen who owned them.

Pagan halted before a stall and examined its varied contents with great solemnity.

"What shall we buy, Charles?" said Baron. "Black ribbed stockings, gingerbread, toffee apples or a pair of pink stays?"

"Stay me with flagons; comfort me with apples," sighed Pagan.

"That's really not a bad idea, Charles—the flagon part," agreed Baron.

Pagan nodded his head sagely. "Such ideas come to me at times," he murmured modestly. "Yonder lies the town and—if only there's a tavern in the town in the town . . ."

"Quite so," said Baron.

They walked towards the great gate of the town, a tunnelled archway, dark by contrast with the glare outside, between two flat and massive buttresses at the foot of a low square tower of scarred brown stone. A coat of arms in faded colours was painted on the stones above the arch; the tower was loopholed and topped by a tiled pyramid roof on the apex of which was perched an enormous stork's nest. Flanking the gate tower was a café with two rows of white, sun-blistered shutters on its yellow-washed walls. Baron nodded towards the little green tables and shrubs in tubs which stood before it. "How will this do, Charles?"

Pagan glanced up apprehensively at the stork's nest on the tower. "Excellently—so long as we don't get an omelette direct from factory to dinner table."

After lunch they shouldered their packs and walked through the narrow streets of the old town and out through the eastern gate-tower across the moat. Then up over the low hill they tramped, through the vines, and down to Kientzeim in the next valley.

This village was smaller and quieter even than Turkheim. In the hot, still, scented air it seemed to doze among the vineyards. An avenue of tall, graceful poplars led to the main gate. Gay clusters of flowers patterned the lush grass on the dry bed of the moat, and rock plants bloomed profusely from the crannies of the crumbling, sun-baked walls.

They walked slowly up the main street of the village. The gables and quaint Alsatian chimneys of the bordering houses cast hard black shadows on its dazzling white surface. In the middle of the road a dog slept undisturbed in the dust.

They asked for lodging at a simple estaminet and were shown a cool, dark, brick-floored room for meals, and upstairs a large, low-beamed room for sleeping. It contained two massive beds and opened on to a covered, vine-entwined balcony above a tiny courtyard.

Pagan went out to the *bureau-de-poste*. The little town was very quiet and peaceful. A clumsy open framework waggon, drawn by a long-maned chestnut horse rumbled slowly along one of the narrow streets; that was the only sound, except the pleasant hum of bees and the chime of the clock on the church tower. The town lay somnolent and passive in the sun, and only a coloured overall, flitting occasionally behind the dark square of a window, and the cats basking on the hot doorsteps showed that the houses were not deserted.

He returned towards the estaminet. The dog still lay stretched asleep in the road with its head sunk on its forepaws, but a car was drawn up before the door, and Griffin drowsed at the wheel.

Pagan opened the door of their little sitting-room. It seemed very dark and cool after the glare outside. Baron sat in one of the stiff high-backed old chairs; in the other sat a girl. She had her back to the light square of the window. Her features were undistinguishable above the pale glimmer of her light-coloured frock; but the dear familiar poise of her head was unmistakable to Pagan. She was silent, but to him the room seemed charged with her personality.

Baron rose slowly from his chair. "Hullo, Charles," he said. "Here's Clare dropped in to pay us a call. She likes our simple quarters."

Pagan murmured, "I'm glad." A pause followed, and then Baron asked, "Did you see Griffin anywhere about when you came in?"

"He is dozing in the car outside," answered Pagan mechanically.

Baron moved towards the door. "Good! I want to have a word with him before he goes." The door closed behind him.

Pagan remained standing in the middle of the room. His eyes were becoming accustomed to the subdued light; he was conscious that she was looking at him. On the mantelpiece a country clock ticked monotonously; from outside came the murmur of Baron's voice.

He broke the long silence. "It was very good of you to come," he murmured.

She answered slowly in her low, clear voice, "Charles, you went without saying good-bye."

He gave an almost imperceptible shrug of his shoulders. "I knew you were very busy and I did not want to bother you."

Silence came again. She rose from her chair and came slowly towards him. A yard from him she halted. "Charles, are you very angry with me?" she asked gently.

He was silent for a moment, and then he shook his head sadly. "Angry! No—what right have I to be angry?"

She shook her head at him sadly. "And you are not bitter, are you?" she pleaded.

He shook his head. On the mantelpiece the clock ticked on monotonously.

"I'm very, very sorry," she said gently. She raised her eyes to his pleadingly, "Think of that poor maimed man; you can't be angry with me, Charles." Her voice was low.

He raised his eyes to hers and shook his head slowly. "Angry—I'm not angry, nor bitter. I think—I think you are wonderful. I think you are the most wonderful woman in the world." His voice was low and vibrant with feeling. "I think—I think I should have been disappointed if you had not done what you have done. My ideal of you was so—so high." He paused with his eyes fixed shiningly on hers, and then he ended in a whisper, "Thank you—thank you for making it come true."

She put her hand to her face. "Don't, unless you want to make me cry," she whispered.

"It's true, every word of it," he said solemnly.

A wasp was droning erratically about the room. The hoarse murmur of Griffin's voice came from the sunny street.

"Charles dear, promise me you will not be very unhappy," she said gently.

He raised his head. "If you are happy, I shall not be unhappy," he said slowly. "Sad, maybe; but there is sadness in most happiness, and some sadness is sweet."

She bit her lip and looked down quickly at the tiny handkerchief she was twisting in her hands. "I see you are determined to make me cry," she said in a low voice.

He put out his hand protestingly, and went on earnestly, "No—I speak the truth. I have lived long enough to know that we have our moments of happiness and sadness and that together they make up all that is worth while in life; and I have learned to thank God for both." He raised his eyes and looked at her with a sad little smile. "And I thank God for you."

In the silence that followed she was very still. When she spoke it was without looking up, and her voice was low but had that peculiarly clear cut quality that always thrilled him. "Charles, do you remember what you said to me that night just before we went to the café and saw Griffin?"

"I said so much that night and it seems years ago."

"You said," she went on in that low clear voice, "you said, 'I am greedy of life; I am greedy of the moment. This moment, the only moment we know for certain we shall ever have.'"

He nodded his head, without speaking.

Without looking up she went on monotonously as though reading from a book, "You said to me, 'Just say, I love you. It shall not bind you beyond the moment; but say it—if you can with truth.'"

He nodded his head and smiled sadly. "And—you did not answer."

Her voice was very low. "Are you still greedy of the moment?"

"I am greedy of every moment with you," he murmured.

"Of the moment that does not bind beyond the moment?" she whispered.

He nodded his head in silence.

She raised hers slowly and allowed him to see her eyes. "Then I will say it—and I can with truth." Her voice was low and clear. "I, I—love you—Charles."

The wasp buzzed nervously on the window pane. The ticking of the clock seemed to fill the whole room. Only, the two human figures were still and silent. She stood before him with a sad, wistful little smile and infinite love and tenderness in her eyes. He half raised his hands and let them fall again to his sides. His eyes clung to hers as though he would cram into those few moments the love and longing of a whole lifetime. Her eyes met his with that wise and wistful smile that spoke more fluently than fumbling speech.

"The most wonderful woman in God's wide world," he murmured hoarsely.

She shook her head ever so slightly and smiled again wistfully. "Good-bye—dear Charles," she said at last. She dragged her eyes from his reluctantly and moved towards the door. He opened it for her like one in a trance. On the threshold she paused and their eyes met and lingered. Then she passed slowly out.

He did not follow. He moved slowly back across the room to the high-backed chair in which she had sat. He lowered himself into it gently and sat staring at the clean bricked floor with bright shining eyes.

From the sunny street came the sudden quick throb of the car starting up. He heard Baron's voice call good-bye, and then the soft crackle of tyres on the dusty road as the car moved off. The hooter purred twice distantly and then was quiet.

Baron's footsteps sounded in the passage. They seemed to hesitate outside the door, and then they passed on and went quietly upstairs.

CHAPTER NINETEEN

I

PAGAN and Baron remained several days among the vine-terraced foothills of the Vosges. They passed from one sunny old walled town to another. They were days for the most part spent in the open air and sunshine, days of tramping through vineyards or over wooded hills, beside swift-running streams and cascades, or by brown castle ruins perched high on some craggy spur above the sun-drenched plain, of welcome midday halts at rustic inns among the woods or beside hill-ringed lakes, and of evening homecomings, tired and dusty, to feudal villages for welcome baths and food and peaceful pipes in the twilight, while the waggons rumbled slowly in from the vineyards and the storks' nests showed dark against evening skies.

They were sunny, healthy, peaceful days such as they had revelled in a few days previously, but now for both of them the keener edge of happiness was dulled. They seldom spoke of Clare or Viger, but ever recurrent in their thoughts was that scarred ridge among the mountains and the shadow which it cast.

One day they found themselves again in Colmar. It was a hot afternoon when the green glazed tiles on the roof of the old Hotel de Ville shimmered like a tropic sea, and on the old historic houses, the inscriptions in florid gothic letters, red, blue and black seemed to waver on the dazzling yellow walls. Down by the canalized Lauch the kneeling washerwomen were rinsing their linen in the sparkling water or rubbing it with soap on the white scoured planks.

The narrow streets through which they sauntered were almost deserted, and they were surprised therefore, on turning a corner, to find a crowd running towards them.

"Hullo, what's the excitement—free drinks!" exclaimed Pagan.

But Baron had caught sight of a familiar squat, blue-painted helmet in the distance. He grabbed Pagan by the arm and dragged him into a doorway.

"Free broken heads by the look of it," he retorted. "This is where we buy picture postcards for Aunt Maud and look innocent, old Charles. Unless you are looking for trouble; which I am not."

Already the van of the crowd was streaming by, men of the loafer type with flushed faces and hands that grasped sticks or stones. Close upon their heels followed the main press of the mob, a struggling, terror-stricken, stampeding horde, driven before a dozen troopers in horizon blue uniforms and steel helmets who urged their horses into the rabble and laid about them with the flat of their swords.

From the little haven in which they stood flattened against the door behind them, Pagan and Baron watched the turbulent flood surge by. The pursuing troopers passed quickly, and at the cross roads, split into three parties, scattering the mob into the side streets and alleys.

"Well, that's that," said Pagan grimly as they stepped out into the sunshine again. The street had resumed its sleepy, deserted air, and but for the solitary figure that rose from the roadway and limped painfully across the pavement to disappear up an alley, the hurrying mob of a few moments before might have been the fantasy of a dream.

"Short and sharp at any rate," commented Baron.

Pagan nodded. "Yes—if that's the end of it. Chiefly froth though that, I should think. No organization behind it. But a properly run show in Strasbourg, for example, might be unpleasant."

"It might—very, if the authorities don't get on to it in time," agreed Baron. "But I expect they are pretty wide awake to what is going on."

Pagan and Baron did not stay long in Colmar. The remaining days of their holiday were growing few in number, and they moved northwards towards Strasbourg which was to be their point of departure. But they dawdled on the way. They turned aside at Ribeauvillé to climb to the three ruined castles, perched high on the wooded hills around the little town, they tramped the winding corkscrew road from St. Hippolyte to the wooded heights above, whereon the pepperbox turrets and battlements of the great Haut-Koenigsbourg look out across the sunny plain, and they lingered in old-world Barr; but they came at last to Strasbourg with still three days to spare.

II

That night after dinner they strolled out into the town. At a café on the corner of the Place Kleber they stopped. Pagan glanced at Baron with one eyebrow raised, and then without a word they sat down at one of the little tables on the pavement.

"I like this French habit of outdoor caféing," declared Pagan, as he leaned back in his chair and glanced up at the narrow scolloped awning above him. "It appeals to my inborn idleness to sit here idly watching the people passing by. And evening is by far the best time to indulge this strenuous pastime. You notice that now the good people saunter by. Something accomplished, something done, has earned an evening's loaf! The day's work is done, so why hurry?" He nodded towards a plump man and woman who were walking by arm and arm. "There's father and mother with shining evening face—fresh from the wash basin—creeping like snail unwillingly to bed. And here in this young blood in képi and corsets we have the soldier, full of strange oaths and pomaded like the bawd, with a woeful ballad made to his mistress' eyebrow. And here, you see, we have a lady of the town with fair round features with good lipstick lined, with eyes demure and legs of shapely cut."

"And very nice too!" put in Baron appreciatively.

"And as you say, very nice too," agreed Pagan.

"And so they play their part. They stroll along the pavements, sit down for a space to drink a coffee or an apéritif and smoke a cigarette, and then saunter on to the next café. Yes, it's a very good system: keeps one young and philosophical."

"It has its points," admitted Baron.

Behind them, within the open doors of the café, an orchestra was playing. When it ceased for a moment, the strain of other orchestras drifted across the square beneath the stars from the various cafés which surrounded it; and their gay lights gave to the night a festive air.

"What do you think about that, Charles?" asked Baron presently with a nod towards a notice which was pinned to one of the posts supporting the awning.

The notice stated that there was a special cabaret performance on an upper floor of the café. Below the notice was a framed photograph of some half-dozen girls with their hands resting on each other's shoulders.

Pagan cocked an eye at the photograph and yawned. "Are they good to look upon?" he murmured.

"I don't know," answered Baron. "I can't see from here. But there seems to be a good display of leg."

"Your tastes are low," retorted Pagan virtuously. "But as you are on a holiday, I suppose we must indulge them," he added with a resigned air. He emptied his glass and rose languidly.

They passed up two flights of stairs, and were directed by a patriarchal waiter to a door labelled "Cabaret." On the other side of the door their first impression was of many red-shaded lights reflected upon the polished floor and a faint blue haze of cigarette smoke. It was a long room, with a bar on a low raised platform at the far end. A few people were sitting on high stools at the bar. On the shelves behind it was an imposing array of bottles in which the various liquids twinkled like many-coloured lanterns. Down one side of the room ran a long, low, comfortably padded seat with short branches jutting from it at right-angles about every two yards, forming a series of little open alcoves in each of which stood a small table. On each of these little tables stood a card bearing the notice, "Reserved for Champagne."

Baron nodded towards them. "There you are, Charles; if you want to get stung, now is your chance. Sweet champagne at two hundred francs a bottle is as good a method as any of chucking your money about."

Apparently other people thought the same; for the little alcoves were unoccupied except for one small party and three or four ladies of the house who sat together combing their shingled hair with the aid of their small handbag mirrors. The other people sat on the long settee on the opposite side of the room or on the chairs and chesterfields at the end.

"Yes, the Englishman may take his pleasures sadly," remarked Pagan as he sank into one of the chesterfields, "but the Frenchman takes his cannily. He is not such a fool as to go there." He nodded towards the champagne-reserved alcoves. "Those notices should read, 'reserved for Les Anglais and Les Américains.'"

The orchestra struck up, and several people rose and began to dance. Pagan ordered drinks and they sat idly watching the dancers.

Suddenly Baron exclaimed, "There's young Cecil over there. By jove, yes, and Clare." He gripped Pagan's arm tightly. "And, my God, yes—Vigers! He's got the mask on."

Pagan had not seen Vigers since that tragic scene in the inn, and he found it difficult to believe that he was the tall, handsome man in dress clothes, sitting between Clare and Cecil. "Looks pretty all right from here," he said at last.

Baron nodded his head abstractedly. "Yes," he answered in a low voice. "It's really very like he used to be; it gave me the devil of a jar for a moment. But it's so . . . so dead. Poor Clare."

They sat in silence for some moments, and then Baron stirred. "Well, hadn't we better go over, Charles?" he suggested.

Pagan hesitated a moment and then nodded abruptly. Avoiding the dancers, they passed along the end of the room and up the other side.

"I am grieved to find you in these low haunts!" chaffed Baron as he halted before Clare.

She looked up at him and smiled. Her eyes travelled slowly from him to Pagan, lingered a moment, and then moved back again.

"Hullo, Dicky," exclaimed Vigers. He nodded to Pagan. "Evening, Pagan. Yes, you find us leading a gay life." His blue eyes smiled, but the expression of his marvellously lifelike face remained unchanged. He made room for Baron beside him. Pagan sat down on the far side of Cecil.

"Now that you have got away from me, Dicky, I hope you are not being too wild and dissolute!" smiled Clare.

"Well, I did think old Charles was a bit young for this sort of thing," laughed Baron. "But having seen that photograph of all those legs outside, wild bison couldn't hold him back."

"I don't believe you tried very hard, Dicky, did you?" she asked with a smile. "Cecil pretends to be bored with the whole proceeding," she went on, "but I believe really he is thrilled to the marrow."

"And so he ought to be," said Vigers heartily. "When I was his age, a good leg shook me to the core."

"Me too," agreed Baron. "Only in those days the girls kept them all covered up."

"Nowadays these young cubs have got blasé about it," declared Vigers. "Whereas in my day when we did by chance catch a glimpse of one, we thanked God for it and looked the other way, didn't we, Dicky?"

"We thanked God for it anyway," agreed Baron.

A dark-haired little lady, beautifully dressed and with a very pleasing and attractive face, halted before them with a tray of roses. The tray was supported round her neck by a dark red ribbon, and she offered it to them very prettily, standing with her little feet close together.

Clare picked a dark red rose, and both Vigers and Baron thrust their hands into their pockets. Baron withdrew his with a grin. "Sorry. Of course it's Roger's prerogative now."

"It is neither his nor yours," retorted Clare with pretended pique. "I am buying this rose myself. I will leave you and Roger to buy them for the leggy ladies you talk so much about."

She pinned the rose in her frock, and paid for it in that attractive way of hers that seemed to receive rather than confer a favour. The girl tilted her tray and offered it prettily to Baron, but he smiled and shook his head.

"You have not bought one, Dicky!" exclaimed Clare when the girl had passed on.

"I don't know any of the 'leggy ladies,'" laughed Baron.

"But if I were a man I simply could not refuse a pretty girl like that," said Clare. "I think she is charming, absolutely charming."

Baron watched the girl walk down the room. "She certainly is very nice," he admitted.

"Of course she is, Dicky. You must dance with her later on."

Presently the floor was cleared, and a troupe of six young girls did their acrobatic dance turn. Then the general dancing began again.

"Ask the pretty rose girl, Dicky," prompted Clare.

"No," replied Baron gallantly, "I am going to ask you."

She shook her head. "I am not dancing to-night. Ask that charming little person."

Baron hesitated, and Vigers exclaimed, "Good lord, Dicky, you used not to be so slow."

Baron grinned. "Ask her yourself," he retorted.

Vigers glanced across the room at the girl, who had laid aside the tray of roses and was sitting in a chair. Then he looked back at Clare. "She is rather nice, isn't she!" he said, and his blue eyes smiled.

She smiled back at him, and her eyes were gentle and kind. She nodded her small head. "Yes, go along, Roger."

Vigers heaved his tall straight form out of the seat and walked across the room. He halted before the little dark lady, and with his heels together, made her a bow. She turned her head quickly and as her eyes fell on his face she shrank back involuntarily in her chair. But the movement lasted but a fraction of a second. A moment later she was on her feet, her head daintily on one side, thanking him prettily and saying that she would be charmed to dance with him.

Back on the other side of the room, Cecil was talking golf to an inattentive Pagan; and Baron and Clare sat in embarrassed silence. Now that Vigers was not with her, he noticed a look of strain and weariness in her face. "Won't you really dance?" he asked gently.

"Just this one then," she conceded.

Cecil's golf biography came to an end at last. "When are you going back?" he asked suddenly.

Pagan told him. "We thought we would have the last three days here," he said. "We both like Strasbourg."

"Not too bad a spot," conceded Cecil. "But I have heard rumours of trouble here before long."

"What sort of trouble?" asked Pagan.

"Political, you know. Things are working up to a head, from all accounts."

Pagan nodded. "We ran in for a spot of it at Colmar," he said. "But it did not come to much; though I thought there was probably plenty more wherever that came from."

"Mostly hot air here too, I expect," said Cecil.

When the music ceased, Clare and Baron sat down again. Vigers came back down the room and picked up his long cigarette holder. Clare looked up at him, and her face relaxed again into a kindly, affectionate smile. His eyes smiled back at her devotedly.

"Well, you have missed a lot, Dicky," he said chaffingly as he sat down. "She dances divinely—almost as well as Clare. Her name is Yvonne, and . . ." He held out his hands and threw back his head in exaggerated rapture. "And she nestles against one like a . . . like a . . ."

"Bird," suggested Baron with a grin.

Clare laughed.

"It was very nice, anyway," said Vigers emphatically.

"I think I shall have to dance with her," said Cecil suddenly. And he rose and strolled languidly across the room amid the subdued cheers of Baron and Vigers. Vigers rose and took Cecil's vacant seat beside Pagan.

Pagan had taken but little part in the conversation. Marooned on the far side of Cecil, he had had little opportunity of doing so, even had that been his wish. He had spoken no more than half a dozen words to Clare, and those of a most banal kind. But now between him and her, he felt, there was no mean between banality and those deeper things that were forbidden.

With Vigers, however, conversation was less difficult. There was the common meeting ground of the war, and they were soon chatting easily about those bygone days in which they had so much in common.

"Vigers seemed very cheerful, I thought," remarked Pagan as they walked back to their hotel through the deserted streets.

Baron nodded his head without conviction. "Yes— almost too cheerful to be genuine," he added gloomily.

CHAPTER TWENTY

BARON and Vigers sat one night at a café on the great square before the station. It was late and few people were about. The cafés at the foot of the tall blocks of buildings threw a cheerful glow upon the pavements and ringed the dim open space with a narrow ribbon of light. Above them, the tall dark buildings themselves showed dimly, cliff-like against the stars. Now and then a brightly lighted tramcar emerged from one of the tributary streets and cruised across the dim deserted space like a liner making for the open sea.

Baron smothered a yawn and glanced at the watch on his wrist. Vigers seemed loath to move. He lounged in his chair with one arm hanging loosely over the back and gazed across at the distant lights that twinkled on the long front of the station.

"I like that fellow Pagan," he said at last.

Baron nodded and blew a smoke ring from his pipe. "Yes, old Charles is one of the very best," he affirmed.

Vigers pulled out his tobacco pouch and leaned forward to fill his pipe with his elbows resting upon his knees. "Do you think, Dicky," he said presently without looking up, "that if you had not run across me again, he and Clare might have made a match of it?"

Baron glanced at him sharply. "What makes you ask that?" he said at last.

Vigers went on filling his pipe very deliberately. "I don't know—just an idea, that's all. What do you think?"

Baron sucked jerkily at his pipe. "How should I know?" he said evasively. "There was no understanding whatever between them, if that's what you mean. I know that."

Vigers rolled up his pouch and returned it to his pocket. "I know that too," he said. "But I ask you, Dicky, as man to man, do you think that anything might have matured if I had not turned up again?"

Baron leaned forward in his chair. "Look here, Roger old boy, what is the point of all this? Does it matter now, anyway?"

Vigers paused with a lighted match held above the bowl of his pipe and looked at Baron with his clear blue eyes. "Dicky," he said quietly, "you used to be a friend of mine. In those old days in the line when I had plenty of pals you never let me down. Are you going to let me down now when you are the only pal I have?"

Baron stirred uncomfortably in his chair. "Roger," he mumbled, "you know damn well I'd never let you down."

Vigers nodded. "I know, old lad," he said kindly. He struck another match and lighted his pipe. "Tell me then, do you think they would have made a match of it?"

"They might have," answered Baron reluctantly.

"You think they would have? Come now, Dicky—as man to man."

Baron's troubled eyes met Vigers'; he gave an almost imperceptible nod of his head. "Yes—I think they would have," he answered miserably.

Vigers nodded without speaking. A lighted tramcar was slowly ploughing its way across the deserted square. He watched its progress with blue, inscrutable eyes. "Is Pagan the good fellow he appears to be—all through, I mean?" he asked suddenly.

Baron took his pipe from his mouth and frowned at the bowl. "I have known old Charles getting on for twenty years now," he said earnestly. "In fair weather and in foul: in the line and out of it: and except you, old Roger, there is no man I would rather have with me in a tight corner. He may talk like a damned fool at times, but Charles Pagan never let anyone down in his life."

Vigers nodded. "I'm glad of that."

"But why all this, Roger," protested Baron earnestly. "There is nothing wrong, is there?"

Vigers shook his head, and his eyes smiled at Baron's troubled face. "No, nothing wrong. Only I realize more than ever that I was right all those years ago when I chose to stay—up there." He jerked his head southwards towards the invisible mountains.

"I think you are talking rot," said Baron miserably. "Clare loves you and always has loved you. You know that."

Vigers raised his fearless blue eyes to Baron's face. "I know that. I believe she always will love me—God bless her," he said simply. He stared out across the dim square and went on after a moment or two. "But the love she has for me now cannot be the same as the love she had. How could it be? The one was the love of a young healthy girl for a healthy man—the mating love, Dicky, that comes to most of us at least once in a lifetime. The other love isn't like that; it can't be. It is more like the love of a mother or a sister or of an old friend. That is the only sort of love a fellow like me can inspire."

Baron fidgeted in his chair. "Don't be an ass, Roger," he said gruffly. "You are getting morbid about—about that knock you got and you are imagining things."

Vigers shook his head. "No, Dicky. Believe me, I am not morbid, nor bitter nor any of those things," he said quietly. "I am just facing facts. And the fact is that the whole thing is a mistake. Mask or no mask I am not a pretty sight, I know that; and in any case one cannot wash out a dozen years of life and begin again as though those years had never existed. I am not the same man even outwardly; and I am certainly not inwardly."

"Surely it does not make all that difference," mumbled Baron.

Vigers placed his pipe on the table. "Do you think the war changed you much?" he asked.

"I suppose it did a good bit," admitted Baron. "But that was an abnormal experience."

"And was not my life up there abnormal?" persisted Vigers with another jerk of his head towards the invisible mountains. "How much of the war did you have?"

Baron moved restlessly in his chair. "From the end of 'fourteen to the armistice, with a break of six months in hospital."

"Four years at the outside," commented Vigers. "I had three times as long as that up there. Do you think it has not made any difference? Twelve odd years alone with one's thoughts in a dug-out isn't too good a training for modern life."

Baron stared out gloomily across the square. A torn newspaper flapped forlornly at the foot of a lamp post. In the distance an engine whistled shrilly.

Vigers took up his pipe again. "I was right all those years ago when I made my decision, and I knew it. I ought to have stuck to it; only I was persuaded against my better judgment."

Baron roused himself. "I think you are talking rot," he protested with some show of conviction.

"You don't think so at all, Dicky," retorted Vigers quietly. "You know I am talking sense, and you agree with me."

Baron turned his glass round and round on the table and stared at the pavement. "I don't know why you should think that," he said without looking up.

Vigers regarded him for a moment in silence, and his eyes smiled kindly. "Dicky," he said presently. "It was my handwriting which gave me away, wasn't it?"

Baron nodded.

"But it was Griffin's babbling that gave the show away to Clare." He paused, and then went on in accusing tones,

"Then it was Charles Pagan who for his own reasons persuaded you not to tell her?"

"He was all for telling her," retorted Baron quickly. "There is nothing like that about old Charles."

Vigers blue eyes smiled at the success of his little trap. "I know that," he said. "Then it was you who agreed with me?"

Baron was silent.

"It only showed your common sense, Dicky," went on Vigers kindly. "And showed that you were the good friend to Clare and to me that I always took you to be. You were absolutely right. It would have been far better if neither Clare nor I had ever known."

He gazed out again across the open square. "But the difficulty is to get back to the *status quo*. Unfortunately one cannot cut out the last fortnight any more than one can cut out the last twelve years.

"You see, if I put it to Clare that it would be better for us to go our separate ways, she would never consent; and even if she did, the idea that I might not be happy up there would always stick in her throat. Of course if I were the hero of a play," he went on with a little mirthless laugh, "I should go the pace, get tight and all that in order to put her right off me. But I fancy she would see through that, and if it did come off it would cause her a lot of pain." His eyes smiled sadly. "And in any case I am not altruistic enough for that sort of thing, I'm afraid. I would like her always to think well of me." He struck another match and went on calmly and thoughtfully. "You see, almost anything I could do, Clare would guess I was doing it for her; and then she wouldn't have it. If I pretended to fall in love with another girl, for instance, she would see through that . . . unless I married the girl. There is one I could. But that wouldn't be cricket to the girl." He stared at his glass. "There does not seem to be any way out of it; unless I die gracefully!"

Baron sat up sharply. Vigers laughed and brought his hand down on Baron's knee. "You need not worry about that, Dicky," he cried. "Suicide has never been in my line. That has always seemed to me such an unintelligent way out of a mess. And wasteful too. If there were a good war going now, that would be a different matter. One could go west and feel that one was doing some good by it."

Baron looked up miserably. "What *are* we going to do about all this, Roger?" he said.

Vigers shrugged his shoulders helplessly. "I don't know, Dicky," he said at last. Then he glanced at his wrist watch and sat up briskly. "Meanwhile we will go to bed. It is long past the hour when youngsters like you and me should be asleep."

CHAPTER TWENTY-ONE

I

BARON and Pagan stood in the south transept of the great cathedral. They had gone there to see the famous astronomical clock of Strasbourg strike the hour. But they were not the only visitors who were there for that purpose. At least three hundred people were assembled in the dim prismatic light that filtered through the traceried, stained-glass windows. The throng was congested five deep against the north wall of the transept facing the clock, and whenever the front rank, under pressure from behind, attempted to gain a little more elbow room, it was unceremoniously pushed back by the tall cassocked verger patrolling in front, who performed his duties as efficiently if not as tactfully and good-naturedly as a London policeman.

"I'm fed up with this," growled Pagan whose chest was tightly wedged against the knobbly rucksack on the back of the German holiday tramper in front of him. "And if that cove in the cassock comes and leans on me again I shall kick him in the stomach."

"Still another ten minutes to go," sighed Baron.

"Yes, but I'm not going to wait," said Pagan. "I vote we clear out and go up the tower."

"But we have been up there already," objected Baron.

"Only up to the platform," retorted Pagan. "I want to go to the top of the spire."

Baron groaned. "Something like a thousand steps, aren't there?"

"You stay and see the pretty clock strike," grinned Pagan. "I will see you later."

"Right 'o—much later," agreed Baron. "After this I am going to buy some toys for my kiddie nephews."

Pagan pushed his way out of the crowd, nodded cheerfully to the scowling verger, and passed out of the transept door into the sunlight. He walked along the pavement to the great west front and bought the necessary ticket at the little doorway at the foot of the south tower. Then the long climb began. The stone staircase, built in the thickness of the wall, wound round and round in semi-darkness except when an occasional narrow window gave him a momentary glimpse of narrow streets and roof tops far below. It was a long and weary climb up the three hundred and fifty odd steps, but at last he reached the top and emerged upon the great platform above the western front.

This was a stone-paved open space, some thirty yards long by fifteen yards broad, a miniature square poised over two hundred feet above the street level. It stretched across the top of the unfinished southern tower and the great west door and rose window. At one end of the platform was a one-storey house in which lived a caretaker and his family, and in which the complicated mechanism which worked the chimes was housed. There was also the caretaker's little garden and a shop which sold picture postcards and souvenirs. A high stone balustrade surrounded the platform, and from it Pagan looked down upon the tree-bordered river and picturesque Alsatian gables far below.

At the other end of the platform, above the northern tower, rose the steeple, a lofty open, lace-like stone tower, surmounted by an octagonal spire of stone filigree, ending in a rose and pinnacle four hundred and seventy feet above the pavement.

Pagan began the second part of the ascent. The steps wound up around a central column within one of the four open stonework turrets, and so delicate and fine was the filigree tracery of this turret that the staircase seemed to be poised almost unsupported in the air. And as Pagan toiled upwards round and round the giddy stairs he looked now into the long cylindrical interior of the tower, lighted by its eight long, narrow, unglazed windows and now out across the toy-like roofs of Strasbourg to the green open country beyond.

At the top of the tower a narrow balustraded gallery ran round the foot of the tapering spire. Pagan walked slowly round it, pausing a moment on each of the four little spaces above the turrets to enjoy the view, before beginning the final ascent. This took him up eight spiral staircases within the rich open carving of the spire and brought him at last to a narrow space called the lantern, which was barely big enough to hold three people. And there were two people there already. A plump, bare-headed man of German appearance and Clare.

She stood on the other side of the German, furthest from the steps, leaning upon the weather worn stone balustrade. She wore a close fitting little hat, and the red rose which she had bought at the cabaret was pinned on her breast. Her eyes met Pagan's and she gave him a wistful little smile as though it were the most natural coincidence in the world that they should meet up there nearly five hundred feet above the city. The broad chest of the German leant upon the balustrade between them.

"I left Cecil downstairs examining the machinery which works the chimes," she said at last. "He was too lazy to climb up here."

Pagan nodded his head. "Magnificent view," he said banally after a pause.

The German spoke English and was anxious to display his knowledge. With a long sweep of his pudgy hand he traced for them the course of the Rhine and the long range of the Black Forest behind, and pointed out the high peak of the Feldberg. He showed them the double row of poplars that marked the canal that joins the Rhône and the Rhine, and he named the chief peaks visible in the purple line of the Vosges. They should visit the Vosges, he said. They told him they had done so. He pointed out to them the distant towers of the castle of the Haut-Koenigsburg on its wooded bastion, and told them with much detail the story of its restoration by the ex-Kaiser of Germany. But at last he stopped. He shook hands with both of them, squeezed past Pagan, and disappeared down the steps.

Pagan moved up a little and stood beside Clare. Their arms touched lightly as they rested side by side on the stone balustrade. Neither spoke. A strong wind blew in their faces; beneath them the city and the surrounding country lay spread like a map, but so remote were the tiny crawling specks in the tape-like streets below that they might have been alone in the world.

"When—do you go back?" she asked at last in a low voice.

"To-morrow."

She did not look at him. She gazed out towards the distant purple line of the Black Forest. "Then—this is good-bye."

He nodded. They stood in silence for some time, and then she murmured, "I must go."

She took a little handkerchief from her bag, but the wind tore it from her hand and wrapped it round a projecting piece of carving on the stone filigree beside her. Pagan rescued it, but during the few moments that he reached out across the balustrade and unwrapped it from its perch, his body was pressed close to hers. He was shaken by the warm contact. As he slowly straightened himself, their eyes met. In hers there was a half frightened expression.

He looked down at the morsel of silk in his hand. He raised his eyes to hers pleadingly. "May I keep it?" he asked in a low voice.

She looked at him with a sad wistful little smile. "Is it wise, Charles, dear?" she asked gently.

He gave a helpless little shrug of his shoulders. She took the handkerchief from him gently, and then suddenly unpinned the rose from her breast. She held it out to him with a sad smile. "Good-bye, dear Charles," she murmured.

He held the rose between his fingers. "Good-bye."

They gazed mutely at one another for a moment, and then she turned quickly and went down the steps. He did not attempt to follow.

II

Baron was buying a few little presents to bring back to his two small nephews. He and Vigers were dawdling at the shops and stalls under the old colonnade that ran down one side of the corn market. The hot afternoon sun beat down upon the pavé roadway, and seen from the shady arcade, the old lime-washed houses on the opposite side of the street formed dazzling panels of light framed by the dark arches of the colonnade.

They wandered slowly along the cool and shady pavement, stopping now and then at a stall or old bow-fronted shop window to debate the competitive claims upon nephewly fancy of such attractions as a jointed wooden serpent that wriggled as though alive and lead replicas of Napoleon's Old Guard complete with the Emperor himself, bear-skins, band and colour party.

They made their purchases at last and emerged from the shady colonnade into the sunlit square. They sauntered slowly along the hot pavement and came finally to rest at a café near one corner of the square where a short narrow street led out to one of the main roads beyond.

"Too hot to tramp about, anyway," said Vigers as he dropped into one of the chairs in the shade of the awning. Baron placed his hat at a rakish angle on top of the shrub in the green tub beside him. "Too hot to do anything except loaf," he commented.

The square was almost deserted; it seemed to doze in the heat. Two small dilapidated stalls, gay with flowers, stood near the statue in the middle, and the two old market women who owned them dozed on their orange boxes side by side. The only movement was provided by three gendarmes who were holding a very animated conversation among themselves and continually turned their heads to dart glances round the square.

"Trade not very brisk this afternoon," murmured Vigers.

Baron edged round his chair so that his foot came within the shadow of the awning. "No," he grunted. "Perhaps that's what the local sleuths are arguing about—which shall keep cave while the other two come in and have a quick one."

Indeed the half-dozen tables on the pavement outside the café were deserted except for themselves, and there appeared to be nobody indoors either. The little patron himself came out frequently on to the pavement, looked up and down the square and at the gesticulating gendarmes, and then disappeared into the gloom inside again.

"Is he looking for more custom or is that a gentle hint for us to finish this up and have another?" asked Baron as he followed with his eyes the patron's fourth disappearance into the dark interior.

Vigers pulled out his pipe and grunted. "Perhaps he is trying to keep his fat down," he suggested.

A youth on a bicycle with low-dropped handlebars pedalled hastily and erratically up the short narrow street that led out of the square. He dropped his cycle with a clatter on the pavé outside the café and disappeared inside. A moment later he was out again and pedalling erratically across the square. He shouted something to the gendarmes who turned to look at him as he passed and then broke into an argument more animated than ever.

The little patron appeared on the pavement. He carried a pole with a hook at the end. With it he proceeded to pull down the wooden roller shutters that protected the café at night.

"Hullo!" exclaimed Baron. "What's up! Early closing day or something?"

The little patron answered, still heaving on the blind. There was some political trouble, he explained between gasps and heaves. It might come to nothing, but one never knew. Troops had been sent for, but if they did not arrive soon, before the mob got into the square, there might be some nasty incidents; and he was not taking any chances. The shutter dropped into its socket with a bang, and the little patron and his pole disappeared quickly through a side door.

Vigers looked at Baron. Baron grimaced. "Another little rumpus," he said. "Charles and I ran across one in Colmar.

Nothing to worry about. Half a dozen troopers and it was all over in a couple of minutes."

Vigers nodded and glanced round the square. "All the same," he said, "if they got into this square and barricaded the side streets, it would take a lot of shooting to get them out of it."

The sound of a horse's hoofs came from the far end of the square and a moment later a trumpeter in service blue emerged from a side street and clattered across the square to pull up beside the gendarmes. They all talked animatedly for a moment, and then he turned his horse and trotted back the way he had come.

Baron noticed that the square was now quite deserted and that several of the shops and cafés had their shutters down. The two market women had disappeared, though their shabby stalls, bright flowers and empty orange boxes still stood out there in the sunshine. The little street that led from the square was deserted too; but from it came a vague murmur.

Baron turned his head to listen, and he looked at Vigers. Vigers nodded his head and put away his pipe. "Troops will be too late in another five minutes," he said.

Suddenly the lingerie display in the shop window that faced them at the far end of the little street leading from the square, was blotted out. The whole end of the narrow street was blocked from pavement to pavement by a solid wall of humanity.

Baron jumped up. "We had better make ourselves scarce, old Roger," he cried, "or we shall get caught between the troops and the mob."

A mounted officer had clattered in at the far end of the square, but he was alone. The mob was advancing slowly up the street. It made no sound except the rumbling thud of its feet upon the pavé. The gendarmes separated. They flung themselves prone on the hot pavement outside a deserted café and took cover behind some overturned iron tables. They held pistols in their hands.

Baron glanced anxiously behind him and edged towards the side door through which the little patron had disappeared. "The *poilus* will be too late," he jerked out. "There will be a pitched battle in this square in another ten minutes; some of those fellows have rifles. If only the gendarmes could hold them up for a few minutes it might save the situation and prevent a devil of a lot of bloodshed. But they can't." He turned quickly towards the open shop next door. "Come on, Roger; let's get in here out of it."

Vigers did not move. His keen blue eyes swept round the square. He glanced at the mounted officer and at the still empty street from which he had come, and then he looked back at the advancing mob.

He touched Baron's arm. "Tell Charles Pagan to be good to Clare," he cried inexplicably. Then he shouted to the gendarmes, to hold their fire for a few minutes.

He broke into a run, and a moment later was at the head of the street facing the mob. He halted, and Baron saw his hand go to his face and come quickly away. Something fell upon the road and lay there gleaming whitely in the sunshine. It was the mask.

A rumbling murmur broke from the advancing mob. Its leading ranks were violently agitated, like an advancing wave checked by another one flung back from a breakwater. It swayed irregularly along its front, ebbing and flowing with the impetus from behind, but it no longer advanced as a body. The seconds ticked by; the sunshine beat down upon the deserted square. In some belfry a clock leisurely climed the half-hour. Alone in the sunshine in the middle of the street, Vigers' tall form began to advance slowly and silently towards the mob; and the mob, a seething mass of bobbing heads and struggling bodies, contracted before him.

How long that strange tableau lasted, Baron never knew. In that dumbfounded state of coma into which he had been thrown, time had no meaning for him. But the end came suddenly. Half a dozen shots reverberated deafeningly between the high buildings, two almost simultaneously, the others in a straggling fusillade. Vigers swayed. He stood stock still for a moment, drawn to his full height: then his legs crumpled beneath him, and he dropped in a heap upon the road.

Baron came out of his trance; he broke into a run He was aware that a light tank was rattling swiftly over the pavé behind him. A troop of horse had filed from a side street and was moving in line across the square He reached the crumpled form and dropped beside it. The tank was almost upon him. He sat up on one knee and waved his arms furiously to one side; and the tank turned and swung by within a foot of him.

As he bent again over the crumpled form he was conscious that the mob was ebbing in the street like water through a perforated jar. He hooked his arms beneath the doubled figure and dragged the head and shoulders back on to his knee. Then he lowered it gently and rose slowly to his feet. Captain Roger Vigers, V. C., was dead.

THE END

THE LIFE OF WALTER FREDERICK MORRIS
by
David Morris

WALTER Frederick Morris was born on the 31st May 1892 in Norwich. He attended Norwich Grammar School and later went to Saint Catharine's College, Cambridge where he read History. On graduating in 1914, he was due to take up a post with the colonial office in British East Africa, but instead enlisted in the ranks.

That year he was posted to France with the 8th Battalion of the Norfolk Regiment as an infantryman, but was quickly commissioned as a temporary officer. By the end of the war he had been mentioned in despatches, awarded the Military Cross and risen to the rank of Major, commanding the Cycle Battalion of the XIII Army Corps.

In April 1919, Morris and his battalion became part of the occupation army of the Rhineland. It is whilst serving there that he met his wife, Lewine Corney, who was working in Germany for the Catholic Women's League. They were married later that same year.

In January 1920, Morris re-joined the Norfolk Regiment, working as an intelligence officer in Belfast during the "Troubles". Later in 1920 he returned to civilian life and took up teaching, though remaining a Major in the Regular Army Reserve and eventually being appointed commander of the Middlesex Cadet Association. His first teaching post was in Jersey where his two children, Audrey and Peter, were born. In early 1925 he returned with his family to the mainland to take up an appointment as a History master at St Benedict's Priory in Ealing, West London.

It was also in 1925 that Morris's literary career began with publication of his first novel *Veteran Youth*. In 1929 his second novel, *Bretherton—Khaki or Field Grey?* was published by Geoffrey Bles to much acclaim. This was quickly followed by *Behind the Lines* in 1930 and *Pagan* in 1931. Four further novels were published between 1933 and 1937. In 1961 plans to make *Bretherton* into a film, updated to the Second World War, were initiated by his agents Curtis Brown. Sadly, these never came to fruition, though Peter Sellers was said to have been interested in the title role.

After the Second World War, during which he was a Captain of the Royal Artillery Army Search Lights in Norfolk, Morris joined British Industrial Films Limited for whom he worked in London until his early seventies. He remained living in Ealing until 1965 when, following the death of his wife, he returned to Norwich to live with his unmarried sisters Nellie and Vi. He died there in 1969.

Morris, seated on the left, with fellow soldiers (courtesy Morris family).

Captain Morris, seated in the centre, with his platoon officers sometime after 1916 (courtesy Morris family).

Major Morris with Winston Churchill (courtesy Morris family).

W.F. Morris with a "comrade-in-arms" (courtesy Morris family).